MONTANA MAVERICK

BEAR GRASS SPRINGS, BOOK THREE

RAMONA FLIGHTNER

GRIZZLY DAMSEL PUBLISHING

You're my cheerleaders, my sounding board, my comrades in adventure. I would be lost without you, my wonderful friends!

CHAPTER 1

Montana Territory, September 1885

*J*essamine Phyllis McMahon, Bear Grass Springs' recently arrived resident and reporter, nodded to a neighbor as she wiped down the windows of the newspaper office. The latest edition of her newspaper was on full display, and she wanted those passing by to easily read the headlines. However, *"Delinquent Cow Wanders Main Street"* proved of little interest. After another pair walked past with only a cursory glance at the paper in the window, she sighed.

During her first week in town last month, she had published a newspaper daily to drum up interest. Now, a month after her arrival, she printed a twice-weekly paper, and this edition did little to elicit curiosity.

Her print shop, located next to the bank, was often overlooked as people rushed to complete a transaction at the neighboring business. Or, she mused, the townsfolk were too eager to arrive at the Boudoir, the town's whorehouse, which stood just past the bank and at the edge of town. She glanced across the dusty main thoroughfare—aptly named Main Street—to the town's most popular saloon, the Stumble-

Out. The man she had coined the town's most disreputable gentleman was not among the men loitering outside, and she quickly lost interest in those wandering in and out of the saloon.

After a final swipe to polish away an imaginary streak, she reentered her print shop. When she had first arrived, a year's worth of old papers and notes had been stashed in corners and crannies of the one-story building. After collecting most of the excess paper, she decided to keep it on one side of the large room to use as fuel for her fire in the winter. She walked along the front of the shop, with its tall shelves and bookcases blocking the view of the back of the shop and forming a sense of a hallway. Her desk sat between two windows, and a large flat table sat opposite the press where she hand set the newspaper with metal letters.

To the far side of the room, near one window, the press stood on a small raised dais. A lamp hung over the press for dark days or when she wanted to work at night. Covered buckets filled with ink sat near the press, and reams of paper were piled on the floor to one side of her desk. Long rows of wires, like multiple clotheslines, hung across the room for drying the paper after printing. Currently no papers were there, as they were stacked by the door, ready for purchase.

She sat at her desk, pushing aside a stack of article ideas with corresponding research and pulled out a blank sheet of paper. On one side she made a column for what she considered a success in her newspaper so far, and in the other she wrote what she thought were challenges. For success, she wrote N&N. Her *News and Noteworthy* section that came out once a week garnered the most interest from the townsfolk. It made that edition of the newspaper outsell the others three to one.

Her articles about national affairs and global events were rarely remarked upon. However, she always received letters to the editor about the N&N section, along with suggestions for the next edition. "I'll expand that section to include it in every newspaper, and I'll make it longer in each paper. I should have known to play to the townsfolk's vanity and need for gossip," she muttered.

She tapped her pencil on the sheet of paper as she brainstormed other topics that would interest the residents in a small Montana town, with a mining camp in the mountains above and an expansive valley below filled with cattle and cattlemen. She left that thought for later and wrote it in the challenges column. *Little interest in nonlocal affairs. No distribution network. Questionable literacy of townsfolk.*

She dropped her pencil and jerked around as the door burst open. She met the irate gaze of the man she had termed the town's "most disreputable gentleman" since her arrival. "Hello, Mr. MacKinnon. It's lovely to see you today."

Ewan MacKinnon strolled into her office with the grace of a panther. His blond hair with hints of red in it hung to his shoulders, and he was in need of a shave. In his anger, he forgot to doff his hat to her, and he took it off, tracing the brim between his long fingers. Irate brown eyes met her cognac-colored gaze, and his glare intensified as he saw her poorly concealed amusement. "Must ye write about me in every damn edition of yer newspaper?" he demanded.

"You know as well as I do that an *N&N* isn't in this paper," she said with a triumphant smile.

"Oh, ye act all coy. I ken what ye're doin'. Ye're tryin' to make me out to be the town fool. But ye willna succeed. I promise ye that." He took a deep breath. "How can ye write that the cow got the better of me and that I'm lookin' for a rematch?"

She giggled and looked away. "Forgive me. I thought that was what truly occurred. Did you or did you not interact with the cow? And did you not end up in the middle of a cow pie after it … nudged you with its behind?"

He reddened. "Aye, that is what occurred. But ye dinna have to write about it and tell the entire world!"

She laughed. "I doubt the world is interested in the meaningless antics of a cow in our little town of Bear Grass Springs, Mr. MacKinnon. From what I've heard, the rest of the world is busy mourning the death of P. T. Barnum's giant elephant, Jumbo, in a train wreck. I'd be thankful you rate over the death of an elephant in the townsfolk's estimation."

"Ye are a daft woman," Ewan said as he rolled his eyes.

"That may be, but, from what I heard, you had quite a cotillion of women eager to aid you as you struggled to rise."

He flushed red as he turned away from her.

"It's such a pity you pulled Miss Jameson onto your lap rather than allowing her to help you up." She bit her lip as his back stiffened and his hold on his hat tightened. "I don't know as her dress will ever recover."

After a moment, he spun to face her. "Yer articles, an' the actions of women in this town who should ken better, willna force me to marry a woman I dinna like."

She smiled. "Then I suggest you be more careful about whose hand you accept for aid."

"I could barely see!"

She cleared her throat as though swallowing a chuckle. "Yes, I did hear about the unfortunate, uh, splatter that covered your face."

He ran a hand over his jaw but not before she saw a hint of a smile. "Ye enjoy this, do ye no'? The small-town antics that drive most of us insane?"

She nodded. "It's what keeps a small town going and knits everyone together. I have to say, it was a difficult article to write as the Jamesons will not speak with me, and the cow was more interested in chewing her cud. And *you*, well, I know better than to ask you for an interview. So I listened to others describe what they saw as I ate my meals at the café."

Ewan snorted. "Why should the Jamesons speak with ye when ye started speculatin' about Helen's respectability in one of yer first papers?" Any humor hidden in his gaze disappeared as he sobered. "Ye can write articles about me, an' I will no' be affected. I'm a man. But ye canna write about a lass. 'Tisn't right, Miss McMahon."

"If she is acting outside the bounds of propriety, Helen is fair game for a reporter."

Ewan cocked his head to one side as he stared at her. The light glinting in through the windows cast a reddish tint to his dark blond hair. "Do ye no' care what ye could do to that girl? Do ye not ken how hard her life already is, livin' with her mother and brother?"

Jessamine shrugged. "Life is hard, Mr. MacKinnon. It's the one truth we should all understand and accept."

He took a step toward her as his gaze hardened. "Aye, 'tis. But that means ye should no' go around attemptin' to make it harder for those who canna defend themselves. Yer cow story is entertainin' until the point ye make Helen a laughingstock. Then ye go too far. Ye always go too far."

His irate glare met her indignant, defiant stare, and then he spun on his heel and stormed away. The door rattled as it slammed shut behind him.

She picked up her pencil from her desk and sighed. "You're wrong, Mr. MacKinnon. I never go far enough."

That afternoon Jessamine locked the front door to her newspaper office and walked along the town's boardwalk. The mid-September sun shone brightly, and she drew down her wide-brimmed hat to shield her eyes from the glare. It was a tactic she had learned in her early days as a journalist as it made her appear a meek woman, and many were willing to speak freely as she lingered in front of storefronts. She smiled as the strategy had proved as successful in Bear Grass Springs as in New York or Saint Louis. However, little of interest was to be learned as she walked past the bakery, café, and Watering Hole Saloon on her way to the General Store.

She jumped out of the way as a patron was propelled from inside the saloon through the open door by two men. She frowned, as she knew them to be cardsharks and reticent to speak with a reporter, with or without her hat. She heard the man mumble about going to the barbershop farther down the boardwalk and next to the General Store, but he refused to say more after he saw her.

She smiled and continued her journey to Tobias Sutton's General Store, or the Merc, as the townsfolk called it. When the bell over the door jingled upon her arrival, she hid a contented smile. The Merc, the larger of the two mercantiles in town, had everything she could wish to purchase. Tobias was the only one of the two general store proprietors who had successfully ordered ink for her after the unfortunate spill by her former assistant. She squared her shoulders and raised her chin as she walked inside, her ochre satin skirt shining in the sunlight. She smiled at the other woman present, Ewan's sister, Sorcha MacKinnon, ignoring the woman's scorn.

After Sorcha left, Jessamine walked with controlled grace to the front counter. Under the glass she saw delicate lace and a china teacup. "Are you hoping the townsfolk will invest in the finer things with their hard-earned money?"

He met her mocking gaze with a scowl. "Miss McMahon. There is no reason that a respectable wife, living in a town such as ours, should not expect or deserve such beautiful refinements."

Jessamine laughed. "That's not what makes a woman stay." She raised an eyebrow. "As you well know."

His gaze became arctic as he watched her. "You have no right to speak to me in such a manner." He looked her over from head to toe. "You should be restricted to the whore's hours for shopping."

She laughed and shook her head. "That's rich, coming from a man who's rarely at home at night because he's so busy at the Boudoir." She leaned forward, a light flush on her neck and cheeks enhancing the red of her hair. "I may be a reporter, but I have honor."

"As do I, miss."

She studied him. "I've recently learned differently. I wonder if your family believes the same?" She smiled as he stilled. "You shouldn't cast aspersions when you are guilty of your own sins, Mr. Sutton."

He paled. "What would a woman like you know of such a situation?"

She tapped her finger on the polished glass. "More than you could imagine. Treat me with respect, and your story stays buried. Don't cross me, Tobias." She watched as his eyes flared at the threat and the use of his first name.

He stiffened and then nodded, his gaze flicking to the door as the bell overhead chimed. "What can I do for you today, Miss McMahon?" he asked in his most obsequious voice.

She placed her order, her gaze filled with a warning and a promise for retribution if he attempted to cross her. He nodded his understanding and glared at her as she left the store.

She walked to the nearby café for an early supper. Although she had a small kitchen in the rear of her print shop, she rarely ate there. She smiled at the locals already gathered for an evening meal and chose a table close to two men whose loud voices carried.

Harold Tompkins, the husband half of the duo who ran the Sunflower Café, approached with a glass of water and a friendly smile. He accepted her order of fried trout, boiled potatoes, and pickled beets. He raised an eyebrow as she stared straight ahead as she listened to the conversations around her. After a moment, when she failed to engage in conversation with him, he sighed and entered the kitchen.

Jessamine half smiled as the men behind her argued.

One with a baritone voice said, "I tell you. I saw it again last night!"

His friend, with a slightly higher-pitched voice, snorted. "It was the moonshine Herbert poured down yer gullet. That weren't no ghost."

Baritone said, "You got no idea what I saw!"

Her gaze jerked upward as a plate *thunk*ed in front of her. "Hello, Mrs. Tompkins." She smiled as Irene Tompkins watched her with unveiled curiosity and waited for Jessamine to pick up her fork.

"Hello, Miss McMahon. Nice of you to stop in here again." She shook her head as the men behind Jessamine dug their heels in about what they had or had not seen. "Those two will argue until they're dead an' buried." She nodded to Jessamine. "I wouldn't look to them as a source for any of your stories. Neither of them knows east from west, and they barely know how to don pantaloons."

The sound of scraping wood sounded as Irene pulled out a chair and sat across from Jessamine. "You know, miss, I've always considered what I heard here as a sort of sacred confessional." She stared hard at Jessamine when she snorted in disbelief. "You might think that a ridiculous comment, but it's true. It's none of my business what others discuss while they eat a meal, and I have no right to bandy it about town."

"That is because you are the proprietor of this fine establishment," Jessamine said. "I, on the other hand, am a reporter. Nothing that is said in my presence is deemed sacred."

Irene huffed out an agitated breath. "You are wrong. However, that's a lesson you must learn for yourself." She paused a moment and then smiled as she watched her husband chat with a group of miners who had come to town for entertainment. They had arrived for an evening meal after a barber's visit as their beards were trimmed and their hair wet around the collar.

"He seems a good man," Jessamine murmured.

Irene chuckled. "No need to sound so surprised. He *is* a good man, and I'm thankful he's put up with me all these years. Many men wouldn't have."

The reporter watched the older woman with frank curiosity. "Why? You are an astute businesswoman. I would think any man would value such a trait."

Irene sighed. "Perhaps that is an attribute valued here in the Territory. However, most men would want a docile woman, content to sit at home, knitting, cooking, and caring for a family. I always resented being excluded, and Harold understood." Her knowing gaze met Jessamine's guarded one. "If you are very fortunate, you will meet such a man one day."

Jessamine shook her head and laughed. "I highly doubt that. Few would celebrate a journalist in the family. And few men appreciate a woman with intelligence."

The older woman tapped Jessamine's hand and rose. "If you weren't so intent on showing all of us how superior you were, perhaps you'd have a better chance at forming friendships." She moved away to the kitchen to prepare dinners as more diners entered the café.

Jessamine sipped her coffee and ate her slice of cake, her thoughts distant as she was unable to shut out the echo of Irene's words.

∾

The following day Ewan strode to Warren Clark's office and, before he entered, scraped his boots on the boot cleaner outside the door bracketed by two windows. Warren was the town lawyer, and his office had a large front room with a desk along one wall where he conducted most of his business and a potbellied stove in the corner. A doorway led to a small back room that he used as a private office when discussing delicate or confidential aspects of a case.

Ewan nodded to his second eldest brother, Alistair, and then to the lawyer, Warren Clark. Ewan gave the town banker, Mr. Ambrose Finlay, his mischievous smile before he joined them at the round table Warren had set up in his large front office space near the small stove. It pumped out warmth on this cold September day, and Ewan glared at the banker for taking the seat nearest the heat.

Alistair noted his glare and fought a smile. "'Tis typical."

"Yes, typical of you to be late," Mr. Finlay said as he glared back at Ewan. "I remain unconvinced as to the necessity of this wastrel's presence. Simply because he thought of the whore tax, due to his penchant for lascivious activities, does not indicate we should continue to consult him."

Ewan sat back in his chair with his characteristic impish half smile as he stared at the affronted banker. "Perhaps if ye focused less on the cut of yer clothes an' more on the town and its needs, ye'd come up with similar ideas."

"Listen, you little whelp, we did just fine until you came along. We were able to have our meetings at the café."

"Aye, where ye never paid for a single meal," Alistair said with a raised eyebrow. He glared at Mr. Finlay until he slouched in sullen silence. "My brother has ideas on how to raise revenue for this town. Revenue we need for projects to improve this town."

"I want this to be minuted. *I am deeply offended that my council members believe I would shirk my responsibilities to pay my part of a bill. I thought the committee's bills were covered by a fund supplied by the townsfolk.*"

Warren pinched the bridge of his nose. "How in God's name would there be a fund to feed us meals when there's no money for anything else? It wouldn't be honorable to accept the money even if there were such a fund!" He took a deep breath. "And I am not minuting any of this because the meeting has not been called to order." He glared at all present, spending extra time on Ewan.

After a few moments' pause, Warren said, "Now that those preliminaries are complete, I call this meeting to order." He looked at a sheet of paper in front of him where he had scribbled a rough agenda. "Mr. Finlay, would you be so kind as to inform us of the revenue we have collected in the first weeks of the new tax?" The tax meant that a woman employed at the Boudoir had to shop at specific hours at the mercantiles or face a tax. She could not speak to townsfolk, or be taxed. Finally, the Madam had to pay a small tax each month on profits earned at her Boudoir.

Mr. Finlay sat tall, his satin burgundy waistcoat bulging over his paunch. "Regardless of the revenue generated, it has been a tremendous boon to this town to show that vice is not tolerated." He speared Ewan with a glare. "Those living on the fringes of society should remain there, and we have shown the respectable women of our esteemed town our deep regard."

Ewan sighed as he slumped in his chair. "For God's sake, man, we all ken every man in town has visited the Boudoir."

Mr. Finlay turned beet red with his agitation. "Our women do not need to be exposed to such depravity!" He took a deep breath. "In the first weeks of the tax, we have raised fifty dollars." He smiled at the success of the revenue-raising venture.

Alistair nodded. "Fifty dollars in nearly a month isna bad, although it seems a little low to me." He studied the banker. "Was there a charge for managing the fees?"

Mr. Finlay shrugged. "There are always charges when managing money." He shrugged again as though matters were out of his control. "How else would you expect a bank in such a small town to succeed?"

Warren glared at the banker. "You can read the contract and the proposition about the tax as well as I can, Ambrose. There was a clause in there for no fees to be collected by your bank for some time." He met the banker's blank stare. "Don't make me take you to court. You will not like it, and you will not win."

Ewan looked at the three men who formed the Bear Grass Springs' Improvement Committee as they glared at each other before focusing on the banker. "How were ye voted onto the committee? Ye seem to only have yer best interests at heart, not the town's."

"My interests are the town's interests. Unlike my two uninformed colleagues, who fail to grasp such a notion, the townsfolk are more aware of the realities of life in a town such as ours." Ambrose fingered his satin waistcoat.

Ewan laughed. "I wonder what the journalist would do, should she hear about yer actions." He smiled as Mr. Finlay paled. "I dinna think the townsfolk would take kindly to hearin' the banker, who has many of the townsfolk's prized possessions in a safe as collateral to debts owed, is robbin' them of money meant to improve the town."

"How dare you imply any wrongdoing," Ambrose sputtered. "I merely read the contract incorrectly."

"'No' is a fairly easy word to comprehend," Warren muttered. He sighed and raked a hand through his brown hair. "I will ensure we sort out the tax issue, and I will report back to the committee the full findings at a later date. If there are continued problems with the tax collection, we will find another solution. Perhaps a second bank in town would aid us, just as a second general store has."

Alistair and Ewan shared a grin as Ambrose's eyes grew rounder at Warren's threat.

Warren cleared his throat. "Now, Ewan, if you would care to share with us and list a few of the ideas you have for raising further revenue in the town?"

Ewan sat taller and leaned his elbows on the table. "My ideas are no' very different from what has already been implemented." He met the banker's scoff and indignant roll of his eyes and continued. "I believe that a lot of money could be made if ye were to tax the saloons." He took a deep breath. "And if ye were to tax gambling matches and games. Men spend a lot of money on those matches, and the town should benefit from the winnings."

Warren frowned. "Wouldn't the town benefit twice? Once from the tax by the man who has won, and then again when he buys a drink at the saloon, and his drink is taxed? When we tax the saloon, it will retax the man's money."

Ewan shrugged. "That is an argument you could make about everything and thus never tax a thing. However, many of the poker players are passing through. I've known quite a few who drink little and win quite a bit. The town is losin' money on those men."

"Will the tax no' encourage the men to go to other towns, rather than spend time in Bear Grass Springs?" Alistair asked.

"This is Montana Territory. There aren't many towns nearby." Warren paused. "I think we could make an argument to tax gambling. I fear too many would protest an alcohol tax and believe we are over-stepping our authority."

"What about a hotel tax?" Ewan asked. "Few who lodge at the hotel are local."

Ambrose glared at Ewan. "You do not have a head for business, boy. You will destroy any enterprise we have with your taxes."

Ewan shrugged. "I've thought about this quite a bit. I canna say I'm a fan of taxes. But I see no other way to raise the funds we need for town improvements."

"Those who are able will be generous," Ambrose sputtered.

Alistair rolled his eyes, and Ewan snorted before speaking. "If we wait for those who barely ken how to spell the word, never mind the meaning of it"—he glared at the banker—"then nothing will ever be accomplished."

The banker flicked his hand as though what Ewan said was a mere triviality. "It's nearly impossible to know if we are receiving the correct money from the Madam. How will we ever know if we are receiving the correct money from the saloons or the hotel?"

Ewan shook his head. "I dinna ken. I supply the ideas. 'Tis yer job to implement."

Alistair scrubbed at his head. "Any businessman worth his weight would have two sets of ledgers," he muttered. He watched as the banker shifted in his seat. He ignored Warren's surprised glance. "Do ye think smugglin' an' the like wasna common in Scotland?"

Mr. Finlay shook his fingers at the two brothers. "That's why you have such nefarious minds and can think like common criminals!"

Alistair sat forward with his hands clenched together in front of him. "I would remind ye that I was no' the one found to have swindled the town out of money!" He took a deep breath.

"Bein' smart enough to outwit those keen on keepin' all their cash for their own benefit doesna make one a criminal," Ewan said.

Warren shook his head in dismay. "I'll look into the town bylaws. It was easy to tax the whores and the whorehouse as they are out of the bounds of propriety. However, with a gambling tax instituted, other businesses will begin to worry that we will tax them to help raise funds."

Ewan shrugged. "'Twould only be fair to tax a small percentage of profits or a tax on sales for the town's improvement."

"Yes, but how would you enforce it?" Warren asked. "Would you be willing to participate in this tax scheme?"

"Ludicrous scheme," Ambrose muttered.

"Aye. The town is fine now but 'twill fall apart if we do nothin'," Ewan said. He and the banker shared an intense stare filled with loathing. "I believe we should help each other succeed an' no' hoard our success."

Mr. Finlay slammed his hand onto the table and rose. "I've had enough of this whippersnapper's disregard!" He grabbed his coat and stormed from the room, the door rattling as it slammed behind him.

Warren gave Ewan a reproachful look. "You could learn a bit of tact, Ewan."

"Why bother with one like him? He's already admitted to robbin' the town of hard-earned money. I canna feel badly for showin' him my dislike."

Alistair sighed as he stretched out his legs. He held his hands toward the warmth of the potbellied stove. "At least we have more heat, now he's gone."

Warren laughed. "Yes, now that he's not blocking the stove." He sighed. "And it's a glorious day as we don't have to pay for his meal."

Alistair met Warren's troubled gaze. "Harold wasna happy we were havin' the meeting here. He likes listenin' in, although we never accomplish much."

Ewan shook his head. "Harold should be on the committee, not Mr. Finlay." He glared out the door as though still able to see the banker.

Warren rose and entered a back room that he used as a private office. He emerged with cups in one hand and a coffeepot in the other. After pouring the coffee, he placed the metal pot on top of the stove in the main room and sat again.

"Heaven," Ewan murmured as he took a sip. "Sorcha's is improvin', but she'll never brew a decent cup."

Warren chuckled. "I'd have thought that Annabelle would have taught her by now."

Alistair raised an eyebrow and fought a smile. "Nae. Nae such luck for those living in Cailean's house." He winked at his brother. "Leticia makes a fine cup of coffee. And I hear Miss Jameson does too."

Ewan sputtered into his mug and glared at his brother. "Ye ken I've no interest in the woman. It doesna matter what that vicious journalist wrote."

Alistair glared at Warren a moment. "Can ye no' prevent that woman from writing such stories about us?" He let out a frustrated sigh. "About Ewan?"

Warren tapped his fingers on the side of his mug before he took another sip. "It seems she is taken with young Ewan. If you had shown her courtesy when she had arrived last month, you may not now find yourself in her journalistic sights."

Ewan growled. "The woman misrepresented who she was! Ye ken we all thought we were gettin' a man. Why would we have thought J.P. McMahon was a woman?" He raised his hand as though proving his point. "What woman uses two initials for her name?"

Warren shrugged. "A woman who has had to be intrepid enough to survive in this world. A world run and controlled by men." He met

Ewan's frustrated gaze. "She knew well enough that she would be denied this post, even though she is overqualified for it, simply because she is a woman. I cannot blame her for her actions."

"Her deceit," Alistair said. "Ye are a very forgiving man, Warren."

"About some things perhaps." He watched Ewan. "You have to admit, you do make the paper more lively. And she's yet to report on any falsehoods."

Ewan snorted. "She exaggerates, tellin' just enough of the truth so that I canna complain so much as to shut her down."

Warren rose and filled their cups before topping his off. "Would you want to shut down the paper? It's brought lively discourse to the town."

"Just wait until she attacks someone ye care about, Warren. Then ye will no' consider it innocent or amusin'," Ewan said. "I can handle being the focus of her attention. I look for her snide comments every edition and then prepare for the banter of my men. But she goes too far when she harms the reputations of others in town."

Warren set his cup on the table and held his hands over his stomach, as though attempting to appear relaxed and to not clench them. "She only wrote the truth about how Miss Jameson acted." He forced a smile. "You protest loudly on behalf of the young woman. Perhaps you wish to hide your feelings for her."

Ewan stared at him, slack-jawed, momentarily unable to speak.

"Besides, it seems Miss Jameson has an interest in you. That should be what matters as J.P. will not refrain from repeatedly mentioning it to her readers." Warren watched Ewan intently.

Alistair nodded. "I believe that's Ewan's point. The reporter will harm Miss Jameson even more than Miss Jameson harms herself. 'Tis not right or proper for a journalist to act in such a way."

Warren shook his head. "She is not printing lies or libel. I cannot bring suit against her. If Miss Jameson continues to act in a reckless manner, I can do nothing to save her."

Ewan slumped in his chair. "My brothers were clever enough to avoid Helen's snare. I will be too."

Warren looked into the depths of his coffee cup. "I hope you are."

He cleared his throat. "Another matter has come to my attention, and I thought I would share it with you as I'm afraid it may affect Cailean and Annabelle."

Ewan and Alistair leaned in, concern furrowing their brows at the mention of their eldest brother and his wife, Annabelle. Cailean ran the livery with Alistair and their partner John Runs from Bears Renfrew, and Annabelle owned the bakery. "What is it?" Ewan asked.

"I learned this morning that our doctor has left town." He met their panicked expressions. "I know that Annabelle is in expectation of a fortuitous event months from now, and I can only imagine how this will worry her. However, I have been assured that his replacement is en route and will arrive within days."

Alistair sat back, dumbstruck. "We must have an accomplished doctor. Cailean and Annabelle suffered enough last year." His eyes shone with fear as he recalled Cailean's torment at nearly losing Annabelle after she had miscarried their first child the previous fall.

"As I said, our doctor, who left to expand his practice and fortunes in Butte, has guaranteed that the new doctor is as highly trained. However, I have yet to learn where he attended medical school."

"But ye have received letters of recommendation?" Ewan asked.

Warren flushed. "I have. But we know that those can be forged." He flicked a glance at Alistair who glowered at Warren's reference to his wife, Leticia's, deception that was discovered earlier in the summer.

Ewan frowned at the memory. Leticia had forged letters of recommendation to obtain her Bear Grass Springs' teaching post in an attempt to escape her abusive first husband. Although she had cared for and taught a widowed man's children in Saint Louis upon first escaping her husband, her letters of recommendations had stated she had more experience than she truly had. However, she had taught admirably for years in Bear Grass Springs before her duplicity about her experience and marital status was discovered. After overcoming Alistair's anger, she and Alistair had wed, and they were raising her daughter, Hortence, together. The townsfolk had forgiven her the deception due to their respect for Alistair and the previous regard they had for her as the schoolteacher.

"I willna have her actions held against her again, Warren." Alistair glared at his friend.

"I fully understand your wishes, Alistair, but the townsfolk will not so easily forget her transgressions. And they are less inclined to believe letters due to what happened with Leticia." He shrugged. "It is understandable."

"Then how will we ken if he's an accomplished doctor?" Ewan asked.

Warren shook his head. "Doc was a man I trusted, although he had an interesting work ethic. He considered some patients more worthy of his time and expertise than others, which isn't how I imagined a doctor in a small town to be. I'm hopeful this doctor he has recruited for us will be as talented but with a greater sense of integrity."

"Aye, in that I'll agree with ye," Ewan said. "I'd let that wee demon in the print shop ken what ye know. Would be good for the townsfolk to understand a new doc is on the way. It may make his arrival easier and will ease any fears at the uncertainty."

"That is a good idea. And it may distract her from you for an edition." He laughed as Ewan scowled.

Ewan swallowed his coffee in a few gulps before rising. "Good luck determinin' how to tax the town's businesses. I'm glad I'm not ye." He smiled. "I must return to work. Winter comes sooner than we'd like." He slapped his brother on his back, nodded to Warren, and grabbed his hat before he slipped outside.

J essamine glanced up at the handwritten article on her desk as her hands moved with lightning speed over the tiny metals letters, recreating the words in a metal proof set in a special tray as she prepared the paper for print. For the article to print properly, the proof had to be laid out in reverse. She smiled as her mind had no difficulty envisioning the words backward, and she was a skilled hand-cast printer. After a few hours bent over the metal tray, she stood and arched her back, groaning as it cracked.

She took a sip of water and then carried the metal tray of letters to the printing press, where she rubbed a thin coat of black ink over it. After she set a piece of newsprint over it, she lowered its cover, moved it to the press, and turned the handle on the press. After counting to ten, she released the press and lifted the cover. She smiled as she read the headline *"Fears Mount Silver Played Out in Obsidian Camp."* She clipped it to a clothesline and continued producing this edition of the paper. She had calculated that fifty copies would suffice. For now. She hoped demand for her newspaper would grow and that she would soon distribute it to the miners in the camp and to the numerous ranchers down the valley.

She huffed out a breath at the thought of calling her one-sided broadsheet a *newspaper*. She knew calling it such was misleading; however, for marketing purposes, she would continue as she had begun.

When the copies were printed and hung to dry, she arched her shoulders again and sighed as she stretched them after hours of work. She scrubbed at her fingers, dirtied with ink, in a clean bucket of water set in her kitchen area and then took off her apron.

"I need an assistant," she muttered as she moved her neck from side to side with a groan. "A competent one." She grimaced when she thought of her first attempt at hiring an assistant. Upon arriving in town, she had interviewed the few young men not in the mining camp and decided to hire Horace Martin. She grunted in disgust as she thought of young Horace. Tall, gangly, with an inability to make his limbs move in the direction he wanted them to, he had nearly set the print shop on fire when he had bumped into an oil lamp and then knocked over a bucket of ink.

Far worse was his incessant chatter. She had thought she could survive her loss of peace, but, when she learned his gossip was costing her her livelihood, she had fired him. Few in town saw the need to purchase her paper when they could speak with him and learn the paper's contents free of charge. Now she was forced to run the entire enterprise on her own.

She smiled, wiping her hands dry as the front door opened. "Hello, Mr. Clark."

"Miss McMahon," Warren said with a nod. "How are you?" He glanced at the broadsheet and then shook his head as he read the headline. "Who'd you hear such rubbish from?"

Jessamine's smile turned cagey. "I never reveal my sources."

He met her gaze, his eyes squinting slightly, as she failed to fidget under his harsh stare. "You can't believe everything you hear at the saloons or in the café. Some will speak in hyperbole simply to see their stories in print."

She laughed. "I vet my stories. When numerous townsfolk speak of a similar concern, I deem it a story worth investigating. Unless it is one I witness myself."

"Such a story, especially if it were true, could lead to panic. This town does not need a panic, J.P. It needs stability and a banker willing to be as generous as possible."

She snorted. "That man doesn't know the meaning of the word. He thinks it is spelled s-t-i-n-g-y. I remain hopeful I am never in need of his aid. It's my unfortunate luck that I'm his neighbor."

Warren waved away her words. "He is the only banker we have in town for now"—he raised an eyebrow as her eyes lit with interest—"and thus we must deal with him. Stories like this will only lead to fears that the Recession, which is easing, will return."

"I heard it wasn't as severe here as in other parts of the country," Jessamine said.

"Oh, it was hard enough on the common townsfolk. And it lasted longer than other downturns." He watched her with disappointment. "You should not feed fear, J.P."

She shrugged. "I refuse to print falsehoods and fairy tales."

Warren glared at her a moment and then sighed. "I didn't come here today to argue with you about your upcoming stories. I wanted you to be aware that we are to have a new town doctor."

Her interest in the potential for a new banker faded, as did her irritation about Warren's criticism of her reporting about the

Obsidian silver mines. "Really? What's his name? Where does he come from?"

"He is Dr. Chester, and he comes from the state of New York. Upstate New York."

She frowned. "Why would he come here?"

Warren smiled. "That is a question we ask about all of us, and, for some of us, it remains a mystery." He nodded with approval as she shifted under his gaze. "Now, J.P." He paused at her dramatic sigh.

She raised an eyebrow. "I could set my watch by your visits."

He frowned and took off his hat as he moved farther into her print shop. He ducked under a line of drying broadsheets, maintaining a pristine suit free of ink stains. "If so, a wise person would cease activities that would lead to the arrival of the lawyer."

She rolled her eyes as she fought an amused smile. "Mr. MacKinnon ran to you, complaining again, and now you are here to exhort me to write namby-pamby stories." She raised her hands, palm up. "Am I incorrect?"

"This time your story affects more than just a MacKinnon, Miss McMahon. You should have more sense than to slander a young woman."

"And you should know better than to use a word like *slander* when it is not called for. I did not slander her. I reported what occurred." She stood taller as she recited facts. "Did she or did she not offer her hand?" Her eyes gleamed as his shoulders stiffened. "Did she or did she not fall on his lap?" Her smile spread as he glared at her. "Did she or did she not tarry upon attempting to rise from such a position?"

He swore under his breath and paced away. "Dammit, J.P., you need to cease antagonizing everyone in town. Write stories that you consider namby-pamby for a bit, but at least you'll be a part of this town. Accepted." He stilled as he saw a flash of longing in her gaze that was quickly masked. "You have to know that, if you continue on this path, few will wish to speak with you in the future."

She smirked. "There will always be someone eager to speak with a journalist. The thought of seeing one's name or one's words in a paper is a thrill few are willing to pass up."

He exhaled a huff of breath. "Your cynicism isn't becoming, Jessamine."

She laughed. "I know, but you like me anyway."

He half smiled and nodded. "Be careful what you write. You are angering too many, too quickly. Write something else that will cause the town to talk, other than speculations about their neighbors' actions." He paused a moment as he saw her sober. "Can you attempt that?" When she nodded, he put on his hat. "I wish you good day."

She plopped onto a chair after his departure, clinging to her sense of pride at a job well done, staring at her drying broadsheets, and fighting loneliness.

CHAPTER 2

News & Noteworthy: *It has come to this reporter's attention that a certain gentleman well known in at least two of the disreputable centers of vice in our fine town is in need of a wife. I'd think carefully, ladies, before I'd consider one such as he a suitable husband.*

*E*wan choked on a sip of coffee as he read the latest paper. His eldest brother, Cailean, had left it folded to the column where J.P. spewed her gossip two times a week. He glared at the words on the paper again before setting it aside.

He sat in the large room in Cailean's house that served as the kitchen and dining room. Near the door leading to the hall and sitting room was a good-size round table covered in a light-green cloth with flowers embroidered along the edge. A sink with a hand pump, a large Great Majestic stove, and an icebox were in the kitchen, along with a small wooden table for preparing food. A filled woodbox was by stove, while a hutch with dishes and linens stood along the wall leading to the hallway. Cupboards were filled with cooking instruments, pans and foodstuffs. A door to the side of the kitchen heading outside led to the livery and an outhouse.

"Damn woman," he muttered. Ever since she had arrived in town in the middle of August, she had focused on him in every edition of her newspaper.

His sister, Sorcha, entered the kitchen and saw him reading about himself. "Serves ye right for antagonizin' a woman with a printin' press." Sorcha moved to the stove and poured herself a cup of coffee, sighing with appreciation as she breathed in its scent. Her light-blue eyes shone with amusement as she witnessed her brother's irritation. Her red-brown hair, tied in a loose plait, fell to her waist. Although her brothers were tall, she stood only an inch over five feet.

"How was I to ken she'd be such a pest?" He rubbed at his head. "No matter what she says here, now every mother in town will push her daughter in my direction. It's as though the demon newspaper-woman kent, by sayin' one thing, she'd cause the exact opposite to occur."

Sorcha chuckled. "Aye, she's a canny opponent, and so far ye are losing." Her amused gaze watched her brother as he ran a hand through his hair. "Ye canna spend more time than ye already do at the saloons or the Boudoir, avoidin' every available female and their mothers. Ye'd have to be rentin' a room at either establishment." She frowned as her brother failed to smile. "'Tis no concern, Ewan."

He strode to the stove and refilled his coffee mug. "'Tis, Sorch. I like my life. I want to continue to live it unfettered by the demands of a wife and further responsibilities. I dinna want a gaggle of women followin' me around or attemptin' to trap me." He shuddered. "Ye ken what almost happened to Alistair with that Jameson girl."

Sorcha sobered. "Aye, although we ken it was more the mother than the girl. Because of her mother, Helen will be one of the first to pursue ye."

Ewan shuddered. "Ye ken she's as bad as her mother. I willna be forced to marry her."

After setting down her mug, Sorcha grabbed her brother's arms in a sort of long-armed hug until he looked at her. "Then be on yer guard, Ewan. She's desperate, and ye dinna want her desperation to lead to yer misery."

He nodded before kissing her forehead. "Thank ye, Sorch. Ye've always understood me better than Cail and Alistair."

She shook her head. "Nae, I've accepted ye as ye are, not as how I wished ye were." She squeezed his arms and let go.

He took two big gulps of coffee before leaving his cup in the sink and slipped from the room. He grabbed his hat and a jacket from the pegs by the front door and walked outside. He turned away from the town, walking past the livery and blacksmith shop toward the nearby sawmill. Ewan saw the new schoolteacher, Mr. Danforth, across the road attempting to corral the young children and shook his head as they raced around like wild beasts, ignoring Mr. Danforth's quiet words to calm down.

Ewan walked a short distance along the road that led to the wide valley that spread out below the town. Large cattle ranches filled the valley, although a few intrepid homesteaders had staked their claims. Ewan inhaled deeply, sighing with contentment as the clean air filled his lungs. The scent of fresh pine and spruce permeated the air, while cottonwoods grew near the stream a short distance from the road. He heard the *peck-peck-peck* of a woodpecker but was unable to sight him in the trees.

He approached the sawmill and called out to Nathaniel Ericson who ran it with his friend Karl Johansen.

Nathaniel emerged from inside with a light covering of wood dust on his work-roughened clothes, a smile as broad as his shoulders. "Ewan," he said as he held out his hand. After shaking Ewan's hand, he rubbed at his head, sprinkling more dust on his shoulders. "I've your order ready." He spoke with the long vowels of someone from Norway, although Ewan joked with him that Nathaniel's English was better than his.

"Aye, thanks," Ewan said. He saw his filled wagon, a team of horses hitched to the front, waiting to head into town and looked around in confusion.

"Your worker is flirting with Leena again." Nathaniel laughed as Ewan frowned. "She made apple cake, and he accepted her offer of a piece."

"Yer sister is too friendly," Ewan muttered, earning another laugh from Nathaniel.

"Ya, she is, but she also knows she is to wed Karl soon. Her happiness is …" He squinted as he searched for a word before shrugging.

"Contagious," Ewan muttered. "I canna help but feel my mood lighten when I am near yer sister."

"Ya, and you know she will not be one of the women in the town who wishes to marry you." Nathaniel laughed as Ewan glared at him. Nathaniel clapped him on the shoulder and led him into the small house next to the sawmill. Inside, Ewan watched with amusement as his worker's joy turned to embarrassment at Ewan's arrival.

"Sorry, boss," Stephen said as he gobbled down the last of his apple cake. He rose and thanked Leena before sidling out the door to the waiting wagon full of lumber.

Ewan smiled at Leena who offered him a piece of apple cake. He nodded his acceptance and sat at the table. "I ken ye have work to do," he said to Nathaniel. "Sorry to take ye away from yer duties."

Nathaniel smiled. "We are mainly caught up on our orders. Do you have many new projects starting?"

Ewan took a bite of the cake and closed his eyes. "Delicious," he whispered. "Aye, I've the house I'm workin' on now and two more to try to complete afore winter. The framin' is about done, and then we'll work on the inside." He watched as his friend fidgeted. "Are ye worried about the winter?"

Nathaniel nodded. "Ya, last winter was long, and we didn't have much work. We've saved this summer, but I never know if it will last."

Ewan nodded and took the last bite of the sweet cake. "If I think of anything, I'll let you know." He murmured his thanks to Leena and rose, leading Nathaniel outside. "The town is boomin', but ye have to ken it could end at any moment."

Nathaniel looked down the road that led toward the town's main street. "We have the train here and ranchers. We aren't dependent solely on the miners. Even if they disappeared, we'd still have a reason to survive."

"I always love your optimism, friend," Ewan said as he slapped him on his back. "I'll be by soon when I need to place another order."

He retraced his steps, passing by the livery on his way to a house behind Main Street and a short distance from Alistair and Leticia's home. It was nearly behind the café, and he had a ready excuse to slip inside for his midday meal each day, rather than venturing the short distance home to discover what Sorcha had attempted.

Before Ewan entered the worksite, he was pleased to see his men busy unloading the lumber for this project. Half would travel to the house on the opposite side of Alistair and Leticia's home. He nodded to the men as they piled the lumber inside and joined the man he considered his unofficial foreman. "Hello, Ben."

Ben smiled and pushed a strand of longish pitch-black hair behind one ear. "How are things today, boss?" He watched him with a curious gleam and a hint of mischief in his gaze.

"That damn woman willna cease writin' about me." He glared at his friend as Ben burst out laughing. "It's no' as though I'm searchin' for my ladylove."

Ben wiped at his cheek and fought to maintain his composure. "I hope not. The Beauties at the Boudoir would be sorely disappointed."

Ewan elbowed him in the side, smiling with satisfaction when Ben grunted in slight discomfort. Ewan looked around the room. "Looks as though the walls should go up today, and then we can work on the roof. I want this roughed in by the end of the month."

Ben nodded. "I've got it under control here. You should go to the other worksite and make sure the lumber is delivered." He tilted his head outside where two of the men chatted. "The men you hired this summer are good workers but still in need of guidance."

Ewan slapped him on his shoulder, his boots *thunk*ing on the wide-plank pine floors. He put all thoughts but work out of his mind as he joined his men.

Fact or Fiction? *Since my arrival, I have been besieged by tall tales that the*

tellers insist are true. Thus I have created a new segment in the paper, and I leave it up to you, my most discerning reader, to determine for yourself if it is **Fact or Fiction?**

This first tale comes from the dubious imagination of our most disreputable gentleman. Imagine a man, returning home from a winter's trapping, to discover his home ransacked by a marauding Indian party. His wife and unborn child are dead, and he's filled with rage and a thirst for revenge. Soon scalped members of the tribe begin to turn up dead with his unmistakable calling card: a bite missing from each dead man's liver. Neither traps nor tricks nor ambushes by expert hunting parties foiled him in his twenty-year vendetta against his sworn enemy. I ask you, is this **Fact or Fiction?**

E wan sat in the kitchen and read aloud the new section of the newspaper to Sorcha who glared at the empty coffeepot. She muttered about men who took the last cup and failed to make any more before she brewed another pot. "Ye ken ye'll rip our stomach lining away with what ye brew." He ducked as she threw a drying cloth at him.

"If ye can do better, then ye should make it," she snarled. After a moment she shivered. "'Tis a horrid story ye were tellin' in the saloon. Why would ye make up somethin' like that? An' why would she print it?"

Ewan laughed. "I did no' make it up! All the men in the saloons tell tales about him. He still lives, and his name is Liver-Eating Johnson." He smiled as his sister made a disgusted face. "He's famous for evading capture by the Crow. And he fought for the Union in the Civil War. He's a heroic figure." He frowned for a moment. "I think he's a sheriff somewhere in Montana now too."

"I refuse to believe a man like him lived. I think the story is fiction. No man would act in such a way." She shivered. "I canna imagine eatin' livers like that." She made another face.

"They killed his wife and bairn, Sorcha. He wanted retribution." He smiled. "Life wasna easy in the West forty years ago."

She joined him at the table. "It isna easy now, but we dinna go around carvin' each other up. Nor do we turn them into folk heroes." She pointed her finger at him. "An' I dinna believe that man walked this earth. He's a figment of yer imagination. Why are ye helpin' that spiteful woman when all she does is write horrid things about ye?"

Ewan laughed. "Well, I look forward to hearin' ye admit ye were wrong. And I'm no' helpin' her. The old-timers have taken a shine to tellin' her tall tales. They gather around her stove an' smoke a pipe as they recount how life was here years ago. She only says she heard it from me because it was her way of mentioning me in this paper."

She snorted. "Most of 'em have been here less time than we have. She should ken better than to believe anything they say."

Ewan smiled. "That's the point, Sorch. I dinna think she cares if they are true or not. She just wants good stories that will sell and get the townsfolk talkin'." He shrugged. "It got you riled."

He ducked as she threw a napkin at him. He sobered as his gaze wandered to the door and livery. "I hope her tales dinna lead to problems for Bears."

Sorcha frowned. "Why should they?"

"Ye ken what some say. That we are brave to have such a man as him livin' in close proximity to us." He smiled as Sorcha rolled her eyes. "Many in town are waitin' to find us scalped some mornin'."

"Well, then they'll be waitin' for a long time as Bears is from a peaceful tribe, and, even if he were no', he's a good man," Sorcha said. "They have no right speakin' about him as they do."

Ewan nodded. "Aye, ye're right. But his acceptance here is tolerated at best."

Sorcha grumbled as she rose to pour herself a cup of coffee now that it was brewed. "I will never understand the desire to dislike based on appearances. I would rather ken the person first and have a reason for my distaste."

Ewan smirked. "Like the Jamesons."

She giggled. "Aye. Them and Tobias. An' the Madam." She shivered. "That woman is more horrible every day to her girls." She bit her lip and shook her head.

"What do ye see, Sorch? I ken ye deliver many of the baskets now that Anna is tired with her condition." He frowned when Sorcha shook her head again.

"The new doctor spends quite a bit of time there," she whispered. "He has no reason to be there as Fidelia has no' been abused lately, which is one less worry for Annabelle." She paused as she thought about Fidelia Evans who was Annabelle's sister and worked at the Boudoir where she was known as Charity. She raised troubled eyes to meet her brother's concerned gaze. "I dinna like him. He doesna look at me as a person but as a thing. Do ye ken what I mean?"

Ewan nodded as he frowned. "Aye, an' that's dangerous for the women at the Boudoir. He could be there for other reasons, Sorch."

"He talks about his medicines, their price, and their strength. I dinna ken what they're for."

Ewan shrugged. "Someone must be ill."

Sorcha heaved out a gust of irritated breath. "A sick whore doesna have the money to have the doctor there almost every day, Ewan. I dinna ken what is goin' on, but somethin' is."

Ewan rose. "Aye, well, 'tis good of ye to be concerned about Anna's sister and the other women there, Sorch."

"Will ye try to find out what is occurrin' there?" She flushed at the question and the implied acknowledgment that her brother visited the Boudoir daily.

"Aye." He stroked a hand down her arm. "Now I must away to work." He winked at her and headed to his worksite. He had good men working for him, but he knew they worked more diligently when he was present.

He slipped on a jacket as a cold snap had moved in, killing most of the flowers and heralding an early start to fall. He detoured to the print shop and poked his head in, smiling when he saw J.P. alone, fighting with the old printing press. "How are ye settlin' in then?" he asked. His smile broadened as she glowered at him.

She wiped her hands on a cloth and glared in his direction before she gave up on the press for the moment. "Fine. Just fine. If this old heap of junk worked, it would be even better."

Ewan chuckled. "I heard that, if ye had a gentle touch, it worked better."

She watched him with a flinty glare. "Don't act charming. I don't call you the town's most disreputable gentleman for no reason." She threw down the rag and stepped off the elevated area the press sat on. She zigzagged around piles of old newspapers, reams of paper to be pressed, and bulging file cabinets to sit at her desk. "Why are you here?"

He leaned against the wall. "What do ye think? Fact or Fiction?"

"It doesn't matter what I think. What matters is that it gets people talking and hopefully buying my paper." She pointed to a pile by the door. "When that happens, then I'll be happy."

"Ye should put out an advertisement for tall tales. Ye wouldna have to pay the majority of the folk. They'd be delighted to see their tales in print." He shrugged. "That way ye could mix yer fact with fiction. Most believe today's was fact."

"How can you accept today's story as though it were normal?" She fought a shiver and then frowned at him as he laughed at her reaction. "This is how normal people react!"

"Nae, it's how a soft woman, actin' at bein' hardened by life, acts. Ye'll have to do a better job at convincin' me in the future, now that I ken ye are no' as I thought." His eyes gleamed with triumph as though he had discovered a secret, and he would use it to his benefit.

"You know no such thing. I've seen things that would make someone like you, who's only known privilege and harmony, cringe. You've never seen suffering. Hell, you've never suffered. How can you expect me to worry about your opinion?"

Ewan shrugged and flashed his mocking smile. "Aye, I've lived a charmed life. How could one such as I ever understand loss?" He winked at her, delighting in her aggravation at his actions and his words, and then sauntered out the door.

He entered the nearby worksite and sighed as his men whistled at him as he walked in. They had begun teasing him after his frequent mentions in the paper and his title as "most disreputable gentleman." After a moment he laughed. "Serves me right," he muttered to himself.

"Someone's waiting for you, D.G.," Ben muttered around a mouthful of nails and nodded toward the back of the project.

Ewan frowned for a second and then caught the humor in Ben's eyes and realized this would be his new nickname from his men. "Dammit," he muttered, walking to the rear of the home. The outside walls were up and one interior wall to separate the spaces also stood. Soon they would move to another project before returning here to finish it after it became too cold to work outside.

His frenetic pace slowed when he saw a woman in a deep-blue dress awaiting him. Her wheat-colored hair was pulled in a tidy bun, while her dress and shawl did little to conceal her generous curves. At a few inches over five feet, she stood nearly a foot shorter than Ewan, plus eight years younger than his thirty.

He paused at the entrance to the room covered in wood dust and filled with pieces of lumber he hoped to salvage for another project. A saw lay near her right foot, and he frowned when her swaying brought her closer to it. "Ma'am," he said. She turned to him, and he sighed. "Ye should no' be here, and ye should take care no' to step on that saw."

His words had the opposite effect. She panicked and moved to stand on it. He leaped forward and grabbed her, his long arms tugging her toward him, and she fell forward against him and away from the saw. When she was out of danger, he pushed her from his arms. "Dinna go creatin' fantasies in yer brain that I was so overcome with seein' ye that I had to drag ye into my arms."

She flushed at his harsh words and looked at her well-worn boots. "I'm sorry for intruding on your work. I was hoping to speak with you, but it is difficult to find you away from your usual pursuits."

"If ye wanted to speak with me, ye could come by the house. I'm there every evenin' for dinner." He met her embarrassed gaze. "Of course ye would see my family, and I dinna ken if ye would like to hear all they would have to say to ye. They are none fond of ye an' the way ye are intent on marryin' a MacKinnon."

She nodded. "I understand. However, I think you've failed to consider all I can bring to a marriage." She watched him earnestly before hushing after he growled at her.

"Do ye have no pride?" He glared at her. "My men are all standing behind us, and, if ye havena noticed, they are no' workin'! They are listenin' to our conversation and what ye are sayin'. Ye will be the center of gossip again, Miss Jameson. An' ye will be the topic of pity as another MacKinnon refuses to marry ye."

She blinked away tears. "I refuse to believe I am unmarriageable." She wrapped her arms around her waist.

"Nae, ye are no'. Plenty of men would be willin' to marry ye, but with ye comes yer mother. An' I dinna ken many who would be willin' to take her on too." He tilted his head to one side. "My brother said ye were desperate. Dinna do anythin' foolish, Miss Jameson."

She raised her head, her whispered words emerging with a mixture of defiance and bitterness. "You have no right to tell me what to do. I already have enough people in my life intent on controlling me." She pushed past him and stormed out of the worksite.

Ewan scratched at his head and shook it before returning to work beside Ben. They worked in silence for a few minutes. "I ken ye heard most of it."

"You fool. You said something, and then she started to whisper. We didn't hear the end of your discussion." Ben looked at him as though encouraging him to speak.

"Ye heard enough," Ewan muttered. "I wonder when that lass will ever learn."

Ben shook his head and reached for more nails. "That's not the question, is it?" He met Ewan's curious gaze. "It's when will she have had enough. That's when there will be hell to pay."

Ewan fought a shiver and began to work in earnest, attempting to forget Helen Jameson.

That evening Ewan sat in the sitting room, staring into space as he acted like he was reading a book. He sat on the tufted settee, near the potbellied stove. Two straight-backed chairs were on either side of the stove and a small desk was in a corner. A pitcher of dried flowers sat on a corner of the desk, while a bookcase leaned against a wall next to the desk. He waited for dinner to be announced, and then he would head to the Stumble-Out or the Boudoir. He sighed as ennui filled him.

"Why the long sigh?" Cailean asked. He sat on a chair across from Ewan. Cailean had the tall lanky grace all the MacKinnon brothers shared. His hair was darker than Ewan's but lighter than Alistair's. Concern flared in his hazel eyes as he watched his youngest brother.

Ewan grumbled and set the book beside him. "I'm hungry." He waited a moment, but Cailean was more patient. "That wee woman visited my worksite today!" He shook his head with incredulousness. "She kens no bounds of propriety."

"Helen Jameson visited you at work?"

"Aye, she was waitin' for me when I arrived. Did no' even try to hide from my men that she was there. Who, by the way, have started callin' me D.G." He rolled his eyes as Cailean burst into laughter at that. "I am no' disreputable!"

Cailean swallowed a chuckle. "You'd better hope you are, if the mothers start circling after you. You've always been too charming." He watched his brother with concern. "I know you hide in the saloons and the Boudoir to escape them and to ensure they leave you in peace. However, I fear your plan could be failing."

"A woman should wait for a man to show interest," Ewan sputtered.

"If that's the case, you'll be single forever," Annabelle muttered from the doorway. She rubbed at her belly before rolling her eyes at her brother-in-law. "I've told you before, Ewan, how you need to have slightly more progressive ideas about women."

Cailean shared an amused smile with his wife. "Helen cornered him at work today in front of his men." His smile widened as his wife's mouth dropped open. "Even you find that forward, darling."

"I would never …" she muttered. "What happened?" She moved into the room and sat next to Ewan on the settee.

"She said I had no' fully considered my options an' the good fortune I would have were I to marry one such as she." He glared at his brother and sister-in-law as they burst out laughing. "Ye think this is hilarious. But this is my life, an' I ken the newspaper woman will hear about it."

"Oh, after all the work you've done to cultivate the mystique of a scoundrel," Annabelle murmured as she swiped at a cheek.

"A *charming* scoundrel," Ewan said.

"C.S.," Cailean muttered, earning a glare from Ewan.

"Dinna start," Ewan said. He sighed and blew out a breath. "I dinna like that Helen is so desperate."

Cailean sobered. "Aye, she is. And it seems to be worsening." He flushed. "I know I should have told you this before, but I'd hoped nothing would come of it. Her mother cornered the reporter last week and wanted her to write a story about Helen's upcoming nuptials. She was cagey about who Helen was to marry, but Mrs. Jameson wanted to ensure there would be plenty of newsprint spent on her daughter's triumph."

Ewan groaned. "She canna mean me. I willna marry her. I dinna care how eager she is to leave her mother's home. I am no' weddin' the woman."

Cailean shook his head. "No, you aren't. We'd never want you to wed a woman you did not care for."

Annabelle took Ewan's hand. "We want you to wed for love."

A shadow crossed Ewan's face before he pasted on his carefree smile. "An' ye ken that will never happen." He squeezed Annabelle's hand. "Is dinner ready? I'm starvin'."

"And eager to escape the house tonight," Cailean muttered. He watched as Annabelle rose and moved to the kitchen. "You won't always be able to outrun your demons, Ewan."

Ewan ignored his comment, laughed, and slapped him on the back as he followed him into the kitchen for dinner.

~

News & Noteworthy: *Was it just me, or did you also see a certain young lady exiting the worksite of our town's most disreputable, albeit eligible, gentleman? I had thought sitting in a puddle of cow dung would have dissuaded her in her pursuit; however, it seems I was mistaken. Perhaps she is hoping the third time is a charm?*

The door to the print shop slammed open, the glass in the door rattling before it was pushed shut. "Dammit, J.P., you can't go around publishing this sort of thing," Warren snapped as he paced around piles of paper on the floor. "I thought I had helped the town hire a reasonable reporter with experience, even if you are only twenty-seven years old. I've had one MacKinnon after another in my office badgering me about your articles."

She looked up from typesetting her latest edition and shrugged. "If they were truly concerned, they'd ensure Ewan stopped acting in such a way as to garner the reporter's attention." Her red hair flowed down her back like a river of fire, pulled together with a loosely tied ribbon.

"There are libel laws, J.P. The MacKinnons are smart enough to know about them and to use them if needed." He sighed as he ceased pacing and leaned against a wall near her raised printing press. "You could write about plenty of other stories in town where you didn't have to focus on the MacKinnons."

"So is it that I'm overstepping the boundaries of the law that concerns you or your friendship with the MacKinnons?" She raised an eyebrow, her gaze mocking in her assessment. "I will not be cowed into writing meaningless twaddle simply because there are those in town offended."

"This could harm your status as a serious reporter." He raised his eyebrows as though in warning.

She snorted as she turned away and sorted through a tray, looking for a specific letter. "As though that concerns me. I live in Bear Grass Springs, for heaven's sake." She found the letter and placed it in the typeset. "Do you know my sales have increased threefold since I started writing more on the *N&N* and *F or F* sections?" She smiled as she worked, her hands blackened by ink. "People like gossip."

"They like news too," Warren growled.

She blew out a puff of air. "I write plenty about the goings-on in the world. In the Territory. And I've yet to receive one letter or one comment when I'm walking through town about my news pieces. If the townsfolk want to focus more on the goings-on of their town and neighbors, who am I to complain?"

"You fuel gossip that could harm others, J.P. I thought better of you."

She glowered at him as she leaned over the printing tray. "Then that was your mistake. I am a reporter and a damn fine one. I'm also a businesswoman, and I must make a living off my work. This may not be Saint Louis, but people are the same everywhere. What interests them is what will affect them. I will continue to publish what I know my reading public wishes to read."

Warren clamped his jaw shut. After a moment he asked, "Even if you destroy others' reputations in the process?" He flushed as her sharp gaze focused on him for the first time.

"Is there something more you aren't telling me? Will your relationship with Sorcha MacKinnon be affected by my articles?" She looked chagrined for a moment before amusement shone from her eyes. "I thought her more of a firebrand than that."

Warren pushed away from the wall. "Talking to you is worse than speaking to a brick wall. You'll never see another's point of view."

"Not when you are attempting to prevent me from publishing what I want. I have every right to print my articles, Warren."

He huffed out an agitated breath and spun to leave. He looked over his shoulder at Jessamine. "One day I fear you will regret your actions. And you will have no one to blame but yourself."

~

That evening Jessamine locked up her print shop. She paused on the boardwalk in front of her shop, watching as men entered the Stumble-Out and a few wagons rumbled down Main Street. She nodded to Mr. Finlay as he made a show of locking up the front door of the bank.

As she turned toward the café, she jumped as a figure emerged from the shadows of the buildings. "Gettin' friendly with the banker?" Walter Jameson drawled as he stood in front of her. Although not a tall man, he loomed over her short frame. The muscles in his shoulders and arms flexed as he crossed his arms across his chest, a testament to the hours he had recently spent toiling in the nearby mines.

"Please allow me to pass, Mr. Jameson." She took a step to walk around him, but he matched her move, his mocking grin meeting her glare.

"Now why should I do that for the woman intent on ruining my sister's life?" He spat a thick wad of chewing tobacco near the tip of her boot and took a step closer to her.

She ignored his attempt to intimidate her and held her ground. "I should think that was your role. You've done a wonderful job of it so far."

He bent down, his fetid breath mixed with coffee and whiskey wafting over her face. "How dare you imply I am not concerned about my sister's welfare." His greasy brown hair fell over his shoulders but did not obstruct the fire in his brown eyes.

"You will never convince me that your concern for your sister is genuine. I know men like you." She shook her head with disgust as that comment made him puff up with pride as though she had praised him. "You see her as valuable as long as you hope to gain something from her."

She gasped as he gripped her arm in a punishing hold. "Your articles are making her a laughingstock in town. They are ruining her reputation. You must cease writing about her."

She jerked on her arm but was unable to free herself. "If you are that concerned, perhaps you should speak with the lawyer about a lawsuit."

Walter scowled. "That man is contemptible and will never be worthy of my sister."

Jessamine frowned in confusion as she attempted to discern the riddle of his words. "Is that because you are unable to manipulate him as you would like?" Her cognac-colored eyes lit with amusement as she saw agreement in his gaze. "I've always wondered why you never encouraged your sister to approach Mr. Clark."

Walter opened his mouth as though to say something and then clamped it shut again.

"There is a story here," she murmured.

He leaned forward until she arched away from him, her arm still in his hand's vise. "You will cease your interest in my sister. She will marry a MacKinnon this time."

"What happens if she doesn't?" Jessamine asked, ignoring the ache in her arm.

"She will discover what happens when she disappoints Mother and me." He smiled malevolently as Jessamine shivered at his words.

After a moment she leaned forward as though desirous of a more intimate conversation with him. She saw interest flare in his eyes a second before her boot heel struck the toe of his boot. She wrenched her arm free as he yelped in pain. "Don't ever think to hold me against my will again, Mr. Jameson. For I believe the lawyer is respectable. Perhaps it is you who is beneath our regard and thus not worthy of speaking to the lawyer."

She pushed past him, walking at a rapid pace toward the café.

Fact or Fiction? *For our latest edition, I have a woodsman's tale from a miner at the Obsidian Camp. Is it **Fact or Fiction**?*

According to local legend, the ghost of a cougar haunts our peaceful town on dark, lonely nights, especially on moonless nights, emerging from shadows when you least expect it. Valuables and perishables disappear after each sighting, and some in town refuse to leave home after dusk due to their fear of meeting with the wretched ghost.

It all began around the time of the town's inception, when Bear Grass Springs was known as Bachson. One day town cofounder Mr. Bachman stumbled into town, bloodied and battered, his clothes in tatters, dragging the carcass of a cougar behind him. The cougar, half starved after the harsh winter and dry summer, had leaped from his perch in a tall tree, tasting success with each bite until the brawny man wrestled with the mad beast and broke its neck. Not one to wait for help, Mr. Bachman emerged from the forest and into the town's only saloon, demanding a stiff shot of whiskey before he was patched up.

*You tell me. Is this **Fact or Fiction?***

E wan entered the café and sat at a table toward the middle of the room. He nodded to Harold and sipped appreciatively from a cup of coffee placed in front of him. He had foregone a lunch at home and had decided to visit with Harold and Irene while also grabbing a quick meal. He leaned back in his chair as he listened to the men near him debate the latest newspaper article.

One man doggedly argued for fact, while the other dug in his heels that it was fiction.

"All's I know is that I've seen that ghost a time or two," the man behind Ewan said in a deep voice. "I hate bumping into it after I leave the Waterin' Hole."

"You see it because you're leaving the saloon! You're too drunk to know what you're looking at," said his friend in a slightly higher-pitched voice.

"No, I've seen that cougar, and it's always a harbinger of ill will," the first man said. "Besides, you should not speak ill of the dead. Mr. Bachman suffered at the hands of Mr. Erickson before he died."

The friend snorted. "They were drunk scoundrels, and you know it. I'll think what I like about our town founders. That journalist didn't even bother to mention our other town founder in her tale."

Ewan fought a smile and met Harold's amused glance as he ignored the bickering friends. "What do ye think?" He nodded his thanks for the coffee refill and the bowl of venison stew with a thick piece of bread.

"What I think and what I know are two entirely different matters," Harold said with a laugh. "That young journalist is smart. Someone fed her a tale about Liver-Eating Johnson, and you all enjoyed it." He watched as Ewan flushed with embarrassment. "He never had no wife living in the wilderness, and the only Indians he had problems with were the Sioux."

Ewan frowned. "Now ye'll tell me that his name was no' Johnson."

Harold shrugged. "It's easy to reinvent yourself in a place like our Montana Territory. I imagine a man such as he did the same." He chuckled. "To make that man's actions sound honorable, oh, what a farce!"

Ewan crossed his arms over his chest as he studied Harold for signs of trickery. "How did he earn his name?"

Harold shook his head. "How would I know? I imagine some fool he was with gave it to him, and it stuck. Why is Fast-Draw Larson called that? We all know he'd be dead before his pistol left his holster if he were ever in a duel."

Ewan huffed in frustration. "Ye'll no' distract me from this discussion. Is that Johnson no' a lawman now?"

Harold shrugged. "I think he was for a time near Billings. He might still be. But he was no hero and he never outsmarted an Indian tribe."

Ewan blew on a spoonful of the hot stew as he again focused on his meal. "I imagine yer grandsons ken him."

Harold shook his head. "They have no reason to know the sheriff of Red Lodge." Then he laughed. "And, if they do, I don't want to know about it." He watched Ewan. "What do you reckon about the newest tale?"

"Seems fiction to me. I walk home late most nights, an' I've never seen a ghost." He shivered. "But I ken ye shouldna doubt them. That's when they make themselves known, ye ken?"

Harold laughed. "You Scots always were superstitious." He slapped Ewan on the back. "I would say I wouldn't put such a yarn past either one of those men. Except they would have found a way to make money off of it." Harold chuckled. "If it had happened, the poor beast's pelt would be enshrined in the Hall!" He fought another chuckle and moved on to the next table.

After eating, Ewan returned to the worksite behind the café which buzzed with his men working and with conversation about the cougar ghost. Consensus among his men was that there most likely was a ghost but that the man would have stabbed the cougar, not broken its neck. "So ye think it's both fact and fiction?" Ewan asked as he swiped a hand over his forehead, smearing wood dust into his sweat.

Ben nodded. "Yeah, that would make the most sense. Nothing else does."

Ewan laughed. "The whole story sounds like a pile of horse dung to me." He scratched at his head before hefting a board.

Ben shrugged as he held the board in place, and Ewan began to hammer. "Perhaps, but it's a darned good story. I can't wait to see what she writes next week."

Ewan studied Ben a moment, frowning at the excitement in his eyes before he glanced at his men. "Are ye intent on purchasin' her paper now?"

Ben nodded. "It doesn't cost much, and I had to wait until almost noontime to read the copy passed around today. I want to see what she publishes next week." He called out to one of the men to bring Ewan more nails.

Ewan nodded his thanks as he continued to hammer in the board with ease and efficiency. "I wonder if this will finally bring her success."

Ben's smile broadened as he watched his friend. "Among her *News and Noteworthy* column, the town's fascination with you, and now with this newest section, I think she will be as successful as a small-town newspaperwoman can be."

∽

E wan knocked on Alistair's door, slapping his brother on the shoulder as he answered. He shucked his jacket and hung it on a peg by the door before following his brother into the living area to the right of the main hallway. The house was similar to Cailean's, with a sitting room on one side of the house and a large room with a kitchen and dining area on the left. A staircase in the hallway led to three bedrooms upstairs, rather than four as in Cailean's house.

Ewan warmed his hands over the stove for a moment before sitting in a chair beside Cailean. "Why did ye want to meet with us here rather than at the family house?"

Alistair shrugged. "Leticia wanted time with Anna, and Hortence likes to play with her aunt, Sorcha. Seemed easier for us to meet here and to let them have their time without us at the bigger house." He smiled as he thought about his wife, Leticia and daughter, Hortence. "Hortence was restless, and I dinna think she would have been happy remainin' here."

"Ah, wee Hortence. She's a good lass," Cailean murmured.

Alistair nodded as he thought about his daughter, whom he had considered his own long before he had formally adopted her. "Aye, although I worry she's sufferin' due to that journalist."

Ewan frowned. "Why? That woman hasna written more about her after that horrible comment in the newspaper the first week she was in town." He shook his head as he thought about Jessamine picking on a young girl because her father was a thief and a liar. Thankfully, the MacKinnons were well respected, and Alistair had made it clear he considered Hortence his daughter. Few were willing to risk angering Alistair, and Jessamine had never written about her again.

Alistair stared at the stove a moment and swallowed as though trying to control his rage with as much ease. "I'd forgotten how cruel we were when we were children."

Cailean furrowed his brow. "Were we cruel?"

Ewan shrugged as he stretched his legs in front of him and slouched in his chair. "We teased wee Angus MacDonald for believin' his father a great war chief."

Alistair winced. "Poor wee bugger was naught but a bastard. Needed to believe in somethin', and we lorded over him that we went home to our own da every night." He sighed. "This is what I mean."

"Teasin' never killed anyone, Alistair," Cailean said.

"Nae, but it can kill your spirit. An' I'm afraid 'tis killin' wee Hortence's, an' she's just seven years old." He shared a worried glance with his brothers. "Ye ken how Hortence doesna like her red hair? How the children tease her about it?" The brothers nodded. "I learned today it has only worsened since that journalist arrived."

Ewan sighed. "Ye canna blame the poor woman for havin' red hair!"

"Nae, but she isna makin' friends. An' she acts outside the bounds of propriety. There are whispers she kens more than she should about the Boudoir." Alistair glared at Ewan as he burst out laughing.

"I've never seen the woman there, an' I'm there most nights. I imagine those rumors were started by men she spurned. Or by Mrs. Jameson."

Cailean tilted his head to one side as though in deep contemplation. "Either way, it doesn't help Hortence. She already battled terrible teasing with her red hair last year. What do the children say now?"

Alistair clenched his jaw and then his fist, his eyes a molten brown. "That she willna ever marry, as no man could love a red-haired woman. That she will end up alone, like the journalist, despised and unwanted."

"*Eejits!*" Ewan yelled. "How can they say such things to a wee lass?" He frowned as he looked at Alistair. "Hortence kens none of that's true, does she no'? She kens we love her and always will?"

Alistair shrugged. "I think so, but she has doubts."

Cailean growled. "She should only have certainty."

Alistair rose and paced. "'Tis near to tearin' Leticia's heart out," he rasped. "An' my own. I dinna ken how to soothe this hurt."

Ewan rose and grabbed his brother by the shoulder. "Ye do what ye've always done, Al. Ye show them yer love every day. With yer constancy. Yer kindness. Yer compassion. This will pass."

Alistair shook his head. "I fear too many remain angered over Leticia's deception this summer. I should have kent better than to believe a party and a piece of cake would soothe their ire."

Cailean snorted. "No one in this town is above reproach. If we don't know that, we soon will with all the reporter is publishing." He sat in deep thought a moment. "From what I hear, the new teacher has little control over the classroom, and many parents are yearning for the days when Leticia was the teacher. That sentiment will spread, and her deception will be forgotten as the townsfolk remember her dedication to the children she taught."

Alistair sighed and sat again. "I hope what ye say is true, Cail. But waitin' for that day is a challenge. An' I canna wish for Leticia's agony to ease at the expense of the new teacher."

Ewan shook his head. He remained standing and leaned against a window frame. "Do ye ken I've never seen him in command of his students when I walk by the school? I pass by frequently on my way to the sawmill. All I see is chaos an' mayhem."

Cailean shared a rueful look with Ewan. "I wonder how long he'll remain in Bear Grass Springs?"

Alistair sighed. "An' the problem is no' that we need a new teacher. It's that we need a second. Forty-four students is too much for one, and Leticia kent that. If we had money for another teacher, everything would be different."

Ewan shrugged. "You ken there are those in town who dinna want to spend the money on the one teacherage, never mind two." He shook his head. "How do they think the wee ones will succeed if they are ignorant?"

Cailean snorted. "*Ignorant* and *uneducated* are two different things, and you well know it. Plenty of those same people who would deny the children an education had one, and they are the most ignorant in town." He sighed. "However, from what I hear at the livery, townsfolk are most interested in other improvement projects. If all the tax money were focused on the school, there would be discontent."

Alistair sighed. "Aye, especially considering we are plannin' to add a gamblin' tax." He shook his head. "Timmons eyed my pitchfork with a bit too much interest today when he visited the livery. Seemed interested in stabbin' me with it."

Ewan scoffed as he thought about the owner of the Stumble-Out Saloon. "He's too worried about the profits he makes from the gamblers."

Alistair shrugged. "'Twould be a help if that reporter were less sharp tongued and in favor of what we propose. Instead she seems most interested in inciting unease and mistrust."

Ewan moved to sit next to his brothers. "Aye, Warren couldna have done a worse job in his choice of reporter. However"—he made a motion with his hand as though returning to their original topic—"'tis no' her fault she has red hair, no more than it is Hortence's. An' although I dinna like all she reports, she should no' be judged by appearances any more than anyone else."

Alistair snorted. "Perhaps. But she should ken that someday she will wish for friendship, rather than animosity."

Cailean nodded. "Aye." He smiled as Ewan looked pleased at the prospect of the reporter receiving her just deserts.

CHAPTER 3

News & Noteworthy: *One wonders why a man, who reportedly adored his son, left him at the mercy of others. If the MacKinnon family did not fear having the man at their home, wouldn't they offer him a bed in the house rather than expect him to live in the tack room and to sleep on a cot? It makes one wonder if they are more concerned than they tell the townsfolk that savage blood wins out. The father's death did seem precipitously fast ...*

*E*wan entered the new worksite in mid-October and glared at his men. "I dinna want to hear about anythin' that woman wrote." He stormed to the side of the room, where he had a work-bench and plans tacked on the wall. He leaned on the bench, his hands gripping the wood with such ferocity that his knuckles turned white. After a few deep breaths, he focused on the drawing in front of him.

"Ewan," Ben whispered.

Ewan held up a hand and took a deep breath. "I dinna want to talk about the vile filth spewed in her column today." He glared at his friend and worker.

Ben nodded and lowered his voice to the point Ewan barely heard him. "I understand. But the men are upset. And I've heard mumblings about starting a group to liberate your family from such a danger."

Ewan threw down the pencil and shook his head. "Dammit!" He let out a piercing whistle that sounded over the sawing and nailing. His men spun to face him, ceasing their work. "I will have yer attention."

He waited until each man in his seven-man crew met his gaze. "I ken ye are all good men. Decent men. An' ye want to ensure that we are all safe and secure in our town." He watched as the looks in his men's eyes became calculating and guarded. "However, I must warn ye, just because somethin' is written in a newspaper does no' make it fact."

"Are ye sayin' the lovely redhead is a liar?" a man named Olaf called out.

"Nae. But I would say she was misinformed." He held up his hands as the men muttered among themselves. "Ye ken everything she writes about me is a mixture of truth and exaggeration. If ye canna trust me to tell ye the truth, ye should no' work for me." He stared into each man's eyes, waiting until each man nodded.

"The fact is that Bears is a trusted partner of the MacKinnon family. He works hard, never complains, and has no wish to live in the main house. I've been working in my free time to build him his own place behind the main house and beside the paddock. It's the least the MacKinnons can do for a valued partner."

He paused as the men considered what he said. "Any man who kent Jack Renfrew, who saw him with his son, saw the dedication the man and son had for the other. To doubt it is to dishonor Jack and Bears." Ewan's jaw ticked. "And the townsfolk, with all their gossiping, kent well enough that Jack died of cancer. I want to hear no more talk about any nonsense in that newspaper. I want to hear no more talk of harming Bears."

The men's shoulders stooped, but Ewan could feel the restless energy of the morning dissipating. He half smiled and motioned for them to continue their work. He nodded to Ben and returned to studying the plans for this particular project.

∾

Jessamine looked up from her printing press and frowned as the door slammed open with such force she feared the glass would break. "If you break it, you pay for it."

"I hope the same is true for you, you heartless harpy," Cailean MacKinnon snapped. He slapped the day's paper onto the printing press, ruining the ink and paper waiting to be pressed. He met her irate glare, showing no contrition for his actions. "If I could, I'd throw the *bluidy* machine into the creek and ensure ye'd never print another article again."

She rolled her eyes. "All you would do is ensure I'd obtain a better press where the letters aren't so fragile and it is easier to print my papers." She smiled with triumph. "I have insurance against an angry mob."

"Do ye want to talk about a mob?" he asked, his accent reappearing in his anger. "I had to talk down a group of drunken idiots from the Waterin' Hole, intent on saving my sister and wife from the likes of Bears. With only a pitchfork to match their pistols." He shook his head as she stared at him with a look of innocence. "Do ye no' ken what ye've done?"

She closed her eyes at his bellow. "Yelling at me will not change my behavior."

"I wish something would. Nothing will make ye see sense, will it?" He strode away from her to the door and then back again, unable to rid himself of his nervous energy. "Do ye have any idea what they would have done to Bears had he been alone in the livery?"

She shrugged. "Roughed him up a bit. I'm sure he's suffered worse."

He lunged for her, stopping from touching her by the merest of inches. "Do ye no' have any idea what drunken men are capable of? What they do to a native born they think has been too highly favored?" He let out a long sigh. "How could ye act to flame the fires of their bigotry with no thought to whom ye'd harm?"

"I am not responsible for how others respond to my article."

Cailean slammed his hand onto a tall chest, the sound reverberating around the room and causing Jessamine to jolt. "Dinna act innocent, ye wee demon. Ye kent well enough what ye were doin'." His eyes flashed with enmity, and he took a deep breath. "I laughed and cajoled my brother every time you wrote about him. I assured him that you knew the bounds of propriety. But you don't."

"Mr. MacKinnon, I fail to understand why you are so affronted. Bears is a laborer who works for you. Nothing more."

He squinted at her as though she were a creature he had never seen before. "A *laborer?*" he scoffed. "Bears is one-third partner in the livery. And I'm proud to call him partner. His father was a trusted and valued friend. Bears is my equal and far superior to you in every way." He stormed out of her shop, slamming the door behind him.

When she looked out the window and saw his retreating form down the boardwalk, she took a shaky breath and collapsed onto a chair. After a moment, she swiped at her cheek, letting out a huff of frustration that a few tears had leaked out. "I will not be cowed from writing my stories," she whispered to herself. She cleaned her cheeks, pinched them, and pasted on a smile as she saw the lawyer walking toward her front door.

She rose and smiled impersonally. "Hello, Mr. Clark. How lovely to see you."

He dropped the newspaper at her feet. "I've defended you, J.P. I've assured the MacKinnons that you'd never stoop so low as to write something slanderous. However, I cannot defend what you wrote today. If they ask me, I will sue you."

She paled and tilted her head. "What if I desire to retain your services first?"

He shook his head, placing his hands on his hips. "I would refuse. I have some morals, and taking on a client who willfully disregards my advice while endangering the livelihood, if not the very life, of a man I greatly respect would go against everything I believe."

Jessamine half smiled. "I know it is not as bad as you are making it out to be."

Warren frowned as he looked at her. "Are you truly this naive? Aren't you a hard-nosed reporter from the East Coast? Haven't you faced the harsh realities of discrimination and hatred for no good reason before?"

She shrugged. "There are always two sides to a story."

"And there is a difference between gossip and news. Yet your goal in life seems to be to ensure that those in this town are forced to face the worst in themselves and each other. You could just as easily allow us to celebrate the good fortunes we have." He glared at her, and she remained silent. He started ticking off incidents with his fingers. "Ewan stifled a riot among his own men this morning who wanted to attack Bears. They only had hammers and saws, but they would still have wrought substantial damage to an unarmed innocent man. Cailean met an irate mob head-on with a pitchfork. How do you think pregnant Annabelle would have felt had her husband been accidentally killed by one of the men in the mob?" He waited as Jessamine remained mutinously silent. "Harold locked a group of men in the café until they saw sense. He used Irene's rolling pin to beat men away from the door."

Warren waited, his stance relaxing slightly as he saw guilt in her gaze. "Those are the three incidences that I am aware of so far. However, you have made Bears' life here a living hell. Did you feel he didn't have enough unwanted prejudice before this?" He paused as he glared at her. "You have raised suspicion and doubt where none were due. You have made the townsfolk jealous of his good fortune, which is uncalled for."

He shook his head as she refused to speak. "No matter what you do—an apology, a retraction in your paper—nothing will ever undo what you've done."

∼

Ewan sat at the poker table at the back of the main room of the Stumble-Out, his face impassive as he listened to the muted conversations of those around him. A private room upstairs was reserved for when the Madam joined them, as she preferred not to be seen gambling. A cloud of smoke hovered over the entire first floor, growing thicker as patrons smoked hand-rolled cigarettes and cigars. The wide-plank floors creaked as a drunken patron twirled a Beauty from the Boudoir in an impromptu dance, avaricious gazes of other men following the billow of her skirts as they stood at the long bar along one wall.

Ewan ignored all of this as he focused on his hand. He played with four of the fiercest cardsharks in the area, and he stood to lose a large amount that evening. One man's upper lip twitched involuntarily, and Ewan knew he was bluffing. The other three were a mystery, as he had yet to learn their tells after years of playing poker with them.

The first man said, "Call," and exposed his hand on the table—three of a kind.

Ewan's face remained inscrutable.

The next man groaned and threw in his cards.

Ewan set down his. "Straight," he said, maintaining an impassive expression.

Mr. Lip Twitch threw in his hand and glared at Ewan.

The man next to him set down his cards with a triumphant gleam. "Flush."

Ewan met the man's cocky smile and nodded. "Well done." He rose, grabbing his hat from the top of an empty table nearby, and moved to the bar. He motioned for the bartender to pour him a whiskey as he fought panic. He absently listened to the men next to him argue.

"I tell you," one said, "the poor bastard's never been the same since he got clubbed in the head by a moose hoof."

Ewan snorted and shook his head. He took a swig of whiskey and closed his eyes as he fought returning to the poker table. He stiffened as a hand slapped him on the shoulder.

"Well played but bad luck," a man with a deep voice rumbled.

Ewan nodded to the man who had won but did not motion for the barkeep to pour him a whiskey. *He could damn well pay for himself with his winnings*, Ewan thought. The man raised an eyebrow at Ewan's recalcitrance in sharing a drink with him and motioned for two drinks.

Ewan accepted a refill of his whiskey and saluted the man. "Well done," he said again before tossing back the shot.

The man leaned one hip against the bar, facing Ewan but also able to survey the rest of the saloon. "Thanks, although there's always luck involved in cards." He nodded to Ewan. "Your day will come."

Ewan grunted a noncommittal noise and took a small sip of whiskey.

"I hear a large poker tournament will take place soon. Held upstairs." He nodded up as though indicating the private room above the saloon.

Ewan shrugged. "I'm not certain that interests me."

The man motioned the barkeep for two more whiskeys. "Well, the winner would walk away with at least a year's salary." He looked at Ewan. "You're a MacKinnon."

Ewan gave a curt nod.

"The Madam will participate in that tournament. If rumor is to be believed, there is little she won't wager to win it all." He smiled when he saw understanding dawn in Ewan's eyes.

"I'll have to check my schedule," Ewan murmured.

The man chuckled and admiration lit his gaze. "Do that." He took a drag off a cigarette and then murmured, "I hear the native working for your family is causing you trouble."

Ewan stiffened. "Nae. He's a trusted partner. And friend." He met the man's speculative gaze. "An attack against him is an attack against a MacKinnon. I'd appreciate it if ye let those ye ken know that."

The man nodded, swallowed his whiskey, and then pushed away from the bar. "Better luck next time, MacKinnon."

Ewan watched as the man sauntered toward one of the two Boudoir Beauties on loan that evening to the Stumble-Out to help pay off the Madam's debts. After one last swallow of whiskey, Ewan slipped out the pine doors to home.

~

News & Noteworthy: *It seems Lady Luck is no friend to our favorite disreputable gentleman.*

Ewan joined his brothers at Warren's house the following evening. They declined Warren's offer of a drink and sat around the roaring fire, listening in quiet companionship a few moments as the wood crackled and hissed.

"Why did ye want us to come here tonight, Warren?" Ewan asked.

Warren settled into his high-back chair and steepled his fingers with his elbows resting on the chair's arms. "I wanted to discuss the last two publications released by J.P." He watched as the brothers scowled. "And if you planned on bringing a suit against her."

Alistair crossed his feet at his ankles as he relaxed in his chair. "'Twould serve the woman right." His brothers grunted their agreement. "Her apology, if those few lines could be called such a thing, were barely visible in the corner of the damn broadsheet."

Cailean nodded. "I agree. She has no sense of what she did." He shook his head as though dumbfounded. "And exhibited no remorse when I spoke with her."

"When did ye talk with her?" Ewan asked.

"I stormed into her office yesterday. After I was certain Bears would be safe, and Alistair was present." He took a deep breath as though calming his anger. "She seemed proud of what she had written."

Warren tapped his fingers together. "I think she is. I think she is proud of her ability to cause discourse in the town. Although intelligent, she hasn't learned to tell the difference between that and *discord*."

"An important distinction," Ewan muttered. "I havena spoken with her since she printed either paper. I ken she published the paper today as a way to apologize. However, her headline should have read, *'Journalist a Bluidy Fool and Begs Your Apology*,' rather than the tepid '*Facts May Be Misleading*' rubbish printed in a corner."

Alistair closed his eyes and scoffed, pulling out the latest paper to read directly from it. "*There is a time in every journalist's career when she must admit she was wrong. When she realizes she has harmed another due to misleading facts. Such an instance occurred yesterday, and I beg that Mr. Runs from Bears—and my reading public—will accept my apology.*

Cailean snorted. "Misleading facts? Why not call a lie a lie? Or a mistake a mistake?"

"Woman has too much damn pride," Warren muttered. "It will be her downfall."

Ewan looked at his brothers. "Ye are the two who work with Bears. What does he say? What would he want?"

Alistair shrugged and sat up, leaning on his elbows. "He wants to be left alone. He wouldna want a court case or any such suit against her as it would only cause him to receive more attention."

"I think he hopes the townsfolk will focus on another story or scandal and forget about him," Cailean said. "He has no desire to sue her and knows that he has no standing in the court."

"Aye, but *we* would," Ewan said. "Yer business was threatened yesterday. I had to warn away a cardshark last night."

Alistair and Cailean shared a long look. "We believe the livery is safe. And, in it, so is Bears."

Warren nodded. "What happens when he has his own home? A home that Ewan builds?" He watched the brothers shift uncomfortably. "Many in the town would want Ewan to build them a home but are financially unable to. When they see Bears receive such a home, their resentment will grow."

Ewan scratched his head, inadvertently sprinkling wood dust on the parlor floor. "I dinna ken how to ease their feelings, Warren. Bears is my brothers' partner. He works hard, and he asks for little. He did no' ask for the home. We would build one for any such worthy and reliable partner in need of winter lodgings. Anyone with sense kens Bears is good with horses. None should be threatened by him."

Warren raised his eyebrows. "As we know, too often too few have any sense. Especially when they put their heads together."

The men were silent for a few moments before Cailean nudged Ewan with his foot. "What did she mean when she wrote that Lady Luck is not your friend?"

Ewan flushed. "I've had a short string of bad luck." His carefree smile failed to alleviate Cailean's worried gaze. "I'm sure 'twill turn around soon."

"Or ye could give it all up," Alistair said. He ignored Ewan's glare. "I ken this has been Cailean's battle with ye, but I agree with him. Ye should no' be wastin' yer hard-earned money on such a foolish endeavor."

Warren rose and exited a door down a hallway, granting the brothers some privacy for their conversation.

"I dinna tell either of ye how to live yer lives!" Ewan flushed as he stared at his brothers, his gaze filled with disappointment as they scowled at him.

Cailean took a deep breath and pinched the bridge of his nose. "We have money now, Ewan. If you were to be in financial difficulties, we could help you. But our families will grow. And soon. We will have other responsibilities. There will be no further partnerships. No other ways to make such ready cash." Cailean shook his head. "I will not be able to help you in the future."

"What are you talking about?" Ewan whispered.

"I had a visitor today at the livery. Mr. Timmons." He watched as Ewan paled and slouched in his chair. "It appears you are out of credit, brother."

Ewan clenched and unclenched his hands as he fought panic that the owner of the Stumble-Out, Mr. Timmons, had visited Cailean today. "I'm sure he was merely concerned about his horse."

Cailean frowned at Ewan's words. "Nae. He wasn't. He worried you would be unable to pay him the exorbitant amount you have on credit." Cailean shook his head in wonder. "Do you owe a similar sum at the Boudoir?"

Ewan flushed and swore under his breath. "Do ye think I go around town, beggarin' myself and runnin' up credit?" His eyes flashed with hurt as he saw doubt in his brother's gaze. "Nae. I owe no money to the Madam."

Alistair sighed. "Ye have a good business, Ewan. Ye have a good income. There's nae reason for ye to lose it all on a toss of the cards. I dinna understand this restlessness ye feel."

Ewan glared at Alistair. "I'm not like ye, Al. I need adventure. I need excitement. An' there is little in this town to provide that."

Alistair shared a look with Cailean and shook his head. "Ye were no' like this on Skye. Then ye were never more content than to roam the hills, losing yerself as ye wandered among the streams as ye searched for fairies. Ye never had such desires then."

Ewan stood, his hands clenched and his body visibly vibrating. "I'm no' the lad who lived on Skye." He stormed from the room and slammed the door behind him.

Alistair and Cailean let out long breaths and eased back against their chairs. "That went well," Cailean muttered.

"Seems like it went as it always does when ye speak to him about his gamblin'," Alistair said. He heaved out a breath. "When will ye tell him that ye've paid this debt?"

"When he's calmed down enough to hear me." He paused as he stared into the fire, the logs transformed into embers. He rose and tossed on a new log. "How can I threaten him this will be the last time?"

Alistair raised his eyebrows. "I think it has to be, Cail. Otherwise he'll never change."

~

E wan walked down Main Street the next afternoon, smiling to those he knew and ignoring many curious stares. He entered the print shop, ruefully aware that the town's sense of intrigue surrounding him would only rise at this visit. His smile faded as he saw Jessamine's frown at his entrance. "Ye had to ken I'd visit ye."

She swiped her ink-stained hands on the apron covering her teal dress. Somehow the color did not clash with her red hair but complemented it. "I had hoped, after a visit with your brother and the lawyer, and my apology yesterday, that I would be spared any further interaction with you."

"*Apology?*" Ewan asked, pulling the previous day's special edition from his pocket. "Ye call that twaddle an apology?"

She lifted her chin and nodded. "Yes. I am a journalist. There are times when a journalist must admit to having harmed another due to misleading facts."

"Ye should just call them lies. We ken well enough what they were."

"I did not lie. I was misinformed."

He paced toward her, his face reddening and his breath emerging in pants with his anger. "Ye canna even apologize in a manner that appears contrite. Ye must attempt to make yerself look a victim too." He shook his head. "Ye were a fool, and God only knows why."

She matched his step forward until they were almost chest to chest. "I was not a fool. I made a mistake. Or am I not allowed to make those? Am I to be held to a different standard than other journalists because I'm a woman?"

Ewan sneered at her. "Dinna act offended now because I doubted yer abilities because ye were a woman. If ye want to act as hardened and as mean as a man, that's yer right. But ye'd be far better off showin' this town that ye have soft sensibilities to go along with yer intelligence."

She clamped her jaw shut as she glared at him and breathed out a huff. "No man would be told to highlight his tender side. No man would be damned because he had the daring to challenge commonly held beliefs."

He shook his head in confusion and backed up. "I told ye afore, an' I tell ye again. Ye're daft, woman. Ye try to be a man, when ye have plenty to offer as a woman." He watched as her glower intensified with his comment. "An' I dinna mean as a wife and a mother. I canna imagine a man daft enough to want to wed ye."

He backed up as she punched him in the arm. "How dare you?" she shrieked.

"Oh, so ye dinna like it when someone speaks about ye without knowin' ye? When they cast aspersions on yer character?" He watched her with anger-lit eyes. "Now ye ken just a little what ye did to Bears. Only I'm no' here with a pistol, wanting to harm ye."

She spun away from him and took a deep, stuttering breath. "I've said I'm sorry." Her voice emerged low, with each word carefully enunciated.

"Aye, in your journalistic way, ye have. But ye have no' shown remorse. No' to me, no' to the town. And especially no' to Bears." He waited, but she remained turned away from him. "Are ye crying?" He touched her shoulder gently, stilling his touch when she stiffened.

"There's no excuse for having printed what I did," she whispered. "I knew, deep inside, I knew I shouldn't print it. And yet I did."

"Why, Jessie?" he whispered.

She spun to stare at him in confusion at the nickname. She took another step back to the point she was at the edge of the raised dais. "I, ... I heard the story, and I thought it would make good copy. Almost like another *Fact or Fiction* section."

"It would have been better there if ye must print such trash."

She closed her eyes. "I should have known better."

"Ye have plenty to offer this town without pandering to the worst among us. Ye dinna want to be held in the same estimation with the likes of the town's two meanest gossips, Mrs. Jameson or Tobias, do ye?" He saw her bite her lip. "Ye should ken that."

"This type of story is how I made my name in New York. In Saint Louis. The more sensational, the greater my readership and the greater my salary." She lowered her head. "I never had to face those I affected with my words."

He raised a hand, slowly reaching out to her. He traced his fingertips down her arm, from her shoulder to her hand. After clasping her hand, he gave her a slight tug so she took a step toward him. "Ye should have kent things would be different in a small town. Everyone knows everyone else, and there's always talk. Ye canna lose yerself in the crowds like ye can in a city."

She nodded and sniffled. "I make you no promises, Mr. MacKinnon. This is who I am as a reporter. If I were to change, I don't know who I'd be." She squirmed under his intense stare, finally breaking away from his gaze and looking at her feet.

"Ye might surprise yerself at who ye could be. At who ye would choose to be, not who ye were expected to be." He squeezed her fingers and backed away, pausing as she began to speak.

"I will promise you one thing," she whispered. "I will apologize to Bears."

He nodded, approval and something else he quickly hid glinting in his gaze. "Aye, that's a good start, Jessie." He gave her a quick smile and shut the door quietly behind him.

~

Jessamine crept into the livery, frowning to see no one at work inside the barn. Horses slumbered in their stalls, and the paddock door was only one-quarter open, letting in fresh air but allowing most of the barn to remain warm. She tiptoed down the long center aisle until she reached the last stall, her shoulders slumping as she failed to find anyone present. For some reason, she had no desire to call out and destroy the peace pervading the livery.

She approached a horse in a far stall, reaching out to him. It whinnied and butted at her hand. When it nibbled at her fingers, she giggled and snatched her hand away. "I don't have any treats for you, beauty."

"That's Brindle," a man with a deep voice said from the shadow by the tack room.

Jessamine yelped and spun in the direction of the voice. She held a hand to her chest, her eyes huge as she met Bears' amused gaze. "I beg your pardon. I did not see you there."

He nodded, the amusement never fading from his eyes although he did not smile. After a moment, he moved closer to her, and his long raven-colored hair shimmered in the faint light as though shot with blue. His eyes so dark they appeared black never wavered from her, and he moved with an unconscious grace.

She lowered the hand from her chest and held it out to him. "I'm Jessamine McMahon, and I'm here to apologize."

He looked at her hand and then at her face before shaking his head. He moved to stand next to her and held out a hand to Brindle, scratching behind the horse's ears. "Are you here to write about how a mixed-blood has the audacity to touch a white woman?"

"What?" Jessamine gasped. She flushed with indignation and then embarrassment. "Of course not. I am sincere in my desire to apologize. I truly hope you will be able to forgive me."

Bears made a low noise in his throat before he backed away from the stall's edge. "I don't need to offer my forgiveness, ma'am. You need to forgive yourself." He turned away from her with a nod of his head that appeared deferential but seemed mocking instead.

"Wait," she snapped, grabbing him by his arm as she attempted to spin him around to face her. She grunted with exertion to realize he was much stronger than he appeared with his long-limbed, lanky build. She took a step back as his gaze flashed with fire. "I beg your pardon."

"As you should. You've brought enough chaos upon those I call friends." He waited as the anger left his gaze, and a smoldering derision remained. "If you want to prove your contrition, your actions will show how you've changed." He nodded to her again and walked toward the end of the barn where he pulled himself up a ladder to the loft overhead.

She let out a deep breath and leaned against the stall. "Well, I never," she muttered. She jolted as Brindle bumped her side with her snout, and she turned to pat Brindle on the nose.

Hearing a throat cleared, she looked in the direction of the tack room.

"I imagine you've never been put in your place." Cailean MacKinnon stood there with a half smile, his arms crossed over his chest, leaning on the doorway.

"What is it about you men who work in this livery? Why weren't you about when I entered?" She stomped a foot and flushed as she realized she was acting like a petulant child.

Cailean chuckled. "Our customers know to call out a welcome when they enter. That way they won't have to wait before we attend to them." His smile broadened as he saw how uncomfortable she was. "Of course you were uncertain of your welcome."

She shook her head, her hands on her hips, the horse forgotten. "I did not care to ruin the peaceful atmosphere when I entered."

"*Hmph.* Said like a journalist. Or a lawyer." His gaze hardened, belying his relaxed pose. "We won't allow you to bring harm to Bears."

She glared at him. "I was trying to apologize, but he wouldn't let me!"

Cailean pushed away from the wall and approached her. "So I heard. Now it only remains to be seen if you will take his words to heart."

She pointed to the loft and furrowed her brow. "How could I possibly understand what he meant? If he won't forgive me, I won't beg for it."

Cailean shook his head as though disappointed. "I know you aren't a stupid woman. You have to be remarkably smart and tenacious to do what you do." He paused. "I would think over what Bears said." He nodded as she let out a huff of frustrated breath and marched down the livery's long center aisle.

≈

Cailean joined Ewan and Alistair on the porch as they awaited supper. Sorcha, Leticia, and Annabelle had *shoo*ed him outside when he complained about Annabelle working too much. He met his brothers' amused smiles.

"Seems ye were evicted from yer own home," Alistair said with a chuckle. He smoked his pipe and stared at the paddock and livery, the mountains in the distance.

"They do not understand that Belle should not exert herself."

Ewan laughed, earning a scowl from his eldest brother. "Ye have to be more tactful, Cail. I can only imagine how ye want to protect Anna after last year, but ye have to let her enjoy these last months before ye have yer bairn. Yer life will never be the same again when the time comes."

Cailean nodded as he sat with a *thud* on an upturned log. "I know what you say is true. Most days I can hide the panic growing inside."

Alistair nodded. "Anna understands yer fear, Cail. After last year, she kens."

Cailean nodded. "I dinna want to steal her joy in these moments." He let out a sigh. "What do ye ken about the new doctor?"

Alistair shared a long look with Ewan, as the resurfacing of Cailean's accent showed his agitation and concern. "I dinna ken the man yet."

"He seems intent on aiding the women at the Boudoir," Ewan murmured. "I hear he is there with great frequency."

Cailean frowned. "But what's the man like? Will he be able to help Belle?"

Ewan shook his head. "I wouldna focus on that man. I'd ensure the midwife is here. She's the reason Anna's still alive."

Cailean let his head rest against the side of the house, his eyes closing for a moment. "I wish the two of you had been at the barn earlier today. There was quite a scene." He opened his eyes to meet his brothers' curious, yet concerned, gazes. With a shake of his head he indicated he did not want to speak about his worries as to his pregnant wife anymore that night. "That reporter came by to apologize to Bears. And he wouldn't accept it."

Ewan sputtered. "Bears wouldn't? And she did?" His delighted smile spread. "'Tis nice to ken she keeps her word."

Alistair cocked his head to the side as he studied his pleased little brother. He took a puff on his pipe and then said, "Why should what she did please ye?"

"I confronted her yesterday. About Bears. About her pathetic attempt at a retraction in the paper. An' she promised she'd apologize to him directly."

Cailean laughed. "Bears said he'd not be forgiving her and that she needed to forgive herself." He smiled as his brothers stared at him, stupefied. "And that, if she wanted to prove the truth to her words, she would through her actions."

Alistair smiled and sighed with satisfaction. "Bears is a canny man. Why should he let her believe a simple apology would suffice? He's right. Her actions will speak louder than anything she could print."

CHAPTER 4

A brisk wind blew, scattering golden and reddened leaves with strong gusts. Shorter days and longer nights, with a crisp feel to the air, acted as a harbinger of winter due to arrive earlier and more harshly than the previous year. Ewan scowled as he considered the amount of work needed to be accomplished before the first snow fell.

He entered the worksite and sighed as his men began to work twice as hard once he arrived. Ben worked nearby, and Ewan listened to a conversation the men were having. "I dinna understand what they're talkin' about."

Ben shrugged. "Seems that reporter put out a new paper this mornin' with another tall tale. The men are tryin' to determine if it's true."

Ewan grunted. "Most things that woman writes are blatant exaggerations." After a moment he muttered, "What was this one about?" He glared at Ben as his friend smiled at his question.

"Seems there was once an early settler who one day decided to ride his horse out on the prairie. He was an absentminded man, interested in nature, and he tethered his horse to a rock as he sat near a pretty cliff to look out over the beautiful expanse below him." He grinned at Ewan's snort. "Oh, no, it gets better."

Ewan raised an eyebrow and grinned at Ben. "If she wrote it, I can only imagine." He hammered in a nail and then set about measuring a board as he listened to his friend.

"As he sat, marveling at the wonder before him, a herd of buffalo hemmed him in place. His horse, the only sensible animal in this story, became skittish and broke free, scaring the buffalo. Some tumbled over the cliff to their deaths. Others swerved away, back to the vast expanse of the prairie. Our fine friend jumped off the cliff, to what he thought would be certain death, to escape a trampling by a buffalo."

Ewan raised an eyebrow. "An' there's doubt it's fiction?"

Ben laughed. "It's not over yet. He falls, thinking in an instant how wonderful his life had been and giving thanks for it, when he lands with a *thud* on a soft buffalo carcass. He's speared in the arm by one of the horns but is otherwise unscathed."

Ewan snorted in disbelief as Ben gave a short bow as though he were a fine stage actor. "Ye're as daft as she is." He listened to his men arguing in favor of the story being fact. "Ye all are if ye believe it's true."

Ben smiled as he picked up a handful of nails. "Haven't you seen the scar on Mr. Finlay's arm?" He shrugged. "And he loves nature."

Ewan shouted in pain as he accidentally hammered his thumb. "Are ye seriously insinuatin' that ye believe the banker, the puffed-up man who willna go anywhere if he's no' in satin or silk, would sit in a field and land on a buffalo carcass?" He shook his head and snorted.

"Then what is his scar from?" Ben demanded.

"I dinna ken. I had hoped he had earned it honorably, as many men in this country did when fightin' in their Civil War." He shrugged. "I dinna go lookin' for other people's secrets, Ben."

Ben nodded. "I imagine that's because you don't want them lookin for yours."

Ewan sighed. "Ye ken me. I've nothin' to hide." He shook his hammer at his friend. "An' dinna give me that rubbish about everyone havin' somethin' to hide." He sighed. "At least the story wasna about me this time."

"Her tall tales never are. Although each one is better."

Ewan rolled his shoulders as though attempting to alleviate tension. "I like the real ones. Teachin' us about the history of this place we call home." He met Ben's amused gaze. "I ken they're real 'cause they make sense. But it doesna make them any less remarkable. Someone had to live those stories, and I'm always filled with a mixture of happiness and regret that it wasna me creatin' such tales."

Ben laughed. "I'll always be thankful I wasn't Colter, running from the Blackfeet." He shook his head in wonder. "I can't imagine being stripped and told to run, knowing their fastest braves were behind me, intent on killing me."

Ewan shivered as he thought about the mountain man and explorer, John Colter. He had been an original member of the Lewis and Clark Corps of Discovery and had spent the majority of his life exploring the wild undiscovered-to-whites West. "He killed their fastest runner and then hid among downed logs in a river."

Ben shook his head. "No, he hid in a beaver lodge."

Ewan laughed. "How do ye expect a grown man to fit in a beaver lodge?"

His friend shrugged. "This is why they think all our stories, about men who truly lived, are tall tales."

Ewan nodded as he shared a smile with his friend. "Can ye imagine what he looked like, strollin' into that trader's post on the Little Big Horn River over a week later, naked as the day he was born, with his feet torn to shreds?"

Ben laughed. "I would think he was lucky not to have been shot on sight." He cast a quick glance at his friend. "I thought you'd be irate that the men were talking about the reporter and her stories today after how she treated Bears."

Ewan shook his head. "I ken now she's no' as I feared. An' that makes all the difference." He smiled as Ben looked at him in confusion before he slapped his friend on the shoulder and left him to work alone as he moved to supervise the men he had just hired that summer.

≈

News & Noteworthy: *One must wonder at the future of our beloved bakery as the proprietor can no longer deny the rumors of an impending most "interesting event." I wonder how long her husband will allow her to continue to work such long hours? Who in town will survive without our bakery?*

Annabelle sat at the kitchen table, rubbing her growing belly as she read and reread the *News and Noteworthy* section in the newspaper. She sighed, finally understanding Ewan's distaste for being singled out for comment. "It isn't ridicule," she said to herself.

"What isn't ridicule?" Cailean asked as he leaned down and kissed her nape. He smiled as his kiss evoked a quiver. "That damn woman. Why can't she focus on another family?"

Annabelle set aside the paper and placed a hand over Cailean's that now rested on her shoulder. "We fascinate her for some reason."

"She didn't write anything false, Belle." He half smiled. "Well, except for that part about me allowing you to do anything. She clearly doesn't know you well enough to understand you'll do what you like." After a moment's silence, he said, "I've spoken with Warren, and we can't shut her down." He moved and settled beside her. He frowned when he saw the concern in her gaze. "What is it?"

"She confirmed the town's suspicion that I am to have a child sometime next year. I worry that a new bakery will open, and I will lose my customers during the time my bakery is closed." She lifted a finger to her husband's lips. "I know it will be a challenge to work after the baby is born, but I love the bakery. I love baking."

"You won't have the time, love," he whispered. "Our bairn will take more time and energy than you imagine."

Ewan wandered into the kitchen, rubbing his belly. He stopped when he saw them and backed out. "Sorry to interrupt."

"No, you're hungry, and I'm being foolish," Annabelle said. "There's a plate of sandwiches in the icebox."

Ewan smiled and pulled out a plate for himself before extracting the sandwiches. He took one and then set the full plate in the middle of the round table. It took only a few moments for Cailean to grab one too. "She didna write anythin' terrible, Anna."

Annabelle shrugged.

Cailean swallowed his bite of sandwich and spoke. "Belle's worried that another might start a bakery in her absence."

Ewan nodded as he gobbled up another sandwich. He rose for a glass of water and then leaned against the kitchen counter. "Why should you have to close?"

Annabelle rolled her eyes. "There isn't anyone in town who I'd trust the bakery to. Who can bake what I bake." She flushed. "That sounds terribly conceited, but I know another bakery could spring up if someone could afford it."

Ewan shook his head. "Not everyone has the resources to start up another business. Have you spent much time with Leena Ericson?" When Annabelle stared at him blankly, he said, "Her brother, Nathaniel, runs the sawmill, and I've come to know him well the past few years. She cooks sweets like a dream, Anna. Almost as good as you, and she cooks different items, such as a delicious apple bread."

His gaze moved from Cailean to Annabelle. "Cail and Alistair took on a partner out of necessity this summer. Perhaps ye should consider a partner too. That way, yer bakery could remain open, and the Ericsons would not have to worry as much about money durin' the winter season."

Annabelle stilled. "I've never considered a partner. Other than Leticia, but she doesn't bake sweets like I do."

Ewan shrugged. "I understand ye wantin' to keep the bakery completely in the family, but sometimes that's no' possible. I'd consider a solution where ye could keep the bakery runnin', Anna." He drained his glass of water and left the kitchen.

Annabelle let out a deep breath and stared at her husband. "What do you think?"

Cailean tapped his fingers on the tabletop. "You've been saying for months that you could sell more goods if you had more help. Another baker would aid you. I wouldn't mind having more than one day a week where you were home with me." He brushed aside a tendril of her hair. "Besides, your dream isn't just the bakery anymore, is it?"

She met his gaze, frowning as he failed to hide the insecurity in his. She cupped his cheek, and a full smile bloomed as she looked at his beloved face. "Of course it isn't. It's us and our family and the life we are building. The bakery is only one part of it." She leaned forward and kissed him. "I love you, Cailean."

"I could not bear it if something happened to you or the bairn."

She rubbed her fingers over his stubble. "I know. I couldn't either." She took a deep breath. "Let me think over what Ewan suggested for a few days. If Leena is to work with me, she should start soon. I want her well-established at the bakery and accepted by the townsfolk before I have our baby."

~

Jessamine sat at a small table to the side of the café during a lull in customers. She had forgotten to eat lunch, and it was a short time before the dinner rush. Bright red calico cloths covered the tables, and small vases of dried flowers sat at the center of each one. She smiled warmly as Harold poked his head out of the kitchen doorway.

"I was just sayin' to Irene that you had missed your midday meal, and here you are. Trying to get a two for one?" he asked with a smile and a raised eyebrow.

"No, I was busy and forgot to eat."

"Well, you should never forget to eat if you're going to keep up your strength." He sighed as he looked at the menu board already wiped clean. "We have fried chicken with mashed potatoes and gravy or fish with the same."

"I'll have the chicken." She flushed. "Did Annabelle bring any dessert today?"

He chuckled. "Yes, and, since you are the first of the dinner crowd, you can choose anything you like." He winked before turning to call the order into the kitchen. He came back with the coffeepot and poured her a cup. "Now tell me about what you're working on."

She shrugged. "More tall tales."

He shook his head. "You've got the townsfolk in a dither over whether or not they're true."

She shook her head. "I think most knew of Colter's run." She blew on the coffee. "I shouldn't make them so obvious when they are true."

He laughed. "What you should do is have a piece of paper, like a voting slip, in your newspaper where they could vote if it is fact or fiction. Thataway you only have to write one of those columns a week, but people would buy each paper to see what their friends thought. And everyone would have to buy a paper to obtain an official vote." He wiggled his eyebrows at her.

"I always thought Irene was the brains behind this business, but I can see I might have been mistaken." She smiled with delight as she considered his plan.

He laughed. "I'm a lot like you. I chest my cards."

She frowned and shook her head.

"In poker, just as in life, you never show all you have, or don't have, too soon. That would be a disaster."

She giggled. "You are a rascal." Her smile widened as he seemed pleased by her comment. "I think the townsfolk like the N&N section."

His smile dimmed. "Well, as long as you are not too biting in your wit, it's fine. Don't threaten those who are vulnerable, Miss Jessamine. They will only be made more so, and it makes all of us weaker."

She frowned at his words, but then Irene arrived with her food, and Irene pushed Harold out of his seat and took his place. Irene smiled as Harold grumbled about dishes to be done.

Irene's smile grew as she watched Jessamine devour her dinner. "I knew there was something wrong when you didn't show for the midday meal. Harold told me that I was fussing worse than a mother hen, but I should have ensured you were all right."

Jessamine flushed. "I forgot the time." Her flush deepened when Harold emerged with a large slab of cake. "You don't have to feel responsible for me."

Irene shook her head. "You're determined not to let anyone care, aren't you?" Irene motioned for Harold to put down the dessert and then skedaddle. "However, I don't need your permission."

Jessamine took a bite of the cake and shook her head. "It's not that. It's more about how I'm unaccustomed to it."

Irene stared deeply into her eyes, before Jessamine broke eye contact and used her fork to cut off another piece of cake to eat. "I've all sorts of ideas about you and what happened to you in the past," Irene said. "It will be interesting to see which ones prove true." She rose as supper customers trickled in.

Jessamine finished her cake, left her coins on the table, and departed. She exited the café and paused a moment on the boardwalk, her gaze rising to the mountains above the town. She shivered as cool air replaced the earlier warmth of the mid-October day, and she had forgotten her shawl.

Sunlight glinted on the high mountain slopes above town. Streaks of golden orange broke the monotony of evergreen as the larch gave a burst of color before they lost their needles for the winter. She stared in wonder at the mountains a moment before shivering again and heading home.

Ewan rode back from a homesteader's plot of land and paused. He patted the side of the horse's neck and, closing his eyes, turned his face up to the warmth of the late afternoon sun. He opened his eyes as he heard the call of a gaggle of Canadian geese flying overhead and watched them soar above him. A soft breeze blew, rustling the golden leaves clinging to the cottonwoods that lined the creek.

Rather than rush back to one of his three worksites in town, he breathed deeply and relished the moment. His work would wait for him tomorrow. He dismounted and *clucked* for the horse to follow him to the creek, where he tied the reins to a tree. The horse nickered and then dozed in the sun. Ewan walked through waist-high dried-out yellowed grass and knelt by the creek. After dipping his bandanna in the frigid water, he wiped at his face.

Three merganser ducks flew low to the water, skidding to a landing not far from him. The creek trickled by, the water over rocks like a symphony and as soothing to Ewan. The sunlight enhanced the gold, orange, and red colors of the trees and bushes around him, giving it a mystical feel. He sighed as his stress eased from a hard season of work.

At a strong gust of wind, he looked up and saw gray storm clouds in the distance. He rose with a reluctant sigh and moved toward his horse. The ride into town took less than an hour, and he returned to the livery. Alistair and Cailean were inside as he led the horse to a clean stall. He curried the horse, smiling as his brothers stood in the hallway with their arms over the stall door, watching his movements.

"So, what did you say to Mr. Willems?" Cailean asked.

Ewan sighed. "It's mid-October, ye ken? Snow will be here soon if the last years are of any use in predictin' how things will go. Ye canna start constructin' a house now." He sighed with frustration.

Alistair frowned. "You could if it were a reasonable home."

Ewan shook his head. "He wants to pay me next year. After he sees how his winter wheat does."

Cailean growled. "No, you can't accept that sort of agreement." He nodded at Ewan. "You've always been an astute businessman."

Ewan scratched behind the horse's ear and leaned into its side. "That doesna make me feel better when I ken they'll be livin' in a one-room hut for another winter with two bairns. The poor woman looked desperate to have a better home."

Alistair sighed. "Well, I do know they are no' popular among the ranchers. They fenced off part of their land to keep out the cattle. Did no' want the 'horrible beasts' wanderin' in and ruinin' their crop."

Cailean scratched his head. "Makes you wonder why they ever chose to settle here. It's a land for cattle."

"Aye," Ewan said. "The ranchers are angry, an' I had more than one urge me no' to build them a home." He shook his head in disgust. "It's perfect land for cattle and for farming." His gaze gleamed as he thought of the valley. "'Tis beautiful land with the creek runnin' through it and a natural spring."

Alistair opened the stall door as Ewan emerged with the tack. "Well, they'll only have more trouble afore they're done. Should have chosen another place to settle."

"Ye never ken, Alistair. This area might need more than ranches to survive," Ewan murmured.

Cailean followed him to the tack room. "I'd go to the café for dinner tonight. Belle wasn't up for preparing dinner, and Sorcha is in the kitchen."

Ewan stilled as he rubbed his grumbling stomach. "I dinna eat at midday. I canna eat her food tonight, Cail." He patted his brother on his arm. "I have to check on the worksites. I might be home late."

Cailean laughed and slapped his brother on the back as he watched him go.

Ewan slipped out of the livery and headed down Main Street before cutting to the street behind the town's main thoroughfare. After a few minutes, he arrived at one of his worksites and entered. He frowned as he saw how little had been accomplished during his absence. "I need a site foreman," he muttered to himself. "I canna do this all on my own."

He left the site and walked through town. He glared at the well-lit print shop, imagining the stories concocted while at her desk. "Bothersome woman." He turned into the café and smiled at Harold who pointed to a table near the back.

After Ewan had ordered, and the evening crowd had died down, Harold joined him. "You look like a man who could use a little conversation."

Ewan sighed as he sipped his coffee. "Aye. I should have kent better than to come here when it was busy." He fought a smile and attempted a scowl as Harold laughed. "I'm tired of bein' the topic of conversation for the townsfolk."

Harold slapped a hand on the table as though he had just heard a great joke. "Of course you are. But you have to understand the towns-folk are enjoying how you are the one under scrutiny and not them. What you don't hear, because you are disgusted with the attention, is their relief at not being singled out."

Ewan frowned as he stared at his friend. "What do ye mean?"

"Before she arrived, we had a smattering of political debates, family quarrels, and too many manly boasts. Now, … now there are only discussions about articles in her paper, and no one reveals a secret."

After taking a sip of coffee, Ewan murmured, "Is it because they are concerned they will be the next scandal?"

Harold nodded, his eyes gleaming with appreciation that Ewan had figured out the townsfolk's concerns. "Unfortunately she has caused us to look at each other with suspicion and doubt."

"Would it be better if she rid the paper of N&N?"

Harold snorted. "Now no man is going to tell a woman as strong willed as she is what to do. You should understand that, son. And I think the townsfolk would miss the N&N." Harold met Ewan's confused gaze. "It's more the tone of it. The threat of meanness. If it were more in the way she writes about you, I think the townsfolk would be more at ease."

Ewan sputtered. "She ridicules me every chance she gets!"

Harold laughed. "Yes, but do you feel threatened by her words? Do you worry about what she'll write about you? Or are you amused?"

Ewan half smiled. "More often than not, I'm amused. Until she drags someone else into the story."

"Exactly," Harold said. "One of my favorites is still about you and the cow, before she inserted Miss Helen in the mess." He laughed as Ewan flushed. After a few moments of silence, Harold asked, "Are you going to build those interlopers a home?"

Ewan cocked his head to the side and stared at a man he considered an uncle. "Nae, they dinna have the money to afford one right now. Perhaps next year." He frowned as Harold grunted with satisfaction. "They have as much right as ye to be here, Harold. Besides, they actually own that land."

Harold snorted. "Possession is nine-tenths of the law. Ask that lawyer of ours." He tapped his fingers on the table. "Puttin' up fences, marring our good land with such an abomination."

Ewan chuckled. "Ye're just offended ye do no' own that prime piece of property. Ye canna own it all, Harold."

Harold shook his head. "And that's a damn shame." He looked outside as dusk turned to evening. "I imagine it was a beautiful ride through the valley today."

"Aye, 'twas."

Harold's gaze became distant. "I call this the Golden Season. For a few short weeks, the sun seems that much brighter as it shines on everything that is some shade of red, yellow, or orange. It's a time of possibilities." He met Ewan's gaze. "Everyone always talks about spring as a time of rebirth. I think now has just as much promise. This is a time when anything is possible."

CHAPTER 5

News & Noteworthy: *Imagine my surprise upon glancing out my window long before sunrise to find a woman, wholly interested in our most disreputable gentleman, scurrying home in the waning night shadows as morning neared. One wonders what secret rendezvous she returned from ...*

*J*essamine sat at her desk, her pencil still as she attempted to concoct more stories for her paper. She arched her back, stiffened from a long session typesetting her latest edition. As she massaged one shoulder, she closed her eyes as she imagined strong hands rubbing at the knots that had taken up a permanent residence in her shoulders and neck. As her door twinkled open, she dropped her hand and pasted on a smile as she turned to face her visitor.

"How dare you write such slanderous material about my innocent daughter?" Mrs. Jameson screeched as she marched into the print shop. She walked with stiff precision—probably brought about by her corset being bound nearly to the point of asphyxiation—and an air of entitlement, even though her navy-blue wool dress showed its age with its ragged hemline and worn collar. Her attempt to cover the collar with a scarf failed as it gaped open around her neck.

Jessamine rose, smoothing a hand over her copper-colored satin skirt. "I've never written one slanderous word about Miss Helen. If it weren't true, I would not have printed it." She raised an eyebrow as she met Helen's irate mother's gaze.

"Do you know what your article has done to my daughter's sterling reputation?" Her eyes narrowed as Jessamine scoffed. "She has been tarnished due to your incessant reports of her movements through town."

Jessamine smirked at Mrs. Jameson. "If she had nothing to hide, then she wouldn't act as she did, and I'd have nothing to report. You should keep a better watch over your daughter."

The older woman leaned forward and poked Jessamine in her shoulder, earning a grimace of pain. "How dare you insinuate my daughter is out of the bounds of what society expects from a young unmarried lady. You keep up this way, and she'll never wed."

Jessamine snorted. "Why do you think the townsfolk readily believe what I wrote? She's been on the edge of acceptable behavior for months. And you were the one proclaiming her upcoming nuptials before I arrived!"

"How dare you sully her good name and imply I've in any way harmed her reputation." Mrs. Jameson gasped as though shocked at the implication.

"What name and what reputation?" Jessamine raised an eyebrow. "She shares her name with a woman more concerned with her personal standing in town than with her own daughter's welfare. With a woman who is an inveterate gossip and schemer who attempted to buy the ruination of another couple's happiness for her own benefit." She glared Mrs. Jameson's protestations into silence over her interference in Alistair and Leticia MacKinnon's love affair that summer. Jessamine continued. "Your daughter shares her name with a bully, a whoremonger, and a cheat."

"You leave my son out of this!" Mrs. Jameson growled.

Jessamine's eyes flashed with anger. "Why is it you are more offended at my attacks against your son, Walter, than against your daughter?" She watched the small woman quiver with rage and shook her head before continuing. "Finally Helen shares her last name with Vincent Jameson, a man more enamored with a Beauty from the Boudoir than with his wife. A man with no sense of responsibility or honor as he divorced you and left you penniless. Don't tell me that you still pine for Mr. Jameson?" She smirked at Mrs. Jameson.

By this point Mrs. Jameson was so red that she looked about to explode. She remained mute, as though her rage prevented her from speaking.

"This, then, is the name you are intent on protecting?" Jessamine asked with a sardonic smile. "It seems to me Helen is merely following in her family's well-trodden path." She jerked back, evading Mrs. Jameson's swat. "Strike me, and I will bring charges against you. And make a mockery of you in the paper," Jessamine said as her eyes flashed with loathing.

"You know no decency. You, who have only lived a charmed life. How dare you come to our town and judge us? You don't know us, and you don't care to."

Jessamine shrugged. "You're a few months too late in your attempt to garner my sympathy. I've watched you bully, belittle, and berate your daughter too often to ever believe in the sincerity of your protestations as to your desire to protect her." Jessamine tilted her head forward as though in silent acknowledgment to something Mrs. Jameson had said. "However, no matter how much I detest you and your inability to act as a good and loving mother to your daughter, I should not bring any further suffering onto your daughter, Helen. Having to live with you and your son are punishment enough for one lifetime."

She and Mrs. Jameson shared a long, scathing look before Mrs. Jameson spun on her heel and stormed out.

E wan stood next to his brothers at the town's harvest dance the following week in late October. The townsfolk and ranchers gathered each year to celebrate before winter arrived. This year's harvest had been bountiful, with backyard gardens producing plenty to last through winter. The few farms in the valley had also produced bumper crops, although many of the farmers had recently arrived and would use the profits to pay off debts and prepare for the coming year. The ranchers had shipped their cattle to Chicago on the train, and their beef had sold at a great profit. Thus, there was much to celebrate.

Ewan sipped at a glass of whiskey from a keg the Stumble-Out had snuck into a corner of the Odd Fellows Hall. His gaze tracked the movements of Jessamine, and he watched her pause to exchange a few words with different members of the town, although few were eager to spend much time in her presence. She wore an amber satin dress with a big bustle, and her red hair tied with a ribbon was like a river of fire down her back.

"Ye are fortunate ye are no' married. Ye can get away with drinkin' that wee dram, rather than the punch," Alistair grumbled. He followed Ewan's gaze and hid a smile in his glass. "Why do ye no' ask her for a dance?"

Cailean nudged Ewan in the side with an elbow. "See how she taps her foot? It's obvious she wishes she were dancing." Cailean looked around the room, seeing Sorcha twirling the dance floor with a miner. "Seems no man is brave enough to ask her."

"Ye ken well enough why I dinna ask her," Ewan hissed. "She writes articles about me twice a week. I dinna need to give the towns-folk somethin' else to jabber about."

Alistair chuckled. "Ye already are, the way ye stare at her." His smile widened as Leticia joined him. He ran a finger over his wife's cheek. "Do ye want to dance, love?"

At her nod, he handed his glass of punch to Ewan and led his wife onto the floor.

"Why are ye no dancin' with Annabelle?" Ewan asked Cailean.

Cailean shrugged. "She's too busy at the food table." He nodded to the two tables laden with food. "Seems she's enjoying her conversation with your Miss Ericson."

"She isna mine," Ewan said. "And I think she would help Anna." He met his brother's worried gaze. "She doesna want to give up the bakery …" He clamped his mouth shut as Jessamine approached.

She laughed, although the sentiment did not reach her eyes. "I find it interesting how everyone stops talking as I approach." She took a sip of the punch before setting it down on a windowsill. "Can no one make a decent drink? This is the second event I have attended, and the punch has been horrible both times."

Cailean shared a long look with Ewan and raised his eyebrows.

Ewan cleared his throat. "I ken that would be something ye'd love to discuss in yer paper, but it would hurt the feelings of Mrs. Guerineau. She's an elderly woman, and she takes great joy in concoctin' the punch as her mother did when she lived in New Orleans afore the War." His grave gaze met Jessamine's. "Please dinna embarrass her."

Jessamine sniffed as though he had offended her with his request. "I'm not as wholly without sentiment or sense as you seem to believe." It was impossible to know if the flush on her cheeks was caused by indignation or embarrassment.

Cailean moved so that Jessamine did not storm away from them. "I hope that is true, Miss McMahon. However, many of your recent articles would give rise to doubt." He watched as she lifted her chin. "Your persistent attacks on Miss Jameson, your spurious report about Jack Renfrew's death, and your constant fear-mongering do not fill me with confidence as to your sincerity."

"I already know what you think of me. You've made your opinion plain."

Cailean nodded. "Aye. You've been a disappointment." He paused as he saw a flash of hurt in her eyes before she glowered at him. "However, I hope to be proven wrong in my estimation of you every time I read your paper."

"The fault is in you for having expectations," Jessamine snapped. She glared at him until he moved and allowed her to pass.

Ewan sighed. "That dinna go well."

Cailean chuckled. "No, but she's acting like a cornered bully, and someone needs to stand up to her." He looked across the room to see

Walter Jameson following her movements with an intense glower. "And it's better us than one like Walter."

Ewan nodded. He slapped Cailean on the back and moved to follow Jessamine as she stood alone to the side of the dance floor. After he set his glass on a nearby table, he stood beside her. "Ye ken ye've only made life more difficult for yerself."

"Yes, blame me for everyone else's foibles. Blame me for shining a light on how things truly are." She crossed her arms over her chest and glared at the townsfolk watching them with avid curiosity.

He grabbed her hand, dragging her to the floor as a slow waltz began. "Stop fightin' me, ye wee demon." He grunted as she kicked him in the shin, her pointed shoes bruising even through his boots. "No one asked ye to bring to light our secrets and shames, Jessie." He flushed as she glared at him for the nickname. "Ye could have more success if ye wrote with humor."

"I am a serious reporter. Humor is not what I do." She tugged on her arms but was held tight against him.

"That's not what ye do *yet*," he countered. "Ye are smart enough to ken ye can change. We all can." He pulled her closer, smiling as she growled her discontent. "Ye can do whatever ye want."

She looked up at him, her expression softening for a moment. "You're right. I can." His hold on her eased a moment, and then she raised a knee, hitting him in his crotch. At his groan as he doubled over and fell in the middle of the dance floor, she bent down and whispered in his ear, "Don't ever manhandle me again, *ye ken?*" She marched off the dance floor and out of the Hall amid a humming murmur from the townsfolk.

Ewan gasped and flushed and accepted his brothers' aid off the floor. They pushed him into a chair, forfeited to him by one of the elderly matrons of the town. He bent over to the point he grasped his ankles. "Damn her to hell," he rasped. "I'm goin' to …"

"*Shh*, Ewan," Alistair said as he patted him on the back. "Dinna say much. Too many are curious about what was and wasna said on the dance floor."

"*Bluidy* hell, I forgot how much that hurts." He let out a deep breath and sat up to the point his elbows rested on his thighs.

Cailean handed him a glass of whiskey, and the brothers acted as a shield as the townsfolk craned their necks to obtain a better view of him. After Ewan had taken a swig of whiskey, he held up his hand, and Alistair hauled him to his feet. The three brothers marched to the door and outside.

Once outside, Ewan collapsed against the side of the building and took a few deep gulps of the cool night air. "I canna think what I did to anger her so. I'll never understand that woman."

"I dinna ken why that should worry ye." Alistair shared a confused glance with Cailean. "She's a cantankerous woman." Alistair waited a moment for Ewan to agree and then huffed in frustration. "Ye canna want anything to do with her, Ewan."

Ewan raised an eyebrow as he took another breath, the lines of pain easing around his eyes. He held out his glass to his brothers. "I'll see ye later tonight or tomorrow." He pushed away from the building, and soon darkness enveloped him.

Sorcha watched her brothers leave the Hall but continued her dance with Frederick Tompkins, Irene and Harold's grandson who ran a nearby ranch. She glared at him as he chuckled at Ewan's discomfort. "Have ye no decency?" She raised a brow. "I doubt ye'd find it as amusin' were I to do the same to ye."

He glared at her. "Are you always disagreeable? Can't you just remain silent in my arms as I twirl you around the dance floor?"

She rolled her eyes. "Is that what ye want from a woman? Someone mute and docile to do yer biddin'?"

He tugged her closer as she tried to pull away from him. "Would be more pleasant than having to deal with a woman like you."

She stomped on his foot, the heel of her shoe catching the toe of his boot, and he groaned in pain. She wrenched out of his hold and marched off the dance floor, her head held high as she joined her sisters-in-law.

"Oh my," Annabelle breathed. "I'm just thankful the reporter left and didn't see you act in such a way."

"She wouldn't have any right to comment after how she treated Ewan," Leticia said with a wry smile. "What did Frederick say to enrage you so?" She raised her brows as she looked at Sorcha.

Sorcha exhaled a deep breath, her cheeks reddened from anger and embarrassment at being the focus of attention for all present. "He laughed at Ewan an' then said he wanted someone quiet and docile to spin around the dance floor."

"Oh my," Annabelle repeated. "He doesn't know you at all to say such things." She nudged Sorcha as Irene made her way toward them.

Irene looked Sorcha over from head to foot and then asked, "What did he say?"

Sorcha frowned. "I thought ye'd blame me. He's yer blood."

Irene shook her head in dismay. "I know what he's like. An overbearing brooder at the best of times." She smiled as Sorcha laughed. "At least he did no lasting damage to your spirit."

Sorcha snorted. "That man willna ever have the ability to affect me." She smiled at Harold as he appeared holding a cup of punch. "I fear I do no' much like yer grandson."

"He's an acquired taste. Like this punch." He winked at her. "You'll come to appreciate him." He watched the two eldest MacKinnon brothers reenter the Hall without Ewan. "Seems the youngest brother had the sense to hide out in one of his lairs."

"He's no' a wolf," Sorcha snapped.

Harold laughed. "No, he isn't. But I imagine he feels just as hunted at times." He smiled as the two men joined them. "Seems he got more than he bargained for."

Alistair nodded as he looked around the Hall, relaxing as he caught sight of Hortence playing in a far corner. "Aye, he'll have to learn her ways."

Sorcha tapped her brother on his arm. "He willna! He has no reason to want to ken her any better."

Alistair raised his eyebrows as Cailean laughed. "Not all courtships are smooth, Sorch," Cailean murmured. He watched Frederick glare at them from across the room. "Something I'd think you were learning."

She let out a huff of air before accepting a miner's invitation to dance. "Ye're all daft," she snapped and walked away. She glowered at Frederick as he watched her dance with a miner, her pleasure in the dance increasing as Frederick's scowl intensified when she looked up at the miner as though he were a fount of wisdom.

~

E wan sat downstairs at the Boudoir and watched the antics of the women as they enticed men upstairs. Most men needed little persuasion to follow one of the whores, but a few seemed content to bide their time downstairs. Ewan nursed a glass of whiskey and replayed the scene from the dance over and over in his head. "*Eejit*," he muttered to himself as he remembered her struggles to free herself from his hold only to have him tightening his grip on her.

His self-reflection was cut short as a ruckus from upstairs caught his attention. He leaned over the side of his chair to look around a girl trying to entice him into something more than ogling, and he shook his head. "That wee idiot!" He pushed aside the whore, reaching out to steady her so she did not topple to the ground, and stood.

He fumed as those in the main room watched with openmouthed stupefaction as Jessamine was dragged down the stairs by the Madam's henchman, Ezekial, with the Madam on her heels. Jessamine grimaced as Ezekial's hold on her arm tightened, and he shook her as though she were a rag doll.

"How dare you sneak into my establishment and attempt to … to …" The Madam sputtered to a stop. Her irate gaze fell on Ewan and turned cunning and calculating. "If a woman is that desperate to join my girls, I feel it only proper to allow her most avowed admirer the right to her."

"Nae, Madam," Ewan protested. "She's a journalist. Attemptin' to do what she sees as her job."

The Madam glared at him, her hands on her still trim hips. Her bosom rose and fell in her eggplant-hued satin dress with onyx jewelry decorating her throat, wrist, and ears. "I should have known a man who never partakes of my girls would be unwilling to consort with her."

Ewan flushed with anger but was shoved aside as a burly miner strode to the front.

"I'll take 'er," he said. He swiped his palm along his forehead as though a spit shine would make him more presentable.

Jessamine struggled against Ezekial's hold but was unable to free herself from his iron grip. He whispered something in her ear, which made her pale further and fight harder.

"I like 'em feisty," another man said.

Ewan pushed his way to the front and shook his head. "Nae, lads, ye will no' be with this woman tonight. She is a respectable woman. Look to the others if ye are wantin' a bit of bedsport."

The first man looked Ewan over from head to foot and smiled malevolently. "She's here, ain't she? Any woman in a whorehouse is fair game. That's what the Madam has always told us." He took a step toward Jessamine, and Ewan pushed him back.

"Don't touch me, pansy ass," the miner growled. "You won't like the consequences."

In an instant Ewan cold-cocked the man, and he fell like heavy timber to the floor. The man behind him rolled him out of the way and took his place. Ewan raised his fists as he saw the expectation of a brawl in the man's eyes. He didn't look at Jessamine but whispered, "When ye can, run as fast as yer feet will carry ye."

The next moment he was too busy to concern himself with her. One man attacked from behind while the other from the front. He grunted as he was punched in a kidney and then the belly. He kicked at a man and wrenched his arm free. Soon an all-out brawl engulfed the first floor of the Boudoir. Furniture smashed against the wall as large men crashed into it. Whores scrambled upstairs for safety, and Ewan continued to pummel those who attacked him.

As suddenly as it started, it ended. Men sprawled on the floor, gasping for air, blood trickling from broken noses, gashes on heads, or from split lips. Ewan hissed in a breath as he searched for Jessamine, his gaze frantic as he failed to see her.

A whore sidled up to him and pushed him toward the front door. "Get out. Stay out. Don't let the Madam see you here for a long time."

"But Jessie …"

Charity shook her head. "She fled in the middle of the fight. Zeke had to free her to join the brawl." She looked over her shoulder, her chestnut brown hair in ringlets. "Go!"

He stumbled onto the boardwalk and fell against the hitching post. "*Bluidy* hell," he muttered as he took as deep a breath as he could. He heard raucous music from the Stumble-Out where many loitered on the boardwalk. It was a mild night for late October, and men were enjoying the evening after celebrating the year's bounty.

He walked in the building's shadows as he approached her print shop. He sighed with relief to find the area around her establishment momentarily deserted and tapped on her door. When there was no answer, he banged on it until it rattled. He heard rustling inside and called out in a soft voice, "I ken ye're in there, Jessie. Open the damn door."

He fell inside when it opened with alacrity and shut just as swiftly. He righted himself and stared at her in the dim light of her print shop. He allowed her to tug him toward the back of the space, away from the windows and potentially prying eyes.

"What are you doing here? Why would you come here late at night?" she whispered. Her gaze roved over him, and she frowned. She pushed him into a chair and moved into the kitchen, where she wet a cloth.

He hissed when she dabbed at his bloodied lip and a bruise on his cheek. Her movements stilled when he gripped her wrist. "I had to ken ye were all right, Jessie."

"I fail to see why you'd care." She glared at him.

"Do ye?" he asked as he watched her with a wondrous smile. "I thought ye smarter than that." He sobered. "What could ye have been thinkin' by goin' into a whorehouse?"

She shrugged. "I wouldn't expect you to understand."

He acted as though he would tug her down to sit next to him, and then he shook his head and opened his hands. "I would like ye to sit next to me an' explain, but I will no' force ye." He waited for her to understand his words. "I've thought about tonight, at the dance, an' I think I ken why ye were angry with me."

Her eyes glowed with impotent rage. "Never try to bend my will. Never force me to do something I don't want to do." She relaxed when he nodded. After pulling out another chair and sitting next to him, she laced and unlaced her hands. "I was angry when I left the dance. I was filled with this nervous energy."

"I ken. I was too. What I dinna understand is why ye did no' come back here and write a scathing article about me. That would have been more productive."

Jessamine frowned as she stared at him. "Do you see them as decorative pieces to be used at any man's leisure? Or are they women?"

He frowned at her change of topic. "They are women, aye, although they are rarely seen as more than a whore."

She lowered her gaze. "Do you know why the new doctor has been visiting them with such frequency?" She bit her lip as he canted forward. Her eyes widened as though she had just discovered a secret truth. "You care about one of them. It's why you are there with such frequency but never go upstairs."

He shook his head. "'Tis no' about me. Asides, Anna's sister works there." He challenged her with a harsh stare, but she did not contradict him when he spoke about Fidelia.

"It's the worst job imaginable for a woman, I think," Jessamine whispered. "I've seen the doctor come and go almost daily, but I've been unable to speak with any of the women. Ever since the town instituted the shopping times for the whores last month, it's not acceptable for me to mingle with them at the stores. I'm unable to speak with them, and, if I do, they will be taxed for my impertinence." She frowned with frustration.

"That damn brute the Madam hired is always at the back door, and I can never see my way inside during the day. Thus, I thought to sneak in the back at night when the front was busy. I thought the occasion of the Harvest Festival dance would be the best night as they would be the busiest."

Ewan shook his head. "Ye are the daftest woman. If ye had bothered to make friends with us, ye could have asked to deliver the basket to the Boudoir, and then ye could have been inside during the day." He raised his eyebrows as her forehead furrowed. "Ye never did consider that option, did ye?"

At her head shake, he sighed. "Why would ye want to be upstairs when they are entertainin' the men?"

"I wouldn't call it *entertainment*." Jessamine choked as though attempting to swallow a sob. "It was horrible. And I know why the doctor is there with such alarming frequency." She met Ewan's intent gaze. "He's drugging them. Dulling their senses so they can continue to do this work, day in and out."

Ewan shook his head in denial and then exhaled, seeming to droop in front of her. "Aye, 'tis what they all do in the end." He met her gaze, his eyes filled with a deep sadness. "Poor Fidelia."

Jessamine grabbed his hand and squeezed it before flushing and dropping it. "I beg your pardon."

"There's nothin' to beg, except for startin' a wee battle." He sucked in a breath as he prodded at a sore rib. "I ken I'll be barred for a while."

"I'll never understand why you go to the Boudoir."

He flashed his charming smile, hissing when it pulled on his split lip. "Perhaps I like looking at pretty things."

She shook her head as she peered deep into his eyes, as though seeing him for the first time. She shivered and dropped her gaze to the cloth that had fallen to the floor. "I doubt that's the reason." She forced a smile and rose. "You should be heading home."

She froze as someone pounded on her front door and tried the lock. The door jangled, but the lock held.

"Ye should no' be left alone tonight. Too many have drunk too much, and some will wonder if ye are fair game after what happened at the Boudoir. The report of the brawl will have spread by now and will have been exaggerated." He watched her with concern. "Let me stay with ye."

"That's even more improper than me sneaking into the Boudoir tonight!" She shook her head but jumped as another pounded on her door. Her frightened gaze met his. After a moment she closed her eyes and took a deep breath. "Stay," she whispered.

"Aye, I will," he murmured.

He closed his eyes and stretched his legs in front of him as he listened to her perform her ablutions and slip into bed. "'Night, Jessie," he whispered.

After a minute she said in a barely audible voice, "You shouldn't spend the night in a chair without a blanket."

He turned his head to her, lying on the bed with warm blankets around her and her red hair in a braid. "I see no choice."

She stared at him for a moment. "The town already thinks I'm no better than a whore."

He made a sound of disagreement in his throat. "What matters is what ye ken to be true."

She nodded. "Good night, Ewan."

He let out a deep breath, battling disappointment. "'Night, Jessie. Sleep well." He shifted as he attempted to find a comfortable position. After a few minutes he settled into the chair, tugging his coat around him. He slitted his eyes open to watch Jessamine, curled on her side on her small bed. Although she appeared to sleep, her breathing was not the deep inhales of someone in slumber.

"Lay next to me," she whispered. "You shouldn't be in that chair all night." She flicked up one blanket, leaving a sheet and another blanket as a barrier between them.

After kicking off his boots, he slid into bed beside her. "Thanks, Jessie."

"You really shouldn't call me that," she mumbled as she tumbled into sleep.

He chuckled as he sensed that she had fallen asleep. The sounds of the town festivities echoed in the distance as his breathing deepened, and he also slipped into sleep.

CHAPTER 6

*E*wan woke, his sense of place slowly returning to him as he inhaled the scents of ink, paper, and a warm woman in his arms. He leaned forward, breathing in the subtle scent of Jessamine's perfume. He inhaled again. Rosewater. He stilled in his movement that would bring him closer to her and retracted the hand he held around her waist. Momentary panic eased as he realized they were both fully dressed with a blanket separating them.

He kissed her blanket-covered shoulder in a whisper-soft goodbye kiss and eased out of the tiny cot. He froze when she moved toward his retreating form, but then she curled into the mattress and sighed with pleasure as he tucked the blankets around her. He pulled on his boots and tiptoed around the disorganized space. He sat on a stool and ran a hand over his face, his fingers scratching at the stubble. "What have I done?" he muttered to himself. He scrubbed at his hair and face. "I should have remained in the chair."

The bright moonlight glinting in through the window indicated it was no later than two in the morning. However, he knew it would be difficult to sneak out of the newspaper office unseen, and he had promised her that he would remain to protect her from any unwanted visitors. And yet he knew he needed to leave before dawn. "I have such horrible luck."

He sat for a few moments as he watched her sleep, battling tender and burgeoning feelings for her. He fought an overwhelming desire to crawl into bed beside her again. His fingers tapped on his knee as he suppressed mounting panic.

He rose, looking for a distraction, and moved to her desk. Moonlight streamed in, providing light on part of her desk and allowing him to read without a lamp. He smiled as he saw ideas for tall tales. He set aside a piece of paper and froze as he saw Leticia's name under ideas for the *News and Noteworthy* section and the backbone of a story that had been sketched out.

"Nae," he breathed. "Has she learned nothing?"

He looked over his shoulder at the woman resting peacefully on the bed, her red hair in its braid, and any harmony he felt earlier ebbed away. He clutched the paper in one hand, any thought of sneaking out before dawn forgotten. He sat on a lumpy chair near her miniscule living quarters with the proof of her foolishness in his hands and waited for her to awaken.

⁓

A s the sun began to glint through the windows, J.P. stretched and arched her back. She hugged her arms around herself as she remembered a wondrous dream of being cherished and held in a man's arms.

"Wake up, ye wee demon."

She bolted upright, her braid of red hair falling down her back as she spun to face the irate voice. "Ewan! What are you doing here?" She glanced out the window and grimaced at the bright sunlight that burst through it.

"Did ye think it a dream? Me sleepin' with ye?" He laughed as she paled. "Ye invited me into yer bed."

She ran a hand over her clothes and then frowned at him. "I'm fully dressed."

"Do ye no' ken enough to realize it can be done fully clothed?" he taunted. When she paled even further, he shook his head. "Dinna worry, Jessie. I did no more than lie aside ye in that bed, with a blanket separating us."

"Why are you still here?" she hissed as her gaze sharpened, and recollection of the previous night's threats against her lit her expression. "I thought you'd leave before sunrise. Now the whole town will see you depart!" She shifted her legs to dangle over the side of the cot but stopped from rising when he thrust a piece of paper at her. She squinted once before focusing on the paper. "You had no right to rifle through my things while I slept!"

"I did no' rifle! It was right there for all to see on top of yer desk. I was killing time as I tried to think of a way to escape here unseen. When I saw what ye were considering printing, I realized I could no' leave. No' when ye are hell-bent on ruinin' her life."

J.P. shook her head and stared at him with wonder. "What is it about you MacKinnons that makes you believe—whatever you do, whatever you have done—you are to be protected from the harsh realities of this world? That those around you do not have the right to know the truth about you?"

"An' ye think ye are peddlin' the truth with that vile rubbish?" he snapped as he pointed to the printing press. "If ye print that story, ye'll be perpetratin' lies and half-truths in an attempt to rip open wounds that have barely healed, all to sell a few copies of yer paper."

"What's wrong with titillating the masses?" She rose and moved past him. However, he clamped a hand onto her wrist and spun her to face him.

"Aye, I've complained to all who'd care to listen about how ye've treated me. About how ye write about me. But I'm a man. I can do what I like in this world and no' be affected by its vicious double standards. Ye can no' do this to Leticia!"

Jessamine took the piece of paper and pushed it into his chest. "Doesn't it bother you that she tricked a mourning wealthy man into caring for her so she'd have a place to raise her bastard daughter?

Doesn't it matter to you that the one thing she does well is lie and cheat?"

"Do no' ever again call Hortence that. Do ye want the whole MacKinnon clan against ye? Just try attacking my niece again in yer paper or afore any of us. Ye've caused the poor child enough torment with yer words, causing the schoolchildren to think she must be evil because she has red hair, like ye." Ewan shook his head while Jessamine remained uncharacteristically silent. "All ye care to see about people in this world is the evil. The wrongdoin's. The mean-ness. Ye have no ability to see the beauty, the joy, the hope." His eyes shone with disillusionment as he backed away from her. "Ye refuse to acknowledge the sacrifices and the courage that most in this town exhibit daily to survive. To meet their neighbor's call with a smile."

"I've seen enough to know what it is to make my way in this world. To fight for what I have, even if it's against my family's wishes."

He glared at her scornfully. "I had hoped ye were more than a scared little girl, playin' at bein' a woman, who thrived on the atten-tion her paper brought her because she'd been denied the attention of her family for so long. Seems I was wrong."

The sound of her hand slapping his cheek echoed through the room. "Don't you dare judge me."

"Aye, I will. An' I'll find ye wantin' every time. For ye have no decency. Ye think exposin' the secrets we want hidden means ye are doin' a service for the town. Instead ye're slowly rippin' us apart." He huffed and turned on his heel.

She grabbed his arm, preventing him from leaving. "What do you mean?" she asked, her brows furrowed in confusion.

"No one talks to each other the way we used to. There's no real conversation at the café, the livery, the sawmill. Everyone watches each other with a wary regard, assumin' what they say will end up in yer paper." He shook his head. "Ye've managed to turn this town against itself in a few short months."

She snorted. "That's not my fault. If people didn't have something to hide, they wouldn't be wary."

He bent forward, his face reddening with his ire. "Everyone has something to hide. Includin' ye. Ye'd best hope no one discovers yer secrets because ye've made plenty of enemies, an' many will take joy in seein' ye suffer as ye've made others suffer from yer sharp tongue and ill-advised articles." He shook his head with disgust.

She backed away. "I don't believe you. I am a respected member of this town."

"*Fear* doesna mean ye are respected. Think about that, Jessie."

They watched each other for a long moment, their breaths emerging in pants. His irate gaze subtly altered, and she shivered at what she saw in his eyes. He raised a hand to brush aside a loose tendril of fiery red hair, while she clutched at the front of his shirt. He leaned forward, groaning as their lips met in a featherlight kiss. He fought his better instincts to tug her closer and deepened the kiss, his hand tightening in her hair as she leaned into him.

"God, I've wanted to kiss ye for so long," he rasped as he peppered kisses over her neck as she arched to give him better access.

"I thought you didn't like me." Then she gasped as one of Ewan's hands roved over her backside and the other cupped a breast.

"I wouldna be disappointed, Jessie, if I dinna like ye …" He leaned forward, kissing her deeply again, the words "too much" lost in their embrace.

Someone banged on the glass. They sprung apart and spun to the door. He watched as she hastily tied her hair and took deep breaths. She tugged at a shawl over her shoulders and pulled it high on her neck to hide the scratches his beard had left. He raised an eyebrow at seeing her pale at the implication of someone finding him inside her locked newspaper office.

"Hide!" she snapped. She shoved him toward a cabinet and moved toward the front door, her shoulders back and head held high.

She stood in front of the door, preventing Walter Jameson from entering her office and home. "I am having a slow morning today, Mr. Jameson. If you will allow me time to begin the day before returning to discuss whatever concerns you?"

"I will not!" he bellowed. He held up a recent edition of the paper. "How dare you write these words about my sister! I thought you understood from our previous discussion that such articles were to cease!"

She pushed back against him when he attempted to enter her office. "I have asked you not to enter, and I am serious in my request." She met his glare. "You are not welcome inside."

He leaned forward, his fetid breath washing over her. "Do you have any idea what you have done? You are ruining her chances with another MacKinnon! There are no more after Ewan. What will she do?"

J.P. stood as tall as she could but remained at least half a foot shorter than Walter. "I'm certain your family will concoct some scheme that will continue to humiliate your sister. You never fail in that regard."

She gasped as his hand lashed out and grabbed a fistful of her hair. "You will cease writing about my family, or you will answer to me. Take my word for it that you will not enjoy it."

He released her, pushing her with such force that she slammed backward into a cabinet. She righted herself, closing the door and locking it after his departure.

She moved to the back of her office and to the living area, clutching her side. "Go out the back door," she wheezed.

"I did no' ken ye had a back door." Ewan frowned as he watched her. "He hurt ye."

"I think that man is good for little else." She kept one hand at her side. "I refuse to argue with you further today, Ewan. Please leave. Please be discreet."

He watched her with interest. "Why should I be discreet when ye refuse to be about my family?"

She raised a hand and rubbed at her forehead. "Leave."

"Aye, I will. But here's my bargain. I'll no' say a word about last night if ye refrain from publishin' about Leticia and Hortence. If ye do print that article, then all will ken about our *night of passion*."

She belted him in the shoulder with her free hand. "You know we shared no passion!"

He laughed with no real humor. "Ah, ye ken how to hurt a man. I had hoped ye felt somethin' when I held ye in my arms for our kiss." He watched as she lost her battle with a bright flush. He shrugged as though forcing himself to forget their embrace. "But then the truth is in the eye of the beholder. And, as ye've shown over and over again, the town likes a good story more than it likes the truth." He winked and snuck out the back door.

~

Ewan sat at the dining room table with his family around him. Hortence was in the livery with Bears, helping with the horses. Bears adored Hortence and spoke more with her than with anyone else in the family and had not minded the request to watch her as the family held an emergency meeting.

Alistair sat in a chair next to his wife, Leticia. "Ye ken this is a busy time right now, Ewan. After the Harvest Festival, many need care for their horses, and it isna fair to leave it to Bears for long."

Ewan nodded as he looked from Alistair to Cailean and then to Sorcha. Annabelle sat beside Cailean, her hand on her ever-growing belly. "Aye, I ken this is a busy time for us all. But 'tis a true emergency." He extracted the slip of paper he had pinched from J.P and handed it first to Alistair and Leticia. "Read that."

Alistair read it and growled with anger. "This is no' a regular article. The sentences are short and biting."

Ewan shook his head. "Aye. It's more of an exposé, and it's no' a finished article. As far as she would tell me, she has not set a publication date." He paused as he clamped his jaw shut in anger a moment. "Seems she's keen to show the town her journalistic skills while exposin' Leticia to ridicule."

"What does it say?" Annabelle asked Alistair. She placed one hand over Cailean's and another over Sorcha's.

"It details how Leticia survived, with sordid half-truths and exaggerations, in Saint Louis before she traveled to Montana. After she escaped her husband and was pregnant with Hortence." Alistair tossed the piece of paper to Cailean. "She has no right!" As Leticia began to cry, he pulled her against his side and crooned into her ear.

Cailean read the roughed-out article and tapped at the table. "How did you come to be in possession of a story proof? I thought they were highly guarded."

Ewan flushed. "Jessie was in an unfortunate scrape last night, and I helped her out of it."

"*Jessie?*" Sorcha asked with a raised eyebrow. "Ye hate the woman. Why give her a nickname?"

Annabelle watched as Ewan squirmed. "You spent the night with her."

Ewan groaned and lowered his face to his arms crossed on the table. "Aye, I did, but no' in the way ye all imagine. There was no grand night of passion. We passed out on her cot, fully clothed." He silenced his brothers' snickers with a severe glare. "When I woke, she slept. I wandered the print shop, lookin' for somethin' to read 'cause I kent I wouldna sleep much more. The town was full of those seekin' to make mischief with their harvest money, and too many were interested in the pretty journalist, ye ken?" He nodded to the piece of paper. "Then I found that an' wouldna leave as she expected at dawn until I spoke with her."

"She prints this soon?" Alistair asked.

"Aye, 'tis her plan." Ewan held up his hand when all three of his siblings took a deep breath to speak. "I threatened her with my own exposé about our night of passion if she did publish it, an' I'm hopin' she has enough sense to hold off."

"Why should she?" Sorcha asked. "The townsfolk afford her respect solely because they are afraid of her and what she might write about them. Not because they like her."

"Except for the old men who want to tell her tales and aren't afraid of what she'll write," Annabelle said.

"The townsfolk already believe the worst about her because she traipses after men into whorehouses and saloons. They'll not find it odd that you were her lover," Cailean said. He flushed as he looked at his sister.

Annabelle shook her head in disagreement. "I think you're wrong. She goes where she shouldn't, but she's never been seen breaking the bounds of propriety. Not completely. I think, if she were found to have acted on passion, her life would be very difficult here."

Alistair's jaw ticked. "How do ye ken she willna write about it in another paper? A later edition?" His brown eyes smoldered with pent-up rage. "I willna have anyone disrespecting Leticia again, nor wee Hortence."

Cailean met his brother's irate gaze. "That much is out of your control, Alistair. All we can hope is that the town's regard for Leticia and your daughter will continue to grow. Enough of the women here know what it's like to be pregnant and desperate. They have husbands who'd rather carouse and spend all the family's money than buy food or pay the rent. Look at what happened last night with the men in the saloons until dawn."

Cailean frowned when Leticia kept her face buried in Alistair's shoulder as though in shame. He gripped his sister-in-law's hand. "There's nothing to be embarrassed or ashamed about, Lettie. We do not judge you for it."

"I was not his mistress!" she sobbed. "I ... swear," she murmured.

"Aye, but it willna matter what we ken to be true. It will only matter what the townsfolk want to be true. At least for a time." Ewan scrubbed at his head. "I canna believe she'd write such foul things about ye, Lettie. Not after she swore she'd change after Bears' story."

"No one here likes her. She's abused ye every chance she's had. And yet ye sound disappointed in her." Sorcha studied her brother with abject confusion. "Why do ye care?"

Ewan shook his head, his gaze momentarily filled with panic. "I dinna care about her! I care about the family." He met his sister's mocking gaze and rose. "I'm away to see Warren. I ken it's Sunday, but I hope he'll see me."

Cailean nodded as he pulled his wife close in his arms. "Aye, he'll see you. Although there won't be much he can do." He handed Ewan the piece of paper sitting in the middle of the table. "Careful you don't lose that." He nodded at Ewan as he left the room.

Ewan walked through town, nodding to friends and acquaintances. He stopped to laugh and joke with a few about last night's incident, easily deflecting inappropriate inquiries about how the pretty young reporter was after she had escaped from the Boudoir. He laughed as they related the rumor that he'd escorted her upstairs to a crib last night. He tipped his hat to his friends. "You ken me, a gentleman through and through! Never laid a finger on her or any Beauty. Slept in a cold bed last night." He slapped another on the back and made his way to Warren's house.

The lawyer's residence was on a street behind Main Street, nearly behind his legal practice. In the beginning, he had lived in the small back room he now used as a private room in his main office. However, after Ewan had arrived in Bear Grass Springs, Warren had commissioned Ewan to build him a home.

Warren answered the door in a white shirt rolled up to his elbows and a glower. "Ewan," he said on a long sigh. He motioned for him to enter and had him follow him through the sitting room to his home office down a long hallway. Light entered through three windows, and his desk was an orderly disaster.

"How do ye ken where anything is?" Ewan asked as he sat across from him.

"It's only like this when I'm elbow deep in a case." He stretched before he sat. "Is it too early for a drink?" He shook his head at not knowing the time before he shrugged. "The decanter's in the sitting room if you want something."

"Nae, I need to keep my wits about me." He paused a moment, appreciating Warren's calm patience as he waited for him to speak. "What can ye do to prevent someone from printing something?"

"As I've told Cailean more times than I care to count, very little. If it's an outright lie, we can sue after the newspaper comes out. I can threaten her with a lawsuit beforehand, but she knows she has the right to print what she likes, especially if there is truth to what she writes."

Ewan sighed and dropped his head into a hand. "She mixes lie with truth to the point ye dinna ken where ye're goin'."

Warren nodded. "That's the way of it with most big-city reporters. This town was so excited to have a newspaper and reporter, but I remember too well what it was like in Philadelphia." He watched as Ewan stared into space. "The town is greatly entertained by what she writes about you, Ewan. And by the fact you now have to deflect the interest of so many women."

Ewan raised irate brown eyes to meet Warren's concerned blue eyes. "Aye, if it were about me, I wouldna care. And I would never consider destroyin' a woman's reputation. But it isna about me. She's going to attack Leticia. Attempt to tear her happiness from her. And I canna allow that."

Warren frowned. "Is there truth to what she writes?"

"Aye, enough mixed in with the lies to make it hard to sue her. She kens what she does well." He clamped his jaw shut and flushed with anger.

The lawyer studied him as a friend rather than a client. "Seems to me that you are more concerned than you should be by the fact she has disappointed you." He watched as Ewan flushed even more. "I've heard the rumors from the saloons and the Boudoir. That each time she appears to investigate, you are her shadow. Always there to ensure no one oversteps the mark." He paused. "I never thought to see you in such a state over J.P."

Ewan groaned and dropped his head in his hands again. "Damn interferin' lawyer."

Warren chuckled. "You're the one who came for my advice." He paused. "If you are interested in her, and, by all accounts you are, why don't you speak with her?"

Ewan rolled his eyes. "An' give her something else to print in her *bluidy N&N* section?" His next words mimicked her soft voice. "*How entertaining to discover our most eligible gentleman has a heart. How disappointing for him to discover the woman he desires will never share the sentiment.*"

Warren sobered as he saw his friend's torment. "You'll never know until you speak with her. Doubts can be worse than any certainty."

Ewan stilled and met Warren's tormented gaze as he understood Warren was not referring to Jessamine. "Why do ye no' court Helen?"

Warren snorted out a laugh, half-incredulous, half-despairing. "You always were the brother to not hold back." He pinched the bridge of his nose. "There are things you'll never understand. A past that is complicated."

"The more time ye let come between ye, the more her resentment builds."

Warren nodded, but then his eyes flashed with anger. "Yes, but do you know what it's been like, watching her throw herself at you and your brothers? For years now I've had to witness her make a fool of herself."

Ewan sat up straight as though affronted. "We are no' that bad an option." He smiled when he saw Warren flush with embarrassment. "We do no' want wee Helen, but I think her mother and brother are the ones behind her torment." He frowned. "Her brother came by the print shop this morning and threatened Jessie."

"Jessie?" Warren raised an eyebrow. "And how were you there before it opened? I already had a visit from Helen's miserable brother about not being granted access to J.P.'s print shop this morning and his anger at her excuse it was closed. How would you know about their argument?"

Ewan shifted in his seat. "It doesna matter. What matters is that Helen is but a pawn. One day she'll determine she's had enough and want to break free. Ye need to be ready to help her, or ye could lose her for good."

Warren frowned at Ewan's words before nodding. He tapped at papers on his desk. "As for your problem, I'd speak with J.P. See if you can convince her to see sense."

CHAPTER 7

$\mathcal{E}$wan knocked on the print shop door and waited a few minutes. He then pounded on it. When there was no answer, he tried the handle to find it open. After easing inside, he took off his hat and set it atop a pile of papers by the door. "J.P.? Jessie?" he called out as he moved into the room. He heard a snuffle and walked to her small living area.

The curtain was drawn, and he pulled it back. Jessamine lay on the cot, clutching her side as she dozed. He traced a finger down her arm before kissing the top of her hair, so softly she would not feel it in her sleep. "Jessie," he murmured, tapping her arm.

He reared back as her hand struck out, slapping him across his forehead and nose. He held up an arm to ward off any other attack before grabbing her hands. "*Shh*," he whispered. "'Tis me. Ewan."

She sighed as she settled on the bed and shook subtly. "Can you get the doctor? I don't feel well."

"Aye, but tell me what hurts," he said as he ran a hand over her head.

"Ever since I fell this morning, my side hurts. I think I broke a rib." She clutched at her side with a hand and grimaced with each breath.

"I'll see if he can come, and I'll ensure I obtain something for the pain." He paused as she grabbed his hand with her free one.

"No laudanum. Nothing with opium."

He nodded and then realized she could not see his actions as her eyes were closed. "Aye. I'll find the doctor and return."

He rushed from the print shop and returned home. He found Annabelle in the kitchen. "Anna, I ken it's a lot to ask, but could ye help me?" He motioned for her to follow him and picked her coat up off the peg and helped her in it. He led her outside, walking at such a brisk pace that neither were able to speak. When he glanced back at her, he slowed. "Sorry. Ye should no' rush so in yer condition." When they reached the print shop, he guided her inside and led her to J.P. lying injured on her cot.

"Walter visited her this morning and pushed her. I'm going for the doc, but I did no' want her to be alone." He watched as Annabelle nodded while he pulled a chair over for her to sit next to J.P. He squeezed Annabelle's shoulder. "Thanks."

After he searched the saloons for the doctor, and then finding his home and office empty, Ewan went to the Boudoir. Ezekial met him with a menacing glower. "I thought you understood you were barred after last night's antics."

Ewan stood in the hallway and met Ezekial's glower with a fierce glare. "I do no' understand why ye're mad at me. I dinna cause the ruckus here."

Ezekial crossed his tree-branch-size arms over his chest and half smiled. "You were the one to break the furniture and to cost the Madam a fortune. Until that debt is paid, you are not welcome here."

Ewan leaned forward, although he was still a few inches shorter than Ezekial. "How can ye defend such a woman as the Madam? A woman who allows the women under her charge to be abused? Beaten?" He shook his head. "Do ye no' care that one of them will die under yer watch?"

Ezekial watched him impassively.

Ewan took a calming breath. "Is the doc here? I've need of his services."

Ezekial pointed for him to remain in the hallway before striding upstairs. After nearly twenty minutes, the doctor descended the stairs, buttoning up his waistcoat as he walked.

"What is so urgent, young man?" He thrust his black medicine bag at Ewan and slung on his jacket. He marched outside with Ewan beside him.

"Do ye really have business at the Boudoir midday?" Ewan asked as he led the doctor toward the print shop.

"The whores are always in need of my expert touch," the doctor said.

Ewan snorted and shook his head as he walked the rest of the way in silence. He ignored the doctor's grumbling about being called upon to care for the firebrand reporter and ushered him inside.

Ewan and Annabelle stood on the opposite side of the curtain, which the doctor had pulled shut to afford privacy, and listened to his mutterings and her groans of distress. When Ewan moved to enter the curtained-off area, Annabelle grabbed his arm and shook her head.

"You can't, Ewan. Not in front of a man like that." She nodded toward the shadow of the doctor. "He would spread gossip faster than you can imagine. He already will."

Ewan stilled, stifling a growl of protest. When the doctor pulled back the curtain, Ewan schooled his face into a mask of impassivity.

"She has a broken rib. Give her this three to four times a day to dull her pain. She'll be fine with time." The doctor thrust a bottle at Ewan.

"Wait." Ewan grabbed his arm. "What is in this? Is it laudanum?"

The doctor watched him as though he were duller than a butter knife. "Of course it is. You want to ease pain, that's what you give. You want her to remain in pain, don't give it." He freed himself from Ewan's hold, slamming the door behind him.

Ewan stared at Annabelle. "She doesna want anything with opium. She told me that before I went for the doctor."

Annabelle looked at J.P. sweating on the bed and moved to her, swiping at her forehead. "Ewan, it's the only thing that will help her pain. You must give her some."

He held the bottle in his hand before moving to the small kitchen area. He rummaged before he found a clean spoon. When he sat on the edge of the bed, he held the bottle and spoon in one hand and rubbed a finger over J.P.'s brow. "How are ye, Jessie?" he whispered.

"Hurts," she rasped. She opened pain-dulled eyes to him, eyes that had only ever been full of life. "Every breath is an agony," she breathed in a voice so low he barely heard her.

Ewan watched as Annabelle turned away, battling a sob. "I have medicine for ye. 'Twill take away yer pain." He watched as she closed her eyes as though in agreement. "'Tis laudanum."

"If you give that to me, don't leave me." She gasped as she took a too-deep breath.

"Do ye want the medicine, Jessie?" Ewan asked. He softly placed a palm against her cheek.

"Yes." A tear trickled out.

He frowned, and his hand shook as he measured out a small dose. "I'll give ye a wee amount, and then we'll see if ye need more. Is that all right?" He eased the spoon into her mouth and waited until he knew she had swallowed the medicine. After setting aside the bottle and spoon, he held her hand, his thumb tracing patterns over her skin. "I will no' leave ye."

After a few minutes her breathing evened out and her hold on his hand slackened. He focused on Annabelle. "Are ye all right, Anna?"

She sat on the chair beside him, quiet and drawn. "Yes. It made me realize how much Fidelia had been hurt earlier this year. How much she can be hurt again. And I hate that there is nothing I can do to help her. That she still wants nothing to do with me."

Ewan made a sound of agreement deep in his throat but refrained from saying more.

Annabelle rose. "I should return home. Cailean will be frantic when he realizes I'm gone." She squeezed his shoulder. "It isn't proper for you to remain here, Ewan. Come with me, and we'll send Sorcha over to sit with her."

Ewan snorted and shook his head. "Sorcha would poison Jessie with the medication." He rubbed at his forehead. "I promised Jessie that I'd stay, and I will no' break that promise." His gaze was haunted by memories. "Dinna ask me to."

Annabelle nodded and squeezed his shoulder again. "I'll save dinner for you. If you aren't home at a decent hour, I'll have Cailean bring you a plate."

Ewan nodded his agreement. "Thank ye, Anna. I couldna have asked anyone else to aid me today. The others were too angry."

Ewan barely acknowledged her departure as he remained focused on Jessamine. He told her stories from his youth, about his travels to the United States and his reunion with his brothers. He held her hand as she battled pain and her fear of the medicine that was to aid her. The sky darkened as night fell, and he lit a lamp so as to see her face.

Hours later he jumped as a hand clapped him on the shoulder. He looked up to meet his eldest brother's worried gaze. "Eat." Cailean thrust a plate of food at him and shook his head to dissuade him from arguing. After Ewan accepted the food, Cailean pulled over the lumpy chair Ewan had sat in the previous night and collapsed into it.

"Why are ye here, Ewan?" Cailean asked, his accent stronger in his agitation. "Ye have to ken what this will mean."

Ewan wolfed down the meat loaf and potatoes. He paused before attacking the piece of apple pie. "I ken what I'm doing."

"Do ye? Do ye understand that ye'll have to wed her if ye don't leave here with me? It's night, and the longer ye remain here, the worse it appears." He sighed and clasped his hands together in front of him before meeting his youngest brother's defiant gaze. "She's not Flora."

Ewan jerked as though Cailean had punched him. "Aye, I ken that well enough."

Cailean took another deep breath, calming his emotions. "You don't have to try to save her. Or any of the others. There is no way you can."

"Ye believe that's why I go to the Boudoir?" Ewan asked. "Ye think it's because I'm intent on savin' women who have no interest in leavin' such a place?" He set the plate on the floor with a *thud* and looked at Jessamine who rested on the bed.

"Why else do you go there? Why do you torment yourself when I know you don't go upstairs and partake of the favors they offer?" Cailean's hazel eyes shone with confusion and concern.

"The last time I saw her was at a place like the Boudoir." He shook his head as though in defeat and shrugged. "When I'm there, I feel close to her, if only for an instant."

"You'll never see her again, Ewan," Cailean said, his voice harsher than he intended.

Ewan nodded and clenched his jaw. "Aye, I ken that." He raised bleak eyes, made all the bleaker as his cheerful mask was completely absent. "I've always kent that." He took a deep breath. "She's been dead for years."

Cailean exhaled and gripped his brother's arm. "I'm sorry, Ewan. I didn't know."

Ewan shrugged his shoulders. "When I advised you to find another, before you met Anna, I knew what I was talking about, Cailean." His bittersweet smile did little to ease his long-held sorrow. "I'm a hypocrite though. I willna do the same for myself."

Cailean frowned and looked at Jessamine asleep on the bed. "If you won't do the honorable thing by her, leave with me. Allow her to keep her reputation."

Ewan shook his head. "Nae, I willna leave." He clasped her hand. "I'm honorable, aye?"

Rather than soothing his brother, his words provoked greater agitation. "Think about what you are doing."

Ewan looked at Jessamine. "I have. Dinna worry, Cail. Everythin' will turn out fine. It always does with me." His carefree grin met Cailean's glower. "Ye have to ken I'll never follow the town's dictates."

Cailean sighed and slapped him on his shoulder. "At least sit in this chair. It's got to be a little more comfortable than that bare wooden one." He rose, scooting it to where Ewan sat. When he saw that his brother was as comfortable as possible, he slipped out the front door.

After Ewan had finished eating his pie, he stretched his legs in front of him as he prepared for an uncomfortable night in the chair. When he was about to slip into a half-awake state, he heard her voice.

"Who was Flora?"

He opened his eyes and turned his head to meet Jessamine's alert, pain-filled gaze. She shook her head as he pointed to the bottle on the nightstand by the bed and waited for him to answer her question.

"Flora was the woman I loved on Skye. Her father was poor, which was sayin' somethin' as none of us had two coins to rub together. He was forced off the land afore our family." Ewan's eyes shone with emotion. "I promised her that I'd find her, that I'd wed her, that we'd have a wonderful future together, but that I needed time to save money."

J.P. waited for him to continue, her eyes filled with compassion rather than a reporter's rapacious curiosity.

"Cail sent me money for my journey. I never planned to travel here. I was goin' to use it for my weddin' and to live with Flora. I'd find work in a factory in the lowlands. Do anythin' I needed to as long as I could be with Flora." He cleared his throat and shook his head as though embarrassed by his youthful love.

"What happened?" Jessamine reached out a hand and waited until he held hers. "You're here and not there." When he remained silent, she whispered, "I'm asking as a friend, not as a reporter."

He swallowed and took a deep breath. "I traveled to Glasgow. No easy feat from Skye. I'd never traveled farther than ten miles from our land, so the big city was a shock." He shook his head. "The buildings on top of each other. The waste everywhere. The stench of all those people living together." He shook his head. "After days of searchin', I found my Flora."

Jessamine frowned. "At a whorehouse."

"Aye, a whorehouse. Dyin'." He blinked a few times, although his gaze remained unfocused, envisioning a long-forgotten scene. "She'd caught some nasty disease an' was little more than skin an' bones."

"What did you do?"

He sniffled. "I paid for my time with her. 'Twas a filthy, poorly run place. Nothin' like the one here. When we were in her room, I wrapped her in a blanket and carried her out the back steps. I nursed her until she died, three days later."

"Why didn't she wait for you?" Jessamine squeezed his hand.

"Her family was proud, ye ken, but they had no money. When they arrived in the big city, her father didna find work. He had no skills, little education, an' too many mouths to feed." Ewan bowed his head.

Jessamine grimaced, and Ewan was uncertain if it was from his story or her own pain. "So he sacrificed his daughter for the benefit of the family?"

"Aye," Ewan breathed. "An' robbed me of her." He swiped at his cheek and rubbed his shirtsleeve under his nose. "I would have loved her an' loved her well."

"Oh, Ewan, how tragic," Jessamine whispered. "All this time I thought you were carefree. That you'd been spared the harsh realities of life."

He huffed out a laugh. "No one's been spared harsh realities, Jessie. If ye dinna ken that, then ye are no' a very good reporter."

He saw a shadow flicker over her face and frowned. "Are ye in pain?" When she nodded, he picked up the medicine bottle and raised an eyebrow. After she nodded once more, he gave her a small dose. "Sleep, Jessie. I'll be here next to ye."

By the following day, Jessamine's pain had lessened enough that she no longer requested laudanum. At least that is what she told Ewan. In truth, the pain continued as a hot iron in her side, constantly present. She feared it would always be there. Movement was difficult, but, after telling her lie that the medication was no longer needed, she had to swallow all cries of distress and cover a grimace with a smile.

When seated in bed, with a cup of soup in front of her and one of Annabelle's sweet rolls cut into small pieces, she sighed. Immediately the burning in her side intensified, and she masked the pain with a smile as she looked at the bounty in front of her. "How nice of your family," she murmured.

"I ken ye are in pain, Jessie," Ewan said. "I dinna understand why ye are tryin' to hide it from me."

"The pain is bearable," she insisted as she took a slurp of soup and blushed.

He swiped at her mouth as though she were a child, shaking his head in disagreement. "Nae, I ken what it is to bruise a rib, never mind break one. Ye'll have pain for weeks. Why will ye no' take the medicine offered?"

Her gaze filled with a defiant desperation. "No more medication. Ever!"

He frowned but nodded. "Aye, it's yer choice." He waited as she ate half her soup and a few pieces of the roll. When it was evident she would eat no more, he removed the food and set it in her miniscule kitchen area.

She rested against the pillows with her hands crossed over her waist. "I was never going to print that story," she whispered. She met his surprised gaze and nodded. "About Leticia."

"Why was it on yer desk?"

She shrugged and then winced. "It was a story I'd investigated and considered reporting." She met his intense stare. "It's a good story." When he continued to stare at her and remained quiet, she sighed. "But I realized I'd do as much damage printing that article as I did with Bears' story." She flushed. "And I like Leticia."

Ewan frowned as he leaned against the counter in her kitchen. "So it makes a difference whether or not ye like the person? If ye didna, ye wouldna mind destroyin' their reputation?" His eyes flashed.

She winced again as she let out a deep breath. "I'm learning, Ewan, about how to be a small-town reporter. It's very different from the big city. And, unfortunately, it does matter if I like you. If I were to learn a similar tale about Mrs. Jameson, I would find it difficult not to print it."

Ewan shook his head. "Keep learnin', Jessie. I still believe ye should use yer intelligence to write humor and other such articles."

"Be patient," she whispered. "As it is, I won't print anything for at least a week." She watched as he fidgeted in the kitchen and frowned as he was uncharacteristically uncomfortable. "Whatever it is you think you need to say, will you just say it?" She turned her head and met his chagrined gaze. "It's as though I can feel you tensing more with each second that passes while you consider your words."

"Jessie," he said on a long sigh, his voice tinged with humor. "Ye take the romance out of everything."

Her gaze lost all humor as she sobered. "There is no romance between us. We're barely friends."

"Ye ken that's no' true." He reached for one of her hands, raising it to his lips and kissing it. "I've now spent two nights with ye."

"Nothing happened!"

"Aye, to my everlastin' regret." He frowned as she glared at him. "Jessie, ye ken we must marry."

"I *ken* no such thing." She huffed out a breath, unable to hide her grimace. "What I do know is that I will never marry an overbearing, uncultured, brutish Scot like you. Why would I have to? I've survived plenty of scandals in my past, and I'll survive this one."

He flushed at her perception of him. "The townsfolk will no' be kind to ye. I ken … know they are already talkin' about ye."

"They've talked about me, with your help, since the day I arrived." She snatched her hand away from him. "I have no need of a husband. Not now or ever." Her mocking gaze raked over him from head to foot. "And, if I did, I wouldn't look to you."

His flush deepened, and he took a long breath. "Aye, how foolish of me. I'm sorry to bother ye, Miss McMahon." He rose, grabbed his hat off a cabinet, and stormed for the door.

When the door rattled shut, J.P. closed her eyes, willing the tears not to fall. A lone tear leaked out, and she swiped it away. She took shallow breaths and focused on the pain of her rib rather than the ache in her heart.

CHAPTER 8

*J*essamine stilled while she was in the Merc and listened to the women gossiping behind her. She had bound her ribs as tightly as possible, and the pain was bearable if she moved slowly and did not raise her right arm. She focused on the women rather than her ever-present pain and wondered if they knew she was here, before realizing they did not care if she heard. She feigned interest in ribbons as she focused on their vitriol.

"Slut."

Another woman spoke. "Spent the whole night with him, but they aren't married!"

A third, more righteous than the last, added to the discussion. "We thought the schoolteacher was bad, but this one's worse! I don't want to speak to her again about anything." A snicker followed. "As if I'll believe anything she prints again. Has no common decency."

Jessamine took a deep breath, forgetting about her broken rib, and clutched a hand to her side. She turned to face her detractors in what she hoped was a nonchalant manner and smiled. "Hello, ladies." Her smile lost any friendliness and took on a feral tinge when she saw Mrs. Jameson in the group. "I hope you are having a wonderful day."

Mrs. Jameson marched up to her and poked her in her side.

Thankfully it was her unhurt side as J.P. had had the sense not to call attention to her injury.

"You are a disgrace! You should not be allowed to live in our town."

"I will forever find it fascinating how your standards are different when they pertain to anyone who isn't your son." She gasped as she attempted to take a deep breath. "The only reason Mr. MacKinnon was forced to remain by my bedside ..."

She paused as a woman muttered, "You mean *in* your bed!"

"*By* my bedside," she repeated, "was because your son broke my rib. Mr. MacKinnon insisted on caring for me."

Another woman, unknown to Jessamine, snorted. "As if you'll have us believing that man would care for your injuries after all you've written about him!"

"It's certainly more plausible than your notion that he's desperate to be in my bed." Jessamine smirked and raised an eyebrow.

The women in front of her blushed and tittered and lowered their gazes. Only Mrs. Jameson met her bald statement with a glower. "You are shameless. You refuse to acknowledge the bounds of propriety."

"When they are promulgated by women like you, I have no need to understand *your* version of propriety." Jessamine met Mrs. Jameson's glower, recognizing she was her true foe.

Mrs. Jameson took a deep breath. "You have no right to defame my son! He is a wonderful boy."

Jessamine laughed, gasping at the pain it provoked. "That's his problem. You continue to consider him a boy, and he acts as though his actions will never be punished. One day someone will make him pay for all his wrongdoings."

Mrs. Jameson straightened her shoulders. "I do not have to stand here and listen to the likes of you. Ladies?" she said as she spun on her heel and marched out of the Merc.

Jessamine watched them stomp down the boardwalk and enter the café. She let out a shallow breath, so as not to cause any more pain to her broken rib, and then faced the mocking glance of Tobias. "Hello, Mr. Sutton."

"Miss McMahon," Tobias said with a smirk. "What can I get for you?" He frowned as she set a list on the counter. "And I suppose you want this delivered?"

"Yes, by the end of the day." She met his gaze and smiled when he nodded his agreement. "Thank you."

He called out to her when she approached the door. "You won't always have the upper hand over me, miss. One day I'll find a way to get back at you."

She refused to look at him and slipped outside to return to her print shop.

Ewan wandered to the sawmill on a cold early-November day. He tucked the scarf tighter into his jacket and around his neck before stuffing his hands into his pockets. A thin layer of frost covered the trees and grass, although the area nearest the sawmill remained unfrozen due to the heat from the mill and the activity in the yard.

Nathaniel loaded a wagon with his friend Karl but paused when he saw Ewan approach. He motioned for them to continue to work and helped them finish loading the wagon. "Do you have any more to do?" When Karl pointed to the empty wagon next to the filled one, Ewan smiled and helped them fill it too. The quiet camaraderie and the work eased some of his tension.

When they had finished, Karl muttered his thanks before returning to the sawmill. Nathaniel remained outside, sweat pouring off his brow. He and Ewan approached the nearby creek and rinsed their hands before scooping up some water to drink. Ewan splashed his face and neck, shivering at the freezing temperature of the creek.

"I always forget how cold the water is this time of year!" he said as he dried his face with his scarf.

"Ya, but is refreshing." Nathaniel slapped him on the back. "Thank you for your help. You saved us time, and it will allow Karl to prepare for his evening with Leena."

Ewan raised an eyebrow and half smiled.

"He is taking her to the café tonight. I go too, of course, as it is not proper for her to go only with him. But I talk with Harold the entire time and give them time alone."

Ewan smiled. "You're a good older brother to your sister."

Nathaniel sobered. "Your brothers have not been so good to you." When Ewan frowned, he said, "Why did they allow you to stay with that reporter? The one who abuses you?" He pointed to the bruises on Ewan's face.

"She didn't give me these. I fought in the Boudoir and …" He shrugged.

"Ya, but she abuses you in other ways." Nathaniel watched Ewan with concern.

Ewan shook his head. "She was injured, Nathaniel, and needed my help. It was my decision not to leave."

Nathaniel sighed. "You harmed her more than you helped her. Leena told me that the Jameson woman was quite upset as she marched down the boardwalk today. The mother wants you for her daughter." He laughed as Ewan shivered again.

Ewan sat on a wood stump. "What else have ye heard in town? No one says what they feel in front of me or my family."

"Townsfolk say that, if you do not wed the reporter soon, others will find their way to her bed. Or that you were smart to extract your revenge as you did." He shrugged. "You will not have to suffer due to your actions."

Ewan shook his head. "It's never the men who have to suffer."

Nathaniel nodded. "No, only the women." He slapped Ewan on the back. "Do you need more wood?"

Ewan nodded, quickly discussing the order he needed filled and then departed as Nathaniel reentered the sawmill. Rather than return to his worksite, Ewan made a detour down Main Street to the bakery. The bell tinkled as he opened the door, and he smiled as he saw the finely wrought shelves and space he had helped create for Annabelle. At the time, she and Cailean were adversaries, and Ewan had never suspected that she and Cailean would marry.

Leticia emerged from the back and smiled at Ewan. "We're sold out," she said with an apologetic smile as she pointed to the bare shelves.

"Aye, I should have kent better." He rubbed at his head. "Is Anna around?"

Leticia motioned for him to follow her into the back room where Annabelle prepared baskets for delivery. Leticia hefted two and called out a goodbye as she exited the back door.

"Give me a moment," Annabelle said. Her stomach was ever increasing, and she now walked with a slight waddle. She moved to the front where she flipped the sign to Closed, locked the door, and pulled the curtains. "I should have done that a while ago. Most towns-folk know not to come in after two."

Her smile faded as she looked at Ewan. "Are you all right?" She pointed to a stool, and he collapsed onto it. His customary good mood returned for a moment when she put a plate of cookie pieces in front of him, along with a glass of milk. "I know this doesn't make it all better, but sometimes it makes it all bearable."

"Cailean did no' understand how fortunate he was when he married ye. Nor did we." He smiled as she fought tears. "'Tis the bairn, I imagine, that makes ye weepy."

She nodded and sniffled. "What's the matter, Ewan? You haven't been like yourself for days."

He chuckled and then lowered his head to lean on his forearms crossed over themselves on the butcher-block countertop. "That's where ye're wrong. This is more how I am. Moody and pensive. The carefree ne'er-do-well was no' truly me."

Anna pulled out a stool and sat. "I always wondered what you were running from. Losing your money at the gambling table. Whiling away your hours at the Boudoir." She met his gaze, so much like Cailean's before he had made peace with the death of his first wife and baby. "You're not that different from Cailean or Alistair, and I could never understand why you would lose money, rather than pay them back the funds they had taken out for bringing you to America."

Ewan took a deep breath and closed his eyes. "Cailean isna the only one to lose someone he loved. I did too. I also lost every dime he sent to me."

Annabelle gripped his hand and shook her head. "I don't understand. How did you get here?"

"I stole and then I gambled what I'd stolen." He smirked. "Thankfully Lady Luck didna abandon me that night."

She frowned as she studied her brother-in-law. "It doesn't take away the fact that your brother sent money for you to travel here. That he took out a loan. Why haven't you helped to pay him back?"

Ewan shook his head. "Did ye ken Cailean had promised me money a year afore it arrived?" He looked at Annabelle with leashed anger. "A year."

She squeezed his hand. "I don't understand. What's important is that he sent it. That he never forgot his family and wanted you to be together."

Ewan growled and rose. "Nae, 'tisn't what's important! If he'd done what he promised, I wouldna have lost her! I would never have had to let her go!"

Annabelle sat stock-still a moment in the face of his anger and grief. "Cailean did not cause anyone's death, Ewan. Not his wife's. Not his baby's. Not your love's. He's only ever done what he could to help those he loves." She swiped at her cheek. "If you resent your brother this much, you must speak with him, talk it out. If not, perhaps you should consider living elsewhere."

Ewan spun to face her and stared at her with confusion. "I resent fate. I resent his inability to get a loan earlier. I resent false hopes." He took a deep breath. "Aye, I resented him for a long time, and I can no' lie and say it did no' soothe an ache to see him as miserable as I was." He flinched at her indrawn gasp of air. "Selfish man that I am, it helped to ken I was no' the only one sufferin' the loss of someone I loved."

He paused and looked at his sister-in-law. "But, after I spent time with him, after so many years apart, I kent what I always knew was true. He was my brother, and Cailean had done all he could for me." Ewan took a deep breath. "It was no one's fault but fate's and her father's and ..." His voice broke as tears poured down his cheeks.

"Oh, Ewan," Annabelle murmured as she rushed toward him and pulled him into her embrace. "There's nothing I can say to take away that pain." She rocked him back and forth as she cried with him as she held him in her arms.

When he calmed, she sniffled and patted his back. "I don't think your carefree mask was all a ploy. I think you enjoy your unfettered life and your ability to do what you please."

"Aye, I've enjoyed it for years." He took a deep breath and scrubbed at his face. "But I dinna find the pleasure in it now as much as I used to."

She waited a moment for him to speak and then sighed when his gaze remained unfocused and distant. "Does it have something to do with a certain red-haired journalist?" She smiled when he flushed.

She tugged him to a stool and sat next to him when he remained quiet. "Cailean felt guilty for loving me. He thought he was betraying Maggie and their bairn." She sighed. "Love isn't like that, Ewan. There isn't a quota on how much we can love. If that other woman truly loved you, she'd want you to be happy now that she's not here."

Ewan lowered his gaze. "I ken that. I do." He rubbed at his eyes. "But I couldna have picked a worse woman."

Annabelle laughed, not bothering to wipe the tears off her face or to blink away the ones still in her eyes. "Why do you say that? I think she's perfect for you. She challenges you, which is something I think you need. You'd be bored within a week with an agreeable, docile woman." She met his frown. "I may not always like what she prints, but it is her business." She gripped his hand. "What is important is what you know to be true. You must believe that she is the woman you want to court and marry, not worrying about what others will think." She hugged him again. "Be happy, Ewan."

He let out a long, stuttering breath. "I'm tryin', Anna." He met her gaze, embarrassment and shame in his expression. "I dinna want ye thinkin' I wish Cail harm. That I dinna ..." He shook his head.

"I know how much you love your siblings, Ewan." She squeezed his hand. "I know what it is to wish I'd done something differently for my sister rather than to always have a long-standing rift between us. I'm thankful you haven't put past hurts before your present relationship with Cailean."

Ewan nodded. "I'm glad ye're my sister, Anna." He squeezed her hand and rose. "I'll see ye at home."

CHAPTER 9

The following Sunday, a week after he had spent time with Jessamine, Ewan worked in the livery helping Bears. Alistair and Cailean were still with their wives, and Ewan relished the time alone in the barn with the horses. Bears was a hard worker, but he rarely spoke, so Ewan had no expectation of conversation, and he appreciated the uninterrupted time to think.

The rumors about him and Jessamine had only multiplied during the week, although he had kept his distance. The fact she had refrained from publishing a paper this week had heightened the townsfolk's curiosity as they were interested in the latest *N&N* and what she would write about him. His absence from her life had only seemed to heighten the burgeoning scandal, rather than diminish it. The townsfolk now referred to him as the town's heartbreaker and murmured about Jessamine as the wronged woman.

He sighed before digging his pitchfork into a pile of dirty hay. He loaded up a wheelbarrow and moved the hay outside. He breathed in the crisp fall air, infused with the scent of woodsmoke. The sound of men chopping trees carried on the wind, as many were storing up firewood for the winter. He turned into the barn and met Bears' gaze.

"What else do ye need me to do?" Ewan asked as he swiped at his brow.

Bears shrugged. "You've done enough. You won't outwork your demons here."

Ewan stilled and then glared at Bears. "Ye dinna ken what ye're talkin' about."

Bears' long hair swung over his shoulders as he moved with an innate grace around a stall, spreading hay onto the floor and readying it for another horse. "I know more about it than you think. Loss is the one constant we all share."

Ewan snorted. "I thought love was."

Bears turned and his brown-black eyes shone with intelligence and understanding. "No, that's what the poets tell us. We know better." He turned away and continued his work.

Ewan stared at Bears' back a few moments until he realized he would have no more conversation from Bears. With a muttered curse, Ewan set aside his pitchfork and walked to the side of the barn and the hand pump. He bent low, dunking his head in cold water before rising and shaking his head clear.

He grunted when a towel was thrown at him and scrubbed at his face and head. Cailean stood watching him with a mixture of concern and impatient exasperation, his constant expression when looking at Ewan for the past few years. "What have I done now?" Ewan demanded.

"It's what you've failed to do," Cailean said. He flicked a glance at Bears and then shrugged. "I thought you'd have asked for her hand, but it's been a week."

Ewan sat on the stool Cailean set out for him and continued to absently scrub at his head. "I ken how long it's been since I've seen Jessie," he whispered. Cailean sat in silence, and Ewan met his brother's gaze. "Why ... How did ye ken about Flora? It was after ye left. I never told a soul. Even Sorcha dinna ken about her."

Cailean bent forward, resting his elbows on his knees. "When you arrived, you weren't the brother I remembered. You were damaged." Cailean looked out at the paddock and the horses snoozing in the late fall morning. A soft breeze blew, and a gentle light shone over the mountains. "Alistair told me it was leaving Skye that had affected you, and I realized what leaving had done to him."

Cailean cleared his throat as though trying to alleviate his guilt at his middle brother leaving Skye with him. He met Ewan's shuttered gaze. "I knew it was more than that. One night a few months after you arrived, when I was lonely and missing Maggie to my marrow, I went to the Boudoir. You were there but sitting downstairs, sipping whiskey. Not the watered-down pap the Madam sells but honest-to-God whiskey. And you were muttering about Flora." Cailean took a deep breath. "I sat next to you and shooed away the Beauties. And you told me of who you'd loved. But you never said she'd died."

Ewan groaned and shut his eyes. "I thought no one kent." He rose and wandered to the door of the paddock.

"Why do you think I worry about you gambling and going to the Boudoir?" Cailean watched his youngest brother, unable to hide his concern.

"Ye worry about the money I'm losin'. About the fact I never paid ye back." He growled as Cailean spun him to face him.

"Nae," Cailean rasped. "Never. I worry because I ken ye're livin' in the past when ye go to those places. Not the present. That ye have no dream for the future. Ye cling to ghosts as fiercely as I did."

Ewan's ironic laugh echoed through their part of the barn. "Is that no' what I warned ye of? Clingin' to ghosts?" He watched as Cailean remembered their past conversation. "I only kent what ye were doin' because I'm so good at it myself."

Cailean gripped his brother's arm, refusing to allow him to storm away and to end their conversation. "I know I failed you. I know you blame me for her death." He nodded. "Yes, I spoke with Belle. There are no secrets in our marriage." He waited a moment for Ewan's anger to fade. "I'm sorry, Ewan. I did what I could."

Ewan shook free of his brother's hold. "I ken that. Now. After I arrived and saw how hard ye and Al worked. After I saw the toll yer grief still took on ye and how Alistair fretted." Ewan forced a smile. "I refused to be the youngest brother, brought low by grief too. I would be cheerful, and carefree, everyone's friend."

Cailean's steady gaze caused Ewan to shift and lower his head. "You succeeded."

"Aye, I did. And I have kent joy." He raised his head in defiance.

Cailean tilted his head to the side. "When?"

Ewan rubbed at his face. "When I'm battlin' with Jessie. She's unlike anyone I ever kent. The exact opposite of Flora." He flushed as though he had sullied Flora's memory in some way. "I never ken what Jessie will say or do next, and it's exhiliratin'." He sighed. After a moment he whispered, "She needed me that night, Cail. I couldna abandon her."

"Aye. I understand that. However, the gossip is vicious right now. And I fear her next paper will not be well-received, no matter what is written in it."

"She turned me down," Ewan whispered. He met his brother's shocked gaze and nodded. "Said she'd faced scandal before without having to shackle herself to an overbearing Scotsman who thinks he knows what's best for her."

Cailean laughed. Ewan punched him in the chest, and he stumbled backward. Alistair, who had just entered the barn, grabbed Cailean before he tumbled into a pile of hay.

"Why are ye punchin' Cail?" Alistair asked. His brown eyes shone with a quiet contentment, only adding fuel to Ewan's ire.

"I canna be around the two of ye today!" Ewan growled.

"Get yer own woman," Alistair said with a shrug.

Cailean chuckled and said, "He tried, but she said no." He met Bears' curious gaze as he brushed a horse in a nearby stall, and Cailean winked at him. Bears half smiled and continued his work.

"The reporter turned ye down?" Alistair raised both eyebrows and then shook his head. "When?"

Ewan rolled his shoulders as though uncomfortable about the conversation. "Last week. I asked her Monday afore I left."

Cailean groaned. "She was takin' pain medication. She was half out of her mind with it. You never ask a woman when she's in such a state."

Alistair shrugged. "Ye never ken. If she wasna grateful for all he did, she may never want to marry him."

Ewan glared at his brothers. "Ye are no' helpin'." He kicked at the hay spread about the floor. "She said I was takin' advantage of her. That I should be ashamed that I was more concerned about what others would say than common sense. That I didna ken her and should no' want to marry her."

"Ah," Alistair said with a knowing nod. "The lass is afraid."

Ewan laughed. "That woman has no' been afraid of a thing in her life."

Cailean shook his head. "No, I think Al's right. You scared her. Now you have to woo her if you want her as your wife." His smile spread, mischief glinting from his gaze. "Should be a sight to see."

News & Noteworthy: *I have recently discovered that the town's most disreputable gentleman is not nearly as disreputable as he would like us to believe. In fact, I believe his entire disreputable persona is an act. I have recently discovered that Mr. D.G. is a man of his word who continues to honor his lost Scottish love. Poverty and desperation separated them, but he remained steadfast in his constancy and his determination to find her. He searched the large city of Glasgow, Scotland, for her, long after their separation on the Isle of Skye. Imagine his desolation to discover, after months of dreaming of her, that she was dying in squalor. Never one to abandon those he loves, Mr. D.G. remained with her until she died. One wonders if any woman alive can compete with her ghost.*

E wan hammered a nail with extra force as he muttered to himself. *"I have recently discovered ..."* He swore and hammered in another nail, barely missing his thumb. He reached for his bag of nails, only to find Alistair standing there with the bag in his hands.

"Al." He opened and closed his hand for him to give him the bag, but Alistair shook his head.

"'Tis dusk, Ewan. Come home. Have dinner. Spend time with yer family." He watched as Ewan tossed his tool to a wooden box and strode away.

Ewan moved through the empty space, the vision vivid in his mind that only he saw—of the home he had hoped to create with Jessamine. He muttered to himself, refusing to think of her and her betrayal, and then stopped moving when he came to the back wall.

"Ye can only run so far, brother," Alistair murmured.

"Do ye ken who I was building this house for?" he asked without turning around. He took a deep breath. "Myself. A few weeks ago I began to envision Jessie here with me. That's when I kent I was in trouble."

"The article today doesna mean she's lost to ye, Ewan."

Ewan nodded. "Aye, it does. She betrayed me." He turned and met his brother's worried gaze. "I spoke to her as a friend, and she did no' honor that." He clenched and unclenched his fist.

"Ye seem angry at yerself when she's to blame."

"She's no' worthy of my regard, an' yet I canna stop caring for her."

Alistair nodded. "*Loving* her." He and Ewan shared a long look.

"Aye, I canna seem to stop, even though I'd rather hate her." He let out a long breath. "I ken ye understand what that feels like. The public humiliation. The anger. The desire not to love her." He flushed as Alistair nodded. "But the difference is, ye kent Leticia loved ye. I've only ever had Jessie's disdain."

Alistair rubbed at the back of his neck and shrugged. "Why did ye never speak of yer loss with me?"

Ewan shook his head. "Ye spent a decade with Cailean's sorrow as a constant companion. Ye didna need mine as well." He shrugged. "'Twas easier to have ye believe I mourned Skye an' the life there than the truth."

His older brother strode toward him and gripped his shoulders. His eyes burned with a deep love. "I would've accepted any of yer pain if it would have helped ye."

"I ken, Alistair. I ken." He pushed away from his brother and scrubbed at his head. "Now that woman is makin' my life a livin' hell."

"Aye, ye love her, an' she doesna admit to lovin' ye."

"Nae, 'tis much worse than that." He met his brother's confused stare. "Do ye ken how many women came by the worksite today with pails of lunch, words of concern, and gentle inquiries about my mental state? The damn woman has only made me more popular and enticin' to the womenfolk of this town. Seems there's nothin' women like better than a man who's loved and lost."

Alistair chuckled. "Means they hope he can love again." He watched his morose brother. "Which ye can, Ewan. Why do ye no' go there and have it out with her? 'Tisn't like ye to stay here, lickin' yer wounds."

"I did go by the print shop earlier, after I first read the article. But she was no' there." His jaw ticked. "Perhaps I should go there now." He met Alistair's steady gaze. "Aye, I will."

He grabbed his toolbox and walked down the street behind Main Street with Alistair. After accepting Alistair's offer to leave his toolbox at Alistair's house, Ewan walked to the back door of the print shop. He tried the handle and slipped inside upon finding it unlocked.

J.P sat at her desk, reading an article under a lamp as the day's light waned.

He noticed she now had curtains over the front windows, and those were pulled. He watched as she tapped a pencil on a pad of paper while she frowned at something and then set it all aside to stare into space.

"Thinkin' about yer sins?" he asked, smiling as she jolted in her chair. Her gaze flew to him, and she rose so quickly she stumbled over her long satin skirts.

"How dare you sneak into my office, my home, through the back door! I should scream and …" Her chest rose and fell with her rapid breaths, and she glared at him as she righted herself.

He frowned as he saw the residual pain in her gaze. "I ken ye wouldna have let me in the front door." He shook his head. "How can ye act with righteous indignation when ye are the one who acted to betray me? To betray us?"

"There is no *us*, Ewan. There never has been. There never will be." Her cognac-colored eyes shone with anger. "I acted as I always will. For the benefit of the story. You handed me the perfect headline. How could I not use it?"

He paused and waited a moment before responding. When he did, his voice had lowered, although the anger shone through. "I told ye what I did in confidence. To a friend. Not to a bloodthirsty journalist."

She scoffed. "Journalists don't have friends. That's the first rule my father ever taught me."

He balled his hands at his sides and leaned toward her but refrained from touching her. "Ye have no idea what ye did, do ye?"

"I reported on a story that would ensure the masses would continue to purchase my paper, even though they consider me a social pariah. I turned you into a tragic figure who has yet to overcome his lost love, effectively explaining why you're reluctant to marry one such as I. You may not see it that way, but it has worked out as I planned. And, although you may not believe me, I did take Bears' advice."

He shook his head in confusion. "How did this turn into ye exonerating' me an' my sins when ye're the one who has no desire to wed me?" He held up a hand. "An' 'tis no excuse for betrayin' a confidence. Ye have no decency, no shame, Jessie. I expected better of ye."

"That was your initial mistake. Having any expectations of me in the first place." She tossed her head back in defiance.

"Do ye ken what ye did? Ye set every mother and single woman in town on me, like ..." He bit his tongue and flushed as he bit off what he was going to say.

"Like what?"

"'Tis no' proper to say such things to a lady." He nodded at her even though she snorted. "Ye are a lady, Jessie, no matter what ye were told by yer family." He sighed, and his anger seeped away. "I canna even remain angry with ye."

"I've never been worth strong emotions for long."

His eyes flashed fire. "Whoever filled yer head with such nonsense was wrong." He frowned when he saw the echo of betrayal in her gaze. "I suspect it was yer father, as ye never speak of yer mother, an' he should have kent better." His voice dropped to a caress. "Ye, Jessie, are priceless."

She bit her lip that quivered and boldly met his gaze. "I do not need your pity." Each word came out clearly enunciated, with a hint of bitterness.

"Aye, I think ye do. Ye need that, along with my forgiveness." He moved toward her with the speed and grace of a cat, outmaneuvering her so she was in his arms. "An' my love."

She shook her head. "No! I refuse to need anyone."

He pulled her to him as her tears began to fall and held her against his chest. "Cry, Jessie." After many moments, he walked with her to the bed and sat beside her with an arm slung over her shoulder. "Why do ye believe ye can no' need anyone?"

"It makes you weak. Weaker than love." She gripped her side as her breath stuttered. She glared at him as he watched her with concern. "Do not even consider offering me any more of that vile medicine. I threw it all away."

His brows furrowed, and he shook his head. "I dinna understand ye. Why would ye discard somethin' that will help ye?" He tucked away loose tendrils of red hair and then massaged her shoulder. "What happened to ye afore ye arrived here?"

"I don't like speaking about my past," she whispered as she curled into him.

He sighed, pulling her tight against him, relaxing for the first time in over a week as he held her in his arms. He ran his hands down her back, smiling as he kissed the top of her head while she burrowed farther into him. "I love holding ye."

She murmured her agreement, her arms wrapped tightly around him.

After many minutes he asked, "Why won't you tell me about your past, Jessie?"

She shook her head and pushed against his shoulder. "No, I don't want to remember." She peppered the side of his neck under his ear with kisses. "Make me forget." Her hand roved over his waistcoat, undoing buttons and slipping under his shirt until her hands ran over the warm flesh of his chest.

"Jessie," he said, his voice thickening with passion. "Ye dinna ken what ye are askin' for."

She looked at him a moment, and her seductive smile provoked a groan. "I do." She arched up and kissed him.

He groaned, crushing his mouth to hers, unable to kiss her gently. After a moment, he eased away, bracketing her face with his large callused hands. "Is the front door locked?" he asked as he bent forward to nibble his way down her neck.

"Yes," she gasped as she turned her head to grant him better access. She squealed when he tugged her up, her shocked gaze meeting his delighted one as he slowly divested her of many layers of clothes.

She frowned when he turned from her when she was naked. "How dare you leave me now!"

"*Shh.* ... Dinna fash yerself," he said with a wink and a mischievous smile. He flicked the lock on the back door and pulled his shirt over his head, revealing rippling muscles. He kicked off his boots and stood in front of her again, hissing when she traced her fingers over his warm skin and muscles. He raised an eyebrow and smiled when she nodded as he held his hands at his belt buckle. He released it and shucked his pants and underclothes in one easy movement.

Grabbing her to him before giving her time to panic, he held her close. "There's no need to be afraid, Jessie," he whispered as she shivered in his arms. "We can stop now, if ye want."

She raised defiant, determined eyes. "No, Ewan. Love me." She stood on her toes and kissed him, forgetting everything but this moment as he led her to her small bed.

A fterward he held her in his arms, his hands playing in her long red hair. "Ye ken what this means? That we will marry."

She propped herself on his chest and laughed. "Of course it doesn't. You go to the Boudoir with great regularity. You never propose to any of them." She squealed in surprise and a touch of pain as he growled and rolled her beneath him.

"Dammit, woman, I dinna sleep with them! I flirt. I tease. I cajole 'em, but I do naught else." His brown eyes were lit with anger. "Ye are the first woman I've slept with since …"

She whispered, "Since her."

"Aye." He traced a finger down her cheek and then shook his head as though in regret. "Forgive me for hurtin' ye. I didna think of yer injury when I acted as I did." He flopped to his back in disgust.

"You didn't hurt me, Ewan. Not in any way that matters." She traced a hand over his chest, sighing when his clasped hers and held it over his heart. "I can't be what you want me to be."

He turned and looked at her with a frown. "An' what is that? What do ye think I want ye to be?"

"Like Annabelle or Leticia. Always proper and never doing or saying unscrupulous things."

Ewan propped his head on his hand. "I wouldna want ye to be other than ye are, Jessie. I wouldna care if ye continue to work at the paper, although if ye wrote less inflammatory articles ye might find life more to yer liking." He silenced her with a finger to her lips. "But I would never tell ye what to write or what to do with regard to the paper. Unless ye were to hurt someone I loved. Then I would speak up."

She shook her head. "You have no idea what it is to have a family like yours, do you?"

He shook his head in confusion. "Everyone has family, love."

She glared at him. "You're smart enough to understand what I mean. Not everyone has a family willing to support each other."

"What was yers like?" He kissed her shoulder as she cuddled onto his chest and swallowed a sob.

"Horrible." She fought sobs as he crooned to her and drew patterns on her back. "My father was a married man when he met my mother. She was respectable but gullible to the ways of a sophisticated man. He wooed her, bedded her, and got her with child. When he realized he'd have a baby with her, he was delighted because his society wife was barren. He wanted to take me from my mother and raise me openly as his daughter, but my mother refused." Jessamine shivered. "Her act of defiance cost her dearly."

"Why?" he kissed her forehead.

"My father was a powerful man. He wanted a child to inherit his fortune. Or, as was the case with a daughter, to use his fortune to find a man like him to wed me to and to pass on his wealth that way." She shuddered again.

"What happened to yer mother?" Ewan whispered.

Jessie gripped his arms as though attempting to crawl even closer to him. "When I was five, he visited us. I was already pretty, but he was astute enough to understand I'd be attractive when I grew up."

"Ye're beautiful, an' ye ken it," Ewan whispered as he traced a finger over her tear-stained cheeks.

"Even my red hair made me exotic." She sniffled. "He found a way to get me from my mother. He had his physician visit the house when she was ill with influenza, and, within a few weeks, she was a slave to the little blue bottle the doctor would deliver every three days. If she ran out early, she'd cry and beg me to summon him while she rocked and shook on the bed."

"That's why ye hate laudanum," Ewan whispered.

"He made her a slave to it. Soon there was little she wouldn't do to obtain her daily dose." She let out a sigh. "Including sending me to live with him."

"Oh, love," Ewan said as he kissed her head. "What was it like?"

"Horrible. There were no spontaneous tea parties with crumbs on the floor and dances around the table. There were no days in the park where I ran around and tried to catch butterflies. There were no bedtime stories." She sniffled. "Instead I had to learn how to be a proper young lady from the moment I entered his mansion. Back straight, no opinions, no speaking unless I was spoken to. No laughing. No running. No exuberance or emotion of any kind. And of course his barren society wife wanted nothing to do with me. Only put up with my presence at mealtimes because my father demanded it."

He groaned. "Must have been a livin' hell for ye."

She nodded and held on tighter. "I swore I'd escape." After moments of silence, her grip on his arm loosened. "I resolved to ruin myself. In every way."

Ewan pushed her off his chest and moved so that they laid side by side, staring into each other's eyes. "How? How did ye ruin yerself?" His gaze roved over her, and he smiled. "I already ken I was no' the first man to love ye, Jessie."

"Doesn't that matter to you? That I'm an unwed woman, but I wasn't a virgin?"

He frowned. "I willna let ye rile me. Nor will I judge ye. Tell me yer story."

She sighed and closed her eyes. They fluttered open when he tickled her nose with a feather from a pillow. "You are incorrigible. That is not meant as a compliment," she muttered when he smiled with pleasure. "I vowed to do all I could to avoid marriage to the man my father chose. I knew he'd be a man like him. Controlling. Ruthless. Mean." She shivered as if cold on the inside. "I couldn't imagine more of life like that, dominated by such a man."

Her gaze met Ewan's. "My father had a small interest in a New York newspaper. I played up his investment role, forged letters from him, and talked myself into a reporter's role. They needed a woman's perspective and section, and were delighted with the articles I wrote. Eventually I branched out into seedier territory, weighing in on the state of women nearly twenty years after the Civil War, the lack of job opportunities forcing many into a life of sin. I wrote about the laws against women that forced many into asylums." She sighed. "I was never allowed into an institution, so I wasn't able to report on how they were treated there."

"Thank God," Ewan breathed. "I hear they're horrid places."

"Yes, but that's the point. Places like that should have the light shone on them. Just as I did to orphanages around New York, highlighting the need for more compassion and less corporal punishment for young children."

"Ye go against yer times when ye write such articles."

She shrugged. "My father would read the articles by the radical J.P. McMahon and nearly have an apoplexy." She giggled. "It was a joy to watch his reaction when he had no idea I was J.P."

"Is that no' yer name?"

"My name is Jessamine Phyllis, but my father would never call me J.P. That is too vulgar, Ewan, for an Abbott."

"Who's McMahon?" He shook his head in confusion.

"McMahon was my grandmother's name on my mother's side. It's my name, in a circuitous way." She stroked his jaw. "I'm not a complete fabrication."

"Ye are no fabrication. Ye are in my arms an' true." He kissed her head. He nodded as though encouraging her to continue speaking.

"I knew the time of my betrothal announcement was approaching. My father had chosen a man nearly three times my age, and I was desperate not to marry him." She shivered. "I'd always liked my editor, and I thought he liked me too. One night I worked late and ..."

"Ye made love," Ewan murmured.

She snorted. "There was no love, Ewan. It was a horrible mistake, but I could never blame anyone but myself. The whole thing was over within three minutes."

"*Bluidy* idiot," he whispered as he kissed her along her forehead. "Too stupid to understand the gift he'd been given."

"*I* was stupid. I'd never realized he was married!" Her hands hit his as they both brushed away her tears. "I thought it would mean we had to marry if ... if he ..." Her voice faltered. "He called me a childish woman who should have known better than to look for more than a moment's pleasure. As if I'd had any pleasure!"

Ewan *tsk*ed in the back of his throat. "Take comfort in knowin' he's miserable with his wife right now." He smiled as she burrowed again into his embrace.

She sighed. "I returned home, disheveled and emotional, two states that were never to occur under my father's roof. His prodigy was there, and he was astute enough to surmise what had happened after one glance. My father threw me out of the house without a penny."

Ewan growled in displeasure. "What did ye do?"

"I had some money saved, in a box under my bed. When the house was asleep, I snuck in and took the box and a few clothes. I traveled to Saint Louis, with copies of stories I'd written, and got a job there." She sighed. "But my father casts a long shadow, and he said he found a man who didn't care about my past transgressions. He was sending a man to bring me home."

"So ye fled here." Ewan held her closer. "Why'd ye no' change yer name? It only makes it easier to track ye."

She raised her eyes and met Ewan's gaze. "What good reason would I have to give to the town? *I* write the headlines. I refuse to *be* the headline."

Ewan held her close and kissed the top of her head. "Ye have to live the life ye want, Jessie. Yer father sounds like a horrible man, but ye dinna need to prove yerself anymore." He met her watery gaze. "An' ye dinna want to allow yerself to become so hardened that ye become like him."

He swiped at her cheeks, brushing away tears. "Be more like yer mother. Embrace joy. Chase after butterflies. Laugh with exuberance."

"Ewan," she breathed, arching up to kiss him.

"Marry me, Jessie," he whispered as he stroked a hand over her head. "Marry me, and ye'll have another name. Ye'll have the protection of my family. Ye'll never doubt who ye are again."

She sat up, holding the sheet to her breast. The wonder of a few moments ago disappeared from her gaze, and she glared at him. "How can you have listened to my story and not understand?" When he shook his head in confusion, she said, "I have no desire to be under any man's control again. And I know you. You would want to control me, in little ways that seem innocent, but that would end up destroying my spirit."

"Ye have an inability to distinguish between love and control,

Jessie. I want to love ye. To support ye. To hold ye when ye're sad." He shook his head when she stared at him dumbfounded. "How can ye no' want that?"

"I do not love you," she whispered.

Ewan pushed away and launched himself from her bed. He roamed the back area of the print shop as he searched for his underclothes and pants, unhindered by his nudity. When he found his clothes, he pulled them on, his breaths emerging in agitated gasps. "I'll no' ask ye again, Jessie. I'll no' be a fool three times for ye."

"Ewan," she whispered, her voice filled with a plea.

"Nae, woman, ye are too blinded by fear to ever ken what ye could have had." He stuffed his feet into his boots and slapped his hat on his head. "I hope ye have a good evenin'." He slipped out the back door as soundlessly as he had entered it.

When he emerged behind her print shop, he hugged the shadows and moved a ways beyond her establishment before he paused and leaned against the back of a building, dropping his head forward until his chin rested on his chest. He rubbed at his neck and then strode toward home.

CHAPTER 10

*E*wan curried a horse he had borrowed for an afternoon ride out to see the homesteaders, his movements brusque as he focused on his thoughts rather than the horse.

"If you show no regard for the animal, it will show you none when you need it," Bears said in his deep, wise voice. He half smiled as Ewan jumped at his voice. "Focus on each task set before you, and you will find peace."

Ewan glared at Bears. "Do you ever tire of spouting your nonsense?" When Bears watched him with implacable patience, Ewan heaved out a sigh. Rather than throwing the currying brush across the room as he desired, he gripped it tighter before letting out another breath and then focusing on the horse. The horse whinnied with approval, and Ewan's tension eased further. "I hate that ye are right."

Bears chuckled. "Your woman has more spirit than most. You need to learn to approach her with as much care."

Ewan raised a brow. "Are ye sayin' my Jessie is like this horse?"

Bears shrugged. "Wouldn't you?" For once he seemed content to pause in his work and speak with Ewan. "When have you had success with her?"

Ewan frowned. "When I've treated her with kindness and patience."

Bears nodded, his loose hair flowing around his shoulders like a black waterfall. "She's not like your family. Loud. Constantly arguing. Teasing."

"She is when she's talking about her writing." Ewan focused on the horse for a moment. "But that's when she's in charge. When she feels like she's no' in charge, that's when she becomes …"

"Pricklier than a porcupine defending its soft underbelly," Bears said as he tapped the top of the stall. "Earn her trust, Ewan. Respect her."

Ewan watched as Bears walked away with an innate grace, his back straight, and his head held high and proud. Ewan finished currying the horse before returning the saddle and tack to the tack room and shutting the door behind him.

He paused as a customer entered the livery, lingering in the shadows, as Bears approached the man.

"I don't want no half-breed carin' for my horse," the man said with a spat of tobacco in the dust. He leaned forward. "And, if you touch my horse, it's half price."

Bears stood tall and straight, his impassive gaze meeting that of the customer. "I'm afraid we will be unable to care for your animal. If you are unwilling to have me touch your flea-ridden, mud-fevered horse at the sole price we charge at the livery, you'll have to take your business elsewhere."

The man puffed out his chest. "Listen here. You have no right to turn me away. You're the only livery for miles!"

Bears nodded. "Yes, we are. I am a partner here, not a laborer." He stared at the man, waiting a few moments until the reins were thrown at him. "Your horse will be returned to you when your entire bill is paid."

The man swore before storming out of the livery.

Bears patted the horse, earning a gentle nicker from the horse. "*Shh*, sweet one. You'll feel better soon, although I cannot cure your misfortune in owner."

Ewan laughed, and Bears looked over his shoulder. "Does this happen frequently?"

Bears nodded. "Yes. It occurred before the article, and it was more common for a little while. But men like him will always exist." He shrugged. "The furor after her article has eased."

Ewan watched as Bears *clicked* to the horse, leading him into a cleaned-out stall with fresh hay. After a few moments Ewan left the livery and moved next door to the kitchen, surprised to find Annabelle there. "What are ye doin', Anna?" he asked.

She watched him with amusement. "Preparing dinner or I'll never hear the end of belly aching from all of you." She took a deep breath and arched her back.

"Perhaps ye should take it easy." He held up his hands as she pointed a wooden spoon at him. "I'll say nothin' to Cail."

"You'd better not." She stirred the stew again, turned down the heat, and then sat at the table, smiling when he joined her. "You've seemed out of sorts for days, Ewan. What's bothering you?"

"There's a big poker match tomorrow. It's distractin' me."

She shook her head. "No, you only find that entertaining. What-ever happened has injured you in some way. Your smile doesn't shine as bright."

He flushed. "This is what I get for having a sister who kens so much." He smiled as she continued to frown at him. "I had hoped I would marry." He nodded to her hands covering her stomach. "Maybe have a bairn of my own someday." He shook his head.

"You will, Ewan. You're still young. Barely thirty. You have your whole life to live."

His lips lifted in a mockery of a smile. "She doesna want me, Anna. Twice I've asked, an' twice she's declined." He met his sister-in-law's shocked gaze. "There's no reason to ask her again."

Annabelle grabbed his hand and squeezed. "Oh, Ewan, I'm so sorry. I know how much you care for her."

He shrugged. "I'm the fool. In all the times we quarreled, talked, and shared secrets, I canna remember tellin' her that I loved her. Why should she have faith in me?"

Her eyes glinted with righteous anger for him. "You showed her in every way you could how much you loved her. If she didn't understand, then she's a fool."

"Nae, Anna. I am. For a woman like her, words are important. I should have kent that, but when I stormed out of her print shop, I was so angry, I could barely see." He rubbed a hand over his face, his whiskers now more of a beard.

She sighed. "There are other women in this town, Ewan."

He glowered at her. "Dinna even consider pushing that Jameson woman in my direction. I willna marry her. I refuse to even speak with her."

His sister-in-law smiled. "I know. But there are others."

He shook his head. "No' right now. No' for me. Maybe someday." He rose. "Thanks, Anna."

When he approached the hallway door, she called out. "Ewan?" He paused to face her. "Don't do anything foolish tomorrow night." His mischievous smile resurfaced, and she shook her head in consternation.

"I willna make promises I canna keep." He winked at her, and his boot steps sounded on the stairs as he headed to his room.

Ewan sat at the poker table, ignoring everything but the three players around the table. A miasma of smoke, sweat, and perfume filled the air, but he focused solely on his cards and the other players, searching for any signs or tells that would give him a hint of what they held in their hands. However, they were as experienced as he was and sat with impassive expressions as the hand played out.

A single oil lamp hung from a hook in the center of the room, lighting the table, but casting the rest of the room in deep shadows. Spectators hovered in those shadows, witnessing the intense gambling between the four who had not ceased playing for hours. Outside, dawn's rays peeked over the mountains. Neither Ewan nor the others cared what time of day it was. This final hand would determine if they were bankrupt or rich.

As the pile of money in the center of the table increased, Ewan felt a trickle of sweat run down the middle of his back. He stood to lose his business if he lost this hand. "Call," he demanded in an authoritative voice. He ignored the gasp from the corner of the darkened room as the Madam placed a piece of paper on the table.

"Money, Madam," a man grunted.

"That's better than any amount of money," she snapped. She smiled with satisfaction as the scrap of paper was handed from man to man, and the grunts of agreement confirmed her words.

Ewan glared at her but showed no other emotion as he waited for them to display their cards. One man had a pair of jacks and a pair of queens. The other smiled and laid down a straight. The Madam gave a long-suffering sigh. The man who had laid down the straight ignored her as he assumed she had little of worth in her hand.

Then her gaze turned triumphant as she smiled and made sympathetic eyes at Ewan. "I'm so sorry about your business," she murmured. She laid down her cards with a slight *thwack*ing sound that set Ewan's nerves on end. "Full house."

Ewan met the Madam's jubilant gaze. "I'm sorry about the loss of yer best whore."

The spectators gasped as he dropped his cards on the table.

"I believe four of a kind beats yer full house." He pushed away her hands and pulled the earnings toward him, scooping them into his hat.

The Madam sat in horror at his cards. "You're a cheat!"

Ewan rose, leaning over the table. "Never say that again, unless ye wish to die a painful death." He flushed. "Ye're no' dead now only because ye're a woman." He met the glances of the other two men who glared with equal fervor at the Madam. "I wouldna have been invited here had there been any doubt of my honor."

The Madam stood with false bravado and flung her shoulders back. "I wonder if you would be willing to renegotiate?"

"Nae, Madam, I would no'." He rose, smiling his thanks as someone from the shadows tossed him a burlap sack. He transferred the money from his hat into the sack and stared at the Madam. "I will meet ye at the Boudoir in ten minutes."

"She won't be ready to leave," the Madam protested.

"Perhaps no' but ye have no say on whether she stays or goes." He nodded to the men who had played with him and walked down the stairs leading to the main section of the saloon. When he stood on the boardwalk, he took a deep breath of fresh air before cramming his hat on.

He jumped off the boardwalk, crossed the street, and walked behind the other row of buildings until he approached Alistair's house. He knocked on the door and waited. When his brother opened the door, he met his frown with a smile. "I won," he said as he held up the burlap sack.

Alistair tugged him inside, shutting out the cold. "Are ye daft? Ye should no' boast of yer winnings." He then laughed and pulled Ewan into a bear hug. "Well done, little brother."

"I did no' just win this money, Al. I won freedom."

Alistair shook his head in confusion. "I dinna ken what ye mean." He motioned for Ewan to follow him into the long hallway. He pulled up the loose floorboard under the tattered rug, and he watched as Ewan put the sack of money there. "As ye can see, we dinna have many valuables to conceal in the hideaway ye made for us."

"This will keep it safe until I can go to the bank," Ewan said.

"Aye, although ye should leave here with another bag. Someone will have seen ye come here with it, and I dinna want my home a target for burglars." He led Ewan into the kitchen where Leticia and Hortence were having breakfast. Hortence beamed at Ewan.

"Hello, imp," he said as he ruffled her hair. "Are ye off to school soon?"

"Yes, and we learn what parts we get in the Christmas play today."

"Who do ye want to be?" Ewan asked as he smiled his thanks to Leticia for the cup of coffee she set in front of him.

"A Wiseman."

"Ye ken they were men, no?" Ewan asked as he shared a smile with Leticia.

Hortence bounced in her chair with restless energy. "Girls can be just as wise as boys."

Her uncle laughed. "Aye, ye have me there, wee Hortence." He watched as she jumped from her chair to run upstairs for a moment before school.

After listening to her daughter scamper away, Leticia focused on Ewan. "Now, while we have a few minutes free of little ears, would you like to explain why you show up here in the early morning, smelling worse than the Boudoir and Stumble-Out combined?"

Ewan rubbed at his untrimmed beard and flushed. "I was at a poker match last night. All night." He nodded his thanks as Alistair set a sack filled with rice and rocks next to him. "I won." He smirked as Leticia gaped at him.

"Does this mean you will cease playing?"

He shrugged. "It means I have no desire to play at this moment. I wish I could go home, crawl into bed for the day, and then take a hot bath."

"What was it about winning freedom?" Alistair asked as he took a sip of coffee.

A triumphant smile bloomed on Ewan's face. "The Madam participated last night. And lost." He met their curious stares. "She did no' have enough money to cover her last bet, and she wagered one of her whores."

"She has no right!" Leticia gasped.

"Perhaps no', but, if she is no' an idiot, I have won Fidelia her freedom." He looked at Alistair. "Will ye come with me to the Boudoir as I extract her from the Madam's control?"

Alistair smiled. "Aye." He kissed Leticia on the head. "Perhaps today would be a good day for Annabelle to close the bakery. She will want to be home with her sister."

Leticia nodded. "I'll inform her of your news as I walk Hortence to school." She clasped Ewan's hand. "Well done, Ewan."

Ewan smiled and flushed, grabbing the decoy burlap sack as he and Alistair walked outside. They approached the Boudoir, sharing a long look before they stepped onto the back porch. After their knock went unanswered, they eased the back door open. The kitchen was deserted, as most of the women breakfasted closer to noon.

"Come," Ewan said as he ascended the rear stairs. He paused when he saw Ezekial standing outside of a crib. "Do you think ye can prevent me from collectin' what is owed to me? A bet's a bet."

"I think you are being unreasonable in denying the Madam one of her most important assets." Ezekial glared at the two brothers as he fingered his billy club.

Alistair glared at the brute. "Ye are barely tolerated in town, an' I would think long and hard afore harming either of us. My wife is en route to inform Annabelle about her sister. Enough people in this town are aware of what occurred last night an' this mornin'."

"I believe an arrangement can be agreed upon." Ezekial slapped the club in his palm.

"Aye, the arrangement where I collect what is owed to me," Ewan hissed. He turned to the crib Ezekial guarded and banged on the flimsy door. "Wake up!" he snapped.

Ezekial backed away.

After a moment Ewan poked his head into the room and sighed. "Why in God's name did I win a whore?" he muttered. He approached the bedside, frowning when he saw the small blue vial next to the bed on the miniscule table. "Laudanum," he muttered. "A whore and an addict, all for one price." He shook her shoulder until she woke. "Get up an' get dressed. Ye dinna live here anymore."

Fidelia Evans, known as Charity in the whorehouse, stared at him through bleary eyes. "Go away, Ewan. I saw my quota of customers already."

"Nae," Ewan snapped, his patience at an end. "I'm tired, an' I want breakfast an' another cup of coffee. I'm in no mood to argue with ye. Get dressed, or I'll carry ye through the streets as ye are." He saw his threat penetrate her medicine-dulled mind as she rose and turned to find clothes. "Wear the more respectable clothes. Not the bawdy-house ones." He emerged into the hallway to await her, sharing a look with Alistair. Ezekial stood down the hall, his menacing presence a deterrent to any other Beauty thinking of departing with Ewan. Soon Ezekial disappeared downstairs in the direction of the kitchen.

After a few minutes Fidelia stumbled out of her small crib. Ewan grabbed her hand and tugged her behind him. "Come," he muttered. "We might be in time for breakfast." Alistair walked behind Fidelia, helping her as she walked like a drunken sailor.

The Madam stood with Ezekial behind her in the kitchen. "That's it? You'll take her from me as though she were nothing to me?"

Ewan stared from Fidelia to the Madam and back again. "Aye. She is nothin' to ye. She's earned money to feed yer gamblin' habits. Seems ye'll have to find another way to pay yer debts from now on." He paused as the Madam moved forward and blocked their exit, and he glared at the owner of the Boudoir. "Let us pass, Madam."

She ignored Ewan and focused on Fidelia. "You'll be back here within a month. Within a week. You're nothing more than a two-bit whore, hooked on opium. Not even your sister will want you now."

Fidelia's delayed reaction to move toward Ewan as though to evade the rancor from the Madam's words provoked a scornful snort from the Madam. However, not even the Madam's attempt at bravado could hide her panic at losing her prized whore.

"She isna yers any longer to threaten or abuse," Ewan snapped. He gripped Fidelia by the elbow and towed her behind him. The door slammed shut behind them, and he slung one of Fidelia's arms over his shoulder, while Alistair pulled her other over his. Between them, they half-walked, half-dragged her down the alleyway until they were nearly across from the livery.

"I canna tell if she's shiverin' from cold or from her need for more laudanum," Ewan muttered as he tripped and nearly dropped Fidelia.

Alistair grunted as his hold on her tightened. He waited until Ewan had righted himself. "We'll ken soon enough if it's the cold. I fear it's the laudanum."

As they crossed Main Street, they nodded to those they met and ignored curious stares. When they arrived at Cailean's house, Fidelia dug in her heels like a recalcitrant mule.

Alistair shared an amused smile with Ewan. "I dinna think her aware enough to ken where we were takin' her."

"No," she rasped in a slurred voice. "I will not go in there. You can't make me."

"Come," Ewan attempted in a soothing voice, although he knew he had failed when she flinched. "I'm hungry an' tired, an' I dinna want to fight ye. I have a story to tell, an' I think yer sister will want to hear it." He and Alistair carried her up the steps, into the house and the kitchen.

The quiet morning meal ground to a halt at their arrival. Cailean glowered at him. "I thought you were being lazy, not off at the Boudoir."

Annabelle froze with a teacup halfway raised at the sight of her sister with Ewan. "Fidelia!" she cried, rising to hug her sister. "Oh, you've finally left the Boudoir!"

Fidelia stood like a statue in her sister's embrace. "I was kidnapped this morning by this lunatic and his brother. I have no idea why Ezekial didn't stop him." She sat as Ewan pushed her into a chair. "Will you stop towing and pushing me around? I can choose what I want to do in my life!" She missed Annabelle's frown at her slurred words.

Ewan smiled. "Aye, ye can. Because I just won ye yer freedom from the Madam last night. She bartered ye as part of that poker game."

Fidelia blanched and shrank into herself as she sat on the chair. "She couldn't have. She doesn't own me."

"She believes she does. And the men I was playing with believed she did as they were delighted to accept ye in lieu of money. Ye would have had very little say in what ye wanted had I no' won." Ewan smiled triumphantly with his family members. "But I did win. Finally."

He frowned as they continued to gape at him. He dropped the sack on the table and shuffled his feet. "What are ye doin' home, Anna? Leticia was going to stop by the bakery on the way to school with Hortence."

"I felt unwell this morning and decided to not open today for my general customers. I will go soon to bake for the hotel and café." She smiled at him. "And I'm thankful I am here to welcome you, Dee." Her smile faded as her sister glowered at her.

Cailean tugged the sack toward him and frowned when he saw it was filled with rice and rocks. "Is this a joke?"

"Nae," Ewan said with a laugh.

Alistair smiled at his eldest brother. "We hid the real sack in the cubby Ewan made us at my house. This is to confuse those who are watchin' him."

Ewan met his eldest brother's concerned gaze. "I'll go to the bank soon, and no one will bother ye here at the house or at Alistair's."

Cailean shook his head, in wonder this time. "Ye won, Ewan?"

Ewan smiled, unable to hide the pride in his accomplishment. "Aye. Enough to pay ye back for all ye've done for me."

Cailean waved that away. "There's no need." He searched Ewan's gaze and nodded as though satisfied with what he saw.

"Ye *bluidy* fool," Sorcha hissed. "All this time ye've been playin' with the hopes of winnin' enough to pay Cailean back?"

Ewan shook his head. "No, I love the game. But tonight, ... this morning, finally I won."

Fidelia began to shake in her seat. "What does this mean? I belong to you now?"

"No need to look so horrified," Ewan joked. "Many women would be delighted to have me as a husband." He sobered as his teasing did little to ease her panic. "I do no' consider ye a possession, Fidelia. I wanted to win, especially after I saw what the Madam had bet. Asides, had I lost ..." He shook his head as though that were too terrible to contemplate. He met Fidelia's gaze which remained dulled by the opium. "I wanted to win that game to set ye free. At last."

She shook her head as she swiped at her cheeks. "The townsfolk will see me as your ... whore now. I'll never be free of that."

He looked at her and then at Annabelle. "I dinna consider ye mine, Fidelia. I ... dinna think of ye in that way. I had hoped ye wanted to be free. That this time ye'd leave the Boudoir and never return."

Annabelle sniffled as she lost her battle with her tears. "Dee?" she whispered. "Will you stay here with us? Let us help you?"

Fidelia looked at the MacKinnons in the kitchen, and her gaze narrowed. "What will you want from me?"

Everyone remained silent as they waited for Annabelle to respond. She gripped her sister's clenched hand. "Nothing, Dee." She paused. "Except for you to give up the laudanum." She shook her head. "I want you free, not only of the Madam but of the power of that drug."

Fidelia nodded once, and Annabelle let out a deep breath. She pushed herself up and smiled her thanks as the brothers rose to help Fidelia upstairs. Ewan nodded to Annabelle after he and his brothers settled her on the bed, backing out of the room as Annabelle and Sorcha helped Fidelia out of her clothes. He bumped into Leticia in the hallway.

"They're in there, if ye want to help them." Ewan pointed to Alistair's old room. She nodded her thanks before slipping inside.

He walked downstairs and paused when he saw Cailean waiting for him. "Are ye angry with me, Cail?" He walked to the coffeepot and poured himself a cup.

"No, but I am curious. Does this mean you are done with gambling?" When Ewan remained quiet, taking a large gulp of coffee, Cailean asked, "Now that you've finally won?"

Ewan closed his eyes and let out a deep breath, his body relaxing as though releasing pent-up tension. "I think so," he whispered. "I wanted to win. I kent I could." He met Cailean's nonjudgmental gaze. "An' now that I have, I dinna have this need to go back to the tables."

"Are you sure? Most who win have a thirst for more winning."

Ewan shook his head. "No' yet. I honestly hope no' ever." He met Cailean's gaze, his brow furrowing to see the worry remaining in his brother's eyes. "I canna make promises, Cail."

Cailean nodded as though satisfied with his honesty. "You're a good man, Ewan, and I couldn't be more proud to call you brother. Thank you for what you did for Belle and her sister today." He squeezed his brother's shoulder and left through the side door to the livery.

Ewan took another sip of coffee before setting the cup in the sink. After he had a quick wash and changed into a fresh pair of clothes, he set out for work. He fought his natural desire to head to Jessamine's office to share the news with her, instead walking down the alley and into the home he had hoped to share with her. He had not yet decided to sell it, but he knew of a few townsfolk who would be interested in purchasing the residence.

Ben smiled at him when he entered. He was discussing the finish work around the doorjambs with one of the men. When he was done, he wandered over to the table where Ewan looked at the plans.

"You don't really need those anymore," Ben said. "Now it's only a matter of weeks before it's finished."

Ewan nodded. "Come," he said in a low voice, walking to a back room that he envisioned as his bedroom. Through a window covered in a sheet but which would soon have a glass pane, the rolling hills were visible. He wandered the space and was quiet a few moments.

"I hope I've done nothing to displease you," Ben said.

Ewan looked at his friend in surprise. "Of course no'. Ye are a trusted friend, Ben. When I'm no' here, I ken ye will ensure the work continues. I canna continue to lead all these jobs on my own. I find I dinna want to." He looked at his friend and took a deep breath. "Will ye be my foreman? I ken it's no' as good as partner, but there will be an increase in salary, and the men will understand that ye have my full backing."

Ben stared at him in openmouthed surprise.

"I hope I havena offended ye," Ewan said when Ben remained silent.

Ben strode to him, holding out his hand. "Yes. Yes, I'll be your fore-man. Thank you."

Ewan shook his hand and slapped him on his back. "Ye'll rue the day ye agreed, but I'm relieved ye did." He laughed. "I thought for a second ye were going to belt me."

Ben laughed. "No. I never thought you'd share any of your business with anyone, even if it was to have a foreman."

Ewan leaned against the wall. "Do you know how many times I go from site to site, frustrated at how little has been accomplished in my absence? I may need a foreman at each site, but hopefully, for now, the two of us can work together to meet the challenge of encouraging the men to work faster."

He motioned for Ben to follow him to the main workspace, where interior walls were going up. He whistled for his men, who turned toward him, setting aside their tools after they finished what they were doing.

"I have an announcement. I just spoke with Ben, an' he's going to be my foreman. This means, when I'm no' on the job, he's yer boss. If he asks ye to do something, consider it as though I'm askin' ye to do somethin'." He surveyed the small cadre of men looking at him. "Aye?"

The men nodded; a few smiled, and then they turned back to work, mumbling to themselves.

"It willna affect them much, as the work will wind down as winter approaches. But 'tis good to have them understand this now, afore next spring and summer when we'll be busy again." He slapped Ben on his shoulder, and they joined the men.

That afternoon Ewan slipped out of the worksite and walked the short distance to Alistair's house. He knocked on the door, smiling as Leticia answered. When he stood in the hallway, with the door closed behind him, he motioned to the tattered rug at the end of the hall. "I need to extract the money and bring it to the bank. I dinna want ye to be in any danger."

He flipped back the rug, lifted off the board, and pulled out the burlap sack. After peering inside to ensure the money remained, he winked at Leticia. "Can I sit at yer table a moment?" He moved to the dining room table and slowly counted the coin and paper money in the sack.

He shook his head as he met Leticia's shocked gaze.

"I'm surprised the bag held," she murmured as over $300 sat in front of him.

"Aye, seems my luck is holdin'." He replaced the money in the bag and declined her offer of a cup of coffee. "I need to go to the bank." He gave her a wink and departed.

Sunlight streamed in through the bank's tall windows, the rays ricocheting off the highly polished countertops. He strolled up to the main desk and hit the bell for service. "Hello, Mr. Finlay. 'Tis a lovely day."

Mr. Finlay, sporting a plum-colored waistcoat with gold buttons, glared at Ewan. "It was until you arrived. I have no loans for men who make poor business decisions and who spend their time with cardsharks."

"Aye, 'tis a pity to waste a life such as mine." He met Mr. Finlay's glare. "I need access to the MacKinnon box."

He waited while Mr. Finlay flushed, nodding when Mr. Finlay sniffed his disdain but led him to the back and down a rickety flight of stairs. As far as Ewan knew, the bank was the only building in Bear Grass Springs with a basement. The musty smell of the underground space welcomed him as a lit lantern highlighted the bricked-in vault and rows of safe-deposit boxes. Ewan suspected the majority were empty but said nothing.

When Mr. Finlay extracted his box, Ewan stared at him until the man heaved out a sigh and left. When Ewan heard the door close to the upstairs, he wandered to the stairs, glaring at Mr. Finlay who remained. "Dinna imagine I don't ken yer tricks. If I could have privacy?" Ewan asked. He waited as Mr. Finlay heaved out an affronted breath before walking up the final step and slamming the door behind him.

Ewan moved with speed to the box, opening it with the key Cailean had slipped into his hand that morning. Ewan saw papers for the partnership agreement between Bears and the MacKinnons, and another between Cailean and Annabelle. He set the last down as that was not his business. Although it was difficult, he stuffed the money-filled sack in the box, locking it as he heard the door creak open upstairs.

"Aye," he called out. "I've had plenty of time. Thank ye for yer generosity." He raised an eyebrow as he watched Mr. Finlay reenter the room.

"I'll never understand why your brother, who is a reasonably upstanding member of this town, trusts you with the contents of this box." He looked at it with disappointment to find it locked shut. He picked it up, grunting at its weight. "Leave it to you, you dim-witted carpenter, to fill it with rocks."

Ewan chuckled. "Aye, I've little sense." He waited until Mr. Finlay had replaced the box and locked the entire area before following him upstairs. "Good day."

He strode down Main Street, entering the livery to find Bears singing to one of the horses in an unknown language. Ewan waited in the shadows until Bears ceased and began to hum. "What were ye sayin' to the horse?"

Bears looked at him, no surprise evident in his expression at Ewan's presence. "I sang to him of his fine ancestors. That he was born to run and that he should be proud of all the work he does for his owner."

Ewan fought a smile. "He's a horse. It's what he does."

Bears looked at Ewan with a mixture of humor and pity. "He's allowed us to tame him, and we use him to help us. We must always give him thanks." He patted the horse's side before moving into another stall.

Ewan shook his head, heading to the paddock when he heard Cailean's voice outside. The paddock stood behind the livery, and they exercised horses there, worked with horses who needed more train-ing, and used it as an overflow area when the inside stables were full. "Cail," Ewan called out.

Cailean waved and ducked under the posts. "Are you still cele-brating your win?"

He shrugged. "I just deposited the money in the bank, but I dinna ken if I kept enough out to repay what ye gave to Mr. Timmons." He handed a pocketful of bills to Cailean.

His brother pushed it away. "No need to repay me, Ewan."

"Aye, there is. I've been in yer debt long enough. I will never be able to repay ye for the money ye sent for my travels. An' I've come to realize ye would no' want me to." He met Cailean's gaze and saw his agreement reflected in his brother's eyes. "However, I can and will repay ye for my gamblin' folly."

Cailean glared at him, his hands at his sides.

"Buy somethin' for Annabelle. For the bairn." He saw his brother's eyes flash at that suggestion. He smiled when Cailean unfurled a hand and held it out, palm up. Ewan slapped the bills in his brother's palm and nodded. "Thank ye for always lookin' out for me."

"I always will," Cailean said, pulling him into a quick bear hug.

Ewan laughed, backing away. "See ye tonight, Cail." He waved once before he left the livery to return to his worksites.

CHAPTER 11

News & Noteworthy: *It seems our most disreputable gentleman, who had been wooed by the townswomen searching for a fine husband, has instead come into possession of one of the Boudoir's Beauties. It remains to be seen if the woman he marries will accept such a licentious lifestyle.*

Sorcha read the latest *N&N* section about Ewan and slammed it down on the table. Cailean was in the livery while Ewan had departed early for one of his worksites. He had two sites to finish roughing-in before snow fell.

She stormed over to the print shop and barreled inside. She glared at the old-timers who sat by the warm potbellied stove, weaving tall tales with ease. "Out," she snapped. She pointed to the door, and they heaved themselves up with reluctance.

Jessamine watched with a hint of amusement as she took Sorcha's measure. "This is my shop. I decide who stays and goes. I've never known you to visit me here before."

"I've never wanted to visit the woman who's made my brother's life a livin' hell. The woman who would rather spin lies and half-truths rather than tell interestin' stories about the people who populate our fine town." She gave a derisive shake of her head as she glared at Jessamine. "I will never understand why my brother would think ye deservin' of the MacKinnon name."

Jessamine stood taller under the verbal attack. "I'm more deserving than you'll ever know. But, unlike the majority in this town, I don't want nor need your family. Not for its connections."

Sorcha's look turned pitying as she stared at Jessamine from head to foot. "Ye are a fool. Ye had the love of a good man, an' ye tossed it away as though it were worth no more than a two-bit story." She leaned forward. "How can ye be so heartless?"

"He got what he wanted from me." She gasped when Sorcha gripped her arm.

"Nae, he did no'. Do ye ken who he's buildin' one of those houses for?" When Jessamine watched her with absolute boredom, Sorcha stomped her foot in agitation. "*You*, ye daft woman. He wanted a proper home for ye after he hoped to wed ye."

Jessamine snorted. "Well, now he can bring his whore there, and they can live quite contentedly."

Sorcha shook her head. "Watch ye tongue or I may have to treat you like some errant man. The woman Ewan won is Annabelle's sister. An' there's every chance she willna live through the horrible shakes as she is denied laudanum." Sorcha bit her lip. "We dinna ken what to do for her."

"Fidelia is free?" Jessamine whispered. "I could not obtain confirmation from the Madam or anyone else at the poker match who the whore was who had been bartered."

"The Madam is afeared of losin' her customers. Especially the man who paid the most for time with Dee." Sorcha shook her head. "The new doc says to just give her more medicine. The risk is too great to her without it."

"No!" Jessamine gasped. "Don't give her more. See her through it. Keep her away from it."

Sorcha frowned. "What do ye ken about takin' too much laudanum?"

Jessamine shook her head as she attempted to clear her vision of tears. "Too much. Help her through her nightmares. Help her through her cravings. But don't give her more."

"What if she dies?" Sorcha whispered.

"She would die anyway if you kept feeding it to her." Jessamine turned away and gripped the edge of her desk.

"Would ye come to the house an' help us? It seems ye have a knowledge about such things that we dinna."

Jessamine shook her head. "No, I can't. I can't bear to watch that again." She blinked, a tear snaking down her cheek. "Forgive me."

Sorcha frowned as she watched the previously confident journalist crumble in front of her. "Are ye all right, Miss McMahon?" She let out a deep breath. "I ken I can act beastly, but I thought ye a worthy opponent."

Jessamine half-laughed, half-snorted. "I am on most days. I've not been myself lately." She took a deep breath. "I'm sorry I can't come to your house, but I fear that would only cause problems for me. For Ewan." She met Sorcha's worried gaze. "Take care of Fidelia. Don't leave her alone, for she'll try to sneak out to obtain more. Ensure she has plenty of water." Jessamine shook her head as though banishing memories.

Sorcha nodded. "Aye, I'll do as ye say. If I have need of yer knowledge, I will visit ye again. The doc isna much use."

Jessamine squinted after Sorcha's last statement. "He's of little use except peddling laudanum-laced medicine."

Sorcha shrugged and pulled her shawl tightly about her. "Mind what else I said, aye?" After a few moments of silence, Sorcha left, the door sounding with her departure.

∾

The Story Behind The Punch

If you are like me, you have wondered about the delicious, albeit sweet, concoction offered at every town gathering. After inquiring, I discovered the flavorful libation to be from a secret recipe, handed down over generations in

Mrs. Guerineau's family. Fortunately for the residents of Bear Grass Springs, she has generously shared this drink with us.

Mrs. Guerineau was born and raised on her father's large sugar cane plantation near New Orleans, Louisiana. She recalls running through the canes, playing hide-and-seek with her brothers.

Her family's sugar cane plantation provided one of the main ingredients for the drink shared at our festivities. She remembers joining her mother in the kitchen before parties, memorizing how to make the punch. Her mother admonished her to never write down the recipe, lest it be stolen by a jealous guest, only to share it whenever possible.

Although promised to wed a neighbor's son who would one day run a nearby plantation, Mrs. Guerineau fell in love with his younger brother. He was not wholly acceptable to her father as he had settled in the North, and her father considered her beau to be a Yankee. However, after weeks of silent defiance on her part, her father relented, and she married her love. They settled on a farm in Ohio.

After many years there, her husband thirsted for adventure. Convincing her to travel to Montana with him, they set out in 1876 for the Territory. Tragedy struck on the wagon ride, and her husband of forty years died on a river crossing. Not one to succumb to her grief, she showed the tenacity of spirit needed to continue the journey, handling a team of oxen with help from those on the wagon train. Mrs. Guerineau arrived in Bear Grass Springs with a determination to thrive and to celebrate life. As Mrs. Guerineau said, it's her way of honoring her beloved husband.

She honors him, her native Louisiana and her mother's memory every time she makes her punch for us.

Jessamine smiled as another patron purchased her paper. When she had sold the last copy of her current edition, she closed the door and rubbed at her head in confusion. The day's edition had contained a small section on news updates and the large story on Mrs. Guerineau. There had not been space for an *N&N* or *F or F* section. She moved to her desk and sat as she continued to contemplate the day's successful sales.

She turned as the door opened and frowned at her visitor. "I see no reason for a visit from the lawyer today, Mr. Clark. There could be nothing worthy of complaint in that innocuous edition."

He smiled as he moved around a stack of newsprint toward her cluttered desk. "How do you work in such chaos?" At her shrug, he focused on her. "This is the type of article, the type of paper you should write, J.P."

She frowned as she shook her head in confusion. "I don't understand why this was more of a success than the others. There was no intrigue. No scandal."

"Intrigue and scandal will always sell. However, I've found that, when we champion the moments where we triumph over adversity, we inspire others." He smiled at Jessamine. "Your paper sold out today because you inspired the townsfolk. You showed them an inspirational hidden story. Not one shuttered away out of shame."

Jessamine harrumphed. "I like to believe I understand human nature, but I find I'm more confused than ever here. When I was in Saint Louis, I knew what to write. I knew what was expected of me." She rubbed at her temple. "Everything is more complicated in a small town."

Warren laughed. "No truer words …" He motioned for her to rise. "Come. Join me for a meal at the café and allow the townsfolk to see you enjoying yourself with another, rather than alone and listening in on what they have to say."

She flushed. "I thought I was subtle."

"As a brick through a window." He helped her don her cloak and then opened the door for her.

They entered the café and met the beaming smiles of Harold and Irene. One of Jessamine's papers was on an unoccupied table, and had been handled over and over again by the smudges and wrinkles along its edges. Harold motioned them to a table. "I bet you could have sold twice as many papers today."

Jessamine flushed. "I could always print more for tomorrow, but I think I'll plan better for when I write another article similar to that one."

Irene brought out water glasses. "I'd write similar articles once a week and then have a section for comments in the next paper."

Warren shared an amused smile with the café's patrons. "She's having trouble believing that the current edition could be successful without scandal or intrigue." He nodded to Jessamine. "Her words."

Harold laughed. "Most of us have had enough scandal and intrigue in our lives. Sometimes we need to be reminded of the good that exists among us." He smiled with pride at Jessamine. "And Mrs. Guerineau is a fine woman. She's known hardship, but she refused to become bitter due to it."

Jessamine's eyes glowed with wonder. "She's a fascinating woman to speak with. I thought she'd be filled with rancor, but instead she constantly gives thanks for the time she had with her husband."

Harold sat with them and leaned forward, lowering his voice. "Irene and I always try not to pry, but it seems a shame the poor woman has no children."

Jessamine nodded but remained silent. She took another sip of water and met Harold's curious gaze with a blank stare.

Harold and Warren exchanged a glance, and then both men smiled. "Seems it truly is a momentous day," Harold said as he stood to attend other patrons.

CHAPTER 12

*E*wan entered the kitchen and frowned as the conversation among Cailean, Annabelle, and Sorcha ground to a halt. "What is it?" he asked. He tensed as they shared guilty stares.

"I had to go to the Merc before supper. Right before it closed." Cailean cleared his throat and met his brother's impatient stare. "I saw Jessamine entering the café with Warren."

Ewan shrugged. "It doesna matter who she decides to consort with." He glared at his sister as she snorted at his use of the word *consort*. "She has no interest in me. I willna attempt to force her to change her mind."

"Ye ken the woman wants ye, Ewan," Sorcha said. "She would never have written what she did if she didna."

"Nae, she is a reporter after a story. Mine was the beginning of her sentimentalist twaddle. She used me to show the townsfolk she had changed. After her harsh attack on too many of them, including Bears and Helen, she had to find a way to show her change of heart. I was the perfect candidate as I was her constant target."

Annabelle frowned as she watched him. "I hate that you've become so cynical, Ewan. This isn't like you."

He snorted. "Perhaps this is truly how I am, an' I've finally decided to show ye what I'm like."

Cailean rolled his eyes. "Ye are no' a chameleon, ye *bluidy* idiot." He exhaled through his nose as he attempted to calm his temper. "You are angry with her. With good reason."

"Aye, an' learnin' she's having dinner with another man does no' soothe it." His eyes flashed for a moment with anger and hurt before he pasted on his mischievous smile. Ewan pulled out his chair and sat. "What is for dinner?"

"A heaping of common sense," Annabelle snapped. She waddled to the stove and extracted a haunch of venison, which Sorcha promptly took from her. Bears had successfully killed a deer two days ago, and they had fresh meat for a few days.

Cailean watched his brother and correctly sensed that he would not discuss further the conversation that needed airing. "How long until the smokehouse is finished?" Cailean asked.

"I'll have it done on Sunday." Ewan ignored his siblings' disgruntled stares and helped himself to a piece of venison. "We are lucky Bears is such a good hunter. We've always had to depend on the butcher for meat before."

"Yes, although I must learn new recipes." Annabelle smiled at her family as she sat down, ignoring the empty chair at the table.

"You'll relish the challenge, love," Cailean murmured, smiling when his comment provoked a pleased flush on his wife's cheeks.

"How is Fidelia?" Ewan asked. "I ken ye want to ignore how she refused to come for supper again. I worry I forced her into a life she doesna want and resents me for it."

Annabelle gripped her fork tightly and shook her head. "She is miserable. Says she misses her old life, although she does not make any attempt to return to the Boudoir." She met Ewan's worried gaze. "If she did, I would not stop her. She has been granted the greatest gift, and, if she is not able to recognize it, there is nothing more I can do."

"Nae, I did little except free her from that woman. Yer gift is far more valuable, Anna. For ye love her, no matter what she's done. Few would admit to that." Ewan looked down at his plate as his sister-in-law fought strong emotions.

"I do not know how to cure her of her desire for laudanum. I fear that, when the terrible lassitude filling her eases, she'll try to obtain it any way she can."

Cailean patted his wife's fretful hands. "You spoke of her love of embroidery. Would that entertain her thoughts while she is fighting off the laudanum?"

Annabelle sniffled but sat taller. "I may see if either of the mercs can order some goods for me."

Sorcha shrugged. "I've heard that many of the Beauties at the Boudoir are suffering a similar fate."

Ewan nearly growled. "Don't let that quack doctor near Fidelia or Annabelle. Call the midwife if needed."

"Seems the new doc is having a hard time replenishing his stores, and they've run out of their source of medicine." Sorcha met her brothers' incredulous stares. "They talk to me when I deliver baskets. They are people."

Cailean shook his head in wonder. "I never thought to see the day my sister or wife would visit the Boudoir daily." He grunted as Annabelle elbowed him in the side.

"You know it's for deliveries. Now that Dee is no longer there, I'm considering curtailing the amount I sell them."

Sorcha shook her head. "Dinna do that, Anna. The women love yer treats, even though they might not eat as many due to the Madam and Ezekial."

Ewan frowned. "What happened to her other henchmen?"

"Oh, she didna pay them, and they left. Moved on to other towns. Her finances have only worsened since yer card game." She shrugged. "Ezekial is committed to the Madam for reasons I dinna understand."

The brothers shared a long look. "I will continue to hope you remain in ignorance," Cailean murmured.

Ewan nodded as the rumors of the Madam's intimate relationship with her head henchman were widespread among those who frequented the Boudoir. "Aye, ye dinna need to ken anything further.

An' 'tis her own fault she's having financial problems. She should have a successful business. Instead she gambles away the profits and does little to protect the women who work for her."

Annabelle sighed as she ran a hand over her belly. She looked at the ceiling at a crashing sound. "I fear Fidelia is having nightmares again and thrashing about. I should tend to her."

Ewan rose. "Nae, I will. I brought her here, and I willna have her harmin' ye in an opium-fueled fit, when ye are to have a bairn." He nodded to his brother who smiled his thanks. He walked to the hall and up the stairs. When he turned left to enter Alistair's old room, he paused at the sound of Fidelia's pitiful moaning.

"Fidelia," he murmured as he eased open the door. A glass of water had shattered, and shards of it lay on the floor. He ignored the mess for now and wet a cloth in the water pitcher on the bureau across from the bed. He approached her shaking, shivering form on the opposite side from where she had knocked over the glass.

"*Shh*," he murmured. "Dinna fash yerself so." He swiped at her face and clammy neck, jerking out of range as she swiped an arm in his direction. He chuckled as she muttered swear words under her breath. "Calm yerself, Fidelia."

"Don't tell me what to do," she rasped as her teeth rattled. "Just let me die."

He paled at her pleading words, his jaw firming and any levity fleeing his gaze. "Nae, I willna. Too many care for ye and would be filled with pain and agony at yer passing. Especially yer sister." He sat on the chair by her bed, holding her hand. "Ye are stronger than that damn poison."

"I'm not," she cried, her body convulsing. "I just need a little, and then I'll be better."

He *tsk*ed and continued to talk to her in a soothing tone.

Fidelia swore at him and turned away, but the constant hum of his low voice formed a counterpoint to her moans and trembling. He frowned as she failed to slip into a restful sleep, and he stared at his brother when he poked his head into the bedroom.

"She's bad," Ewan whispered after he rose and joined his brother hovering near the door. "I think one of us should go for the midwife and someone should sit with her tonight. Perhaps tomorrow too."

Cailean nodded. "I'll find the midwife and can remain with Fidelia tonight. I'll see if Sorcha can sit with her tomorrow."

Ewan frowned. "Ye have work, Cail."

Cailean shook his head. "Fidelia's more important. Besides, with Bears and Alistair, they will survive without me for a morning."

Ewan slapped his eldest brother on the shoulder. "Well, sit with her now, and I'll find somethin' to clean up the mess." Ewan watched as Cailean sat beside Fidelia, smiling as Cailean recounted stories from the past year before Ewan left to find a dustpan and broom.

Two days later, after the midwife made a follow-up visit to check on Fidelia, Ewan poked his head into her room. He nodded with relief to find her resting peacefully, no longer shaking or quivering. As he was on the verge of closing the door, her low "Wait," caused him to turn and meet her stare.

Rather than long, shiny chestnut hair that gleamed in candlelight, her dull hair was ratted on her head. Sunken cheekbones, sallow skin, and sky-blue eyes devoid of emotion met his stare. "Have you taken inventory?"

He frowned and shook his head.

"Of how I am different? I would no longer be considered a Beauty if the Madam could see me now."

He smiled at her as he pulled out a chair to sit next to her. "Ye will always be beautiful, Miss Ch ... Fidelia," he stammered as he spoke her real name rather than her Boudoir name. "An' ye should no' look to one such as the Madam for validation. Or to the men there." He met her cynical gaze. "Look to yerself." He frowned as she scoffed and curled into herself as she lay on her side.

"Why did you bother to accept the deals of her wager? You would have been much better off forcing her to pay you money."

Ewan leaned on his elbows propped on his thighs. "I dinna agree.

Ye are worth more than any amount she could have paid." He watched as she picked at a thread on the afghan. "Do ye ken who might have won ye?"

She shook her head. "I don't want to know. I have enough nightmares." She fought a shiver. "I hate that she believed she could wager me."

Ewan tilted his head to one side as he studied her. "Fortunately for ye, she did. Would ye have refused to go with another?"

She closed her eyes and nodded. "She gave me an out. I knew you would not harm me." She flushed with embarrassment. "You would not see me as a piece of property."

"Nae. Never." He cleared his throat. "Although many in the town will never see past what ye were." His somber gaze bore into hers.

"I know." She took a deep breath. "Will you ask if someone can continue to sit with me? I fear I am not as strong as I would like to be." Her flush deepened at her admission of weakness. "I am nearly free of that horrible drug's hold on me, and I do not want to seek out more of it."

Ewan nodded. "Aye, sister, I will." He smiled at her shock at his term for her. "Ye are my sister, Fidelia. Ye have been since my brother married Anna." He ignored her sniffle as he rose and eased out of the room.

Sorcha waited for him in the hallway. "Well, how is she today?"

"Better." They shared a relieved look. "Will ye continue to sit with her? Maybe knit with her or something until her embroidery supplies arrive? She doesna want to be alone as she's afeared she'll try to buy more of that wretched potion if given the opportunity."

Sorcha firmed her shoulders and nodded. "I will. She will no' want for company."

He grinned. "Mayhap silence." He laughed as Sorcha hit him gently on his arm. "Have a good day, Sorch."

166

CHAPTER 13

essamine strolled down the boardwalk, hoping for something of interest to occur. She had little of note for her next *N&N* section, and the old-timers had failed to produce an interesting tall tale for her *F or F* column. "Where's a damn cow when you need one?" she muttered to herself. Many townsfolk had come forward, eager to be interviewed for the newspaper, but she wanted to discover those with a hidden story to tell.

After settling on the bench near the café, she watched the townsfolk, content to be ignored. Little of interest occurred, although she frowned as she saw Helen Jameson with shoulders stooped following behind her mother. It appeared that most of Helen's spirit had been whittled away by her mother's constant criticism.

"Poor woman," a man said next to her, and Jessamine jumped. Harold laughed as Jessamine jolted. "Seems you are more interested in her than you'd like the townsfolk to believe."

Jessamine ignored his comment and focused on the goings-on of the town again. Or the not-goings-on.

"If you're lookin' for something for that paper of yours, I'd consider investigating why a fancy gentleman checked into the Grand Hotel. You know Mr. Atkins is a flirt and would enjoy your visit."

Jessamine bit back a smile. "I should sit in your café all day and learn all I'd ever need for my paper."

Harold chuckled. "We know more than we would like about the goings-on in the town." He nodded with his head to someone striding down the boardwalk across the street. "That's the man who arrived yesterday."

Jessamine stilled before scooting back farther onto the bench and any shadows offered by the café's roof. The man, dressed in a fine gray suit, polished black shoes, and a black wool jacket, turned into Warren Clark's office. "I believe I will join you in the café," Jessamine murmured.

Harold frowned. "I'd think you'd travel to the hotel to ascertain all you can about the man while he's busy with Warren."

"I've no need." Jessamine rose and braced a hand on the back of the bench as she faltered.

Harold leaped to his feet and hitched out his elbow. "Here. I might be old, but I can still help a lady in distress." He led her into the café. Rather than easing her into a chair in the front of the café, he brought her to the kitchen and settled her at the small table he shared with Irene during calm moments.

"Miss Jessamine, whatever is the matter?" Irene asked. She emerged from a store cupboard, carrying a heavy sack of flour. She set it on a workbench and rubbed her hands together before swiping them on her apron. "I have a few minutes before I start the biscuits that go with the meal." She pulled out a chair and sat, smiling her thanks to Harold as he set cups of coffee on the table in front of them all. He pulled out a chair and joined them.

"Nothing. I felt slightly faint when I stood up after speaking with Mr. Tompkins outside." She forced a smile. "Forgive me for my foolishness."

"Your foolishness is thinking that we'll believe that pile of nonsense you just spouted," Harold said. "Who is that man, and why did he unnerve you? You're unflappable."

She flushed at the touch of pride that laced his voice. "Thank you," she whispered. When Harold and Irene remained silent, she let out a deep breath. "That man has the look of my father. How he walks. How he seems to believe everyone should move out of his way because his business is imperative. How he dresses."

Irene frowned. "You sound displeased that he would travel all this way to find you."

Jessamine gripped the handle of the coffee mug, turning her hands white. "I haven't seen him in seven years. I had no desire to ever see him again." She closed her eyes as though ashamed and embarrassed. "Isn't it rich? The woman who exposes the foibles of the town now has something she wishes to remain hidden?"

Harold snorted. "Perhaps it will teach you humility."

"And compassion," Irene said. She held Jessamine's hand. "You've allowed life to harden you. To make you believe that all you need is a story, or some version of the truth, to find a fulfilling life." She shook her head. "I hope you come to understand there is more to life than work and the pursuit of a story."

Jessamine blinked away tears and took a deep breath as she sniffled.

"I don't mean to be harsh, dear, but you have to understand that, although parts of your paper are admirable, you have a caustic intelligence you are too eager to unleash on those who would befriend you." Irene met Jessamine's hurt gaze.

Harold cleared his throat. "It took great courage to travel here from Saint Louis as a single woman. And tremendous tenacity to find success as a woman reporter in a town intent on having only a man fill that role."

Jessamine exhaled and pulled out a handkerchief to rub at her face. "I hadn't realized you disliked me so much."

Harold laughed as Irene let out a snort. "Heavens, we like you just fine. You must learn that it's harder to have someone's regard than disdain. For with their approval comes expectations," Harold said.

Jessamine flushed. "This is why I've never sought friendship. Why put yourself in a position where you will only be disappointed when people continuously fail to meet your expectations? And vice versa?"

Irene watched Jessamine with a mixture of pity and concern.

"Seems to me that you've focused far too long on the negative aspects of friendship. Of relationships. Or that you were told from a young age that you would never measure up." She gripped Jessamine's hand.

Harold shook his head. "For you do measure up, girl. You do. But you must realize that, when you belittle others or make them feel less worthy, you are also diminishing yourself." He met her startled gaze. "You are diminishing the town's inherent goodwill to aid one another and instead encouraging the townsfolk to embrace their baser tendency for mistrust and suspicion."

"We know you can keep secrets." Irene met Jessamine's guarded gaze. "Look how well you've guarded Tobias's, keeping our family shame out of the public sphere."

Jessamine shrugged. "I wasn't being altruistic. It was the only way to ensure he'd not bleed me dry with his prices." When Irene watched her closely, Jessamine shrugged. "It seemed wrong to report that story."

"Exactly," Irene said. "It would hurt far more than Tobias."

Jessamine firmed her lips. "It's not my duty to only report the bright stories. To portray this place as a sort of Eden."

Irene burst out laughing. "Oh my! Bear Grass Springs could never be accused of such a thing. Not with the likes of the Jamesons, the Boudoir, and our own nephew present. But it isn't as harsh a place as it often appears in your paper."

"I want to write important articles. But I also need to sell papers if I am to survive."

Harold took a slurp of his coffee. "A fine dilemma to have. And you are intelligent enough to figure out what to do." He tapped his hand on the table as he rose to attend customers who had just entered the café.

Jessamine took a deep breath. "Thank you for your honesty."

A bemused smile spread as Irene watched Jessamine. "I know honesty can be difficult, but I also know you are one to appreciate it." After Jessamine sat as though in a daze, Irene asked, "What will you do about your father?"

"I don't know." She balled her hands into fists. "I don't want to start again in a new place because of him."

Irene patted her hands. "Sometimes our battles choose us." Her wise gaze met the younger woman's frightened eyes. "You'll know what to do when you see him." She patted Jessamine's clenched hands again and then rose to prepare biscuits for the supper rush.

Ewan worked on a small building on the other side of the paddock, his hammer pounding at an incessant pace. He extracted nails from a pail and continued working in silence until his brother stepped into the small room.

"Heard ye were here," Alistair said.

Ewan huffed out a sound. "Wouldna be hard with all the noise I'm makin'." He set down his hammer and focused on his brother. A lamp lit the enclosed space, with the cut-out windows covered in blankets to keep the cold from seeping inside. "I'm makin' progress an' should have this done soon. Hopefully afore it snows." He looked around the compact room. "Should be a decent space for Bears."

Alistair nodded. "He'll argue with us that he'd be fine in the tack room, but I dinna want a stove near the hay." He shrugged. "Thanks for makin' this for us."

Ewan nodded. "My pleasure." He watched as his brother lingered. "What's the matter, Al?"

"I wanted to see how ye are. Ye've been quieter than usual. An' ye are no' visitin' the Boudoir or saloon like ye usually do."

Ewan snorted. "I've no desire to lose the money I finally won, an' I've been barred from the Boudoir." He shrugged. "The Madam doesna want me there unless I'm to be a true customer. Says I provoke unrest among her patrons and girls."

Alistair laughed. "Ye caused a brawl 'cause someone threatened yer woman."

Ewan shook his head quickly. "She's no' mine. She'll never be mine." He lifted the hammer in agitation and swung it down once onto an already nailed-in nail.

His brother sighed and leaned against the doorjamb. "I ken ye're upset with her, but ye'll forgive her. It's what ye do with someone ye love." He met his brother's defiant gaze. "I heard Helen visited ye again this mornin'."

Ewan groaned. "Aye. Although 'twas a strange visit." He shared a frustrated look with his brother. "She was there when I arrived, an' my men said she'd been there since before they arrived. She made a point of bein' seen with me by the men." He shook his head in confusion. "I dinna ken why."

Alistair frowned and was silent for a few moments. "Why would she already have been there? Ye arrive early, an' yer men only ever get to the site afore ye because ye go to the sawmill." He shook his head. "Why would she be away from her mother's house afore dawn?"

Ewan shrugged and shook his head. "I think there is much we dinna ken about her, but I have no desire to learn more. 'Twould only give her misconceptions."

"Or false hope. An' that's one thing that woman doesna need." Alistair let out a deep breath. "Someone arrived yesterday. I thought ye would have heard about it."

Ewan shook his head and furrowed his brow. "Why should I? I'm no' expectin' anyone."

Alistair met his confused gaze, his brown eyes serious. "'Tis rumored the man's her father."

Ewan stilled. "Jessie's?" At Alistair's nod, he sighed. "'Twill no' be good news to her. But I can do little for her. She doesna want me." He met his brother's doubting gaze. "She made it clear, Al."

"No matter what she says, she'll want a friend, Ewan."

"I ken ye dinna like her. Why should ye want me to act as her friend?"

Alistair shrugged. "Ye're miserable. Ye canna deny that ye are." He looked at his brother before glancing around the small room and then out the door to the paddock and the livery. "We have a good family, aye, an' we ken we'll always support each other." He took a deep breath. "I willna like it the first time she's at Cailean's table. No' until Leticia is comfortable. But I also ken ye have the right to yer own happiness. Yer own life that isna dependent on the family or our approval."

Ewan cleared his throat and rubbed at one shoulder. "Cailean would argue I've already lived that life."

Alistair frowned. "He kens why ye acted as ye did. As do I." He watched his brother with sorrowful eyes.

Ewan shrugged. "What's done is done, an' nothin' will change what occurred." He half smiled. "'Twas easier playin' the jovial fool than havin' ye know what I was truly feelin'."

Alistair grunted. "An' ye will never convince me that ye didna enjoy yer time in the saloons and the Boudoir." He smiled. "Live yer life, Ewan. Cailean married Annabelle even though Sorcha despised her. He didna marry to please anyone but himself."

"I'll consider what ye've said," Ewan said as he lit a lamp.

His brother pushed away from the doorjamb. "Ye have nothin' else to do tonight except stare at a book without readin' it. Ye might as well pay her a visit." Alistair winked at his brother who glowered at him before he slipped out of the small room.

Ewan returned to hammering, but his mind was across Main Street with Jessamine. He swore as he nearly hit his thumb and set down the hammer. With a sigh, he tidied the worksite, grabbed the lamp, locked the front door, and headed for home, uncertain if he would seek her out that evening or not.

Jessamine returned from a long walk along the creek and entered her print shop. She came to a halt as she inhaled the familiar scents of paper and ink mingled with brandy and Bay Rum. "How dare you come here?" She removed her hat and gloves with an unwavering frown at her father.

He raised an eyebrow as he sat in a perfectly tailored gray suit with an ice-blue tie that matched his eyes. His immaculate coat hung on the peg by her door. "Did you truly believe you'd evade me forever?" He watched her with a calculating glint in his eagle-sharp gaze.

"You have no right to be here. Please leave." She thrust her shoulders back and stood as tall as her short stature allowed. When her father, who was over a foot taller than her, rose, she refused to back away or to cower in any fashion. "I freed myself from you, and I am no longer your concern."

"On the contrary, Jessamine, you are very much my concern. You owe me. You owe your mother better than this." His disparaging look took in her small print shop and tiny living quarters. "I thought you would want more from life than to live so shabbily."

"This is my life. The life I chose," she said. She gasped when he grasped her arm and pulled her close.

"I made you. I gave you every advantage a father can give a daughter. You owe me, girl." He grimaced with distaste when he saw her ink-stained fingertips. "You are an Abbott! You hire minions to do such work."

She wrenched her arm free, gasping with the pain as she massaged her bruised wrist. "No, I am a McMahon. A name I chose. A name I can be proud of." She shrieked as he backed her into the wall next to the door, his voluminous coat next to her.

"If you were anything other than that worthless factory worker's daughter, you would know how fortunate you are," he hissed. "You should be married with sons by now. My heirs."

She grunted as he gripped her shoulders and held her in place. "Let me go!"

"No, you are coming with me. You will stay at the room I have reserved for you at the so-called Grand Hotel"—he sniffed in disdain at the only refined lodging establishment in town—"and then you will return with me to the life you should never have abandoned."

She pushed at him until he stumbled back a step. "Who have you picked out for me to marry this time? Some other wretched mirror image of you who thinks of women as playthings, never to be listened to or consulted, but seen as an arm ornament?" She glared at her father and reached into her boot, extracting a sharp knife. "Stay away from me. I will not hesitate to use this on you."

He froze at the sight of the knife. "You're as irrational as your mother."

Her gaze darkened. "Never speak to me about my mother. You destroyed her."

He held up his hands. "At least allow me my coat."

She shook her head. "No, leave and, when you are outside, I will toss it to you." She met his frustrated glare. "I know your tricks, Father."

As he backed away and exited the print shop, he lowered his arms and spoke loudly. "Wonderful to see you again, Jessamine." He caught his thrown coat and slipped it on. "Your hospitality is as I remember it." He nodded at a man walking past before he disappeared from sight.

She locked the door and then raced to the back door and locked it too. After resting her head against it, she slid down it until she sat in a heap at its base, trembling.

Many minutes later, the front door rattled as someone attempted to enter. She ignored it, and the visitor left. When footsteps sounded on the rear stoop, she scooted away from the back door. A loud knock resonated through the room, and she covered her mouth to prevent any sound from leaking out.

"Jessie?" a man called out.

Ewan.

"Are ye all right?" The doorknob jiggled, but the door remained shut.

After sitting dumbstruck for a moment, she rose, tripping over her long satin skirts. She flung open the back door to see Ewan walking away from her print shop. "Ewan," she cried out, her voice breaking and emerging as more of a squawk than a yell.

He heard her and spun at the sound of his name. "Jessie," he whispered, rushing to her. "Are ye all right?" He didn't wait for her to answer but pushed her inside, and shut and locked the door behind him.

She burst into tears, and he pulled her close.

"*Shh*, it canna be as bad as all that," he crooned. He waited until she relaxed, and then he eased her onto a chair. He sat on the edge of her cot and held her hand. "I heard yer da's in town."

She nodded and scrubbed at her face with a handkerchief he offered. "Yes. And he wants me to return to New York City. Wants me to marry a man of his choosing and produce an heir for him."

Ewan made a noise in his throat. "*Ye* are his heir. He needs no other."

She rolled her eyes. "He wants a male heir. I would never be good enough."

Ewan frowned and ducked his head a moment as he thought. "Why no'? Ye do everything the man could want ye to do. Ye run yer own business. Ye are a fine journalist. Ye would make any parent proud."

Her breath hitched as she exhaled. "You don't understand my father. I will never be acceptable as his heir. Because I am a woman. I will always be deemed lacking." She frowned. "I told you about him. About my escape."

He nodded. "Aye, but I have trouble believin' a man who's traveled all the way to the Montana Territory would act for any reason other than love."

She flushed with anger. "Not all men are motivated by good, Ewan. He desires power and control, and this is how he wishes to dominate me and my life." She sighed, leaning into his gentle caress.

"How did ye force him to leave here tonight?"

She smiled. "I pulled my knife on him." She motioned to her boot. "I always have one hidden, although I haven't been able to use it at every occasion." She shared a chagrined smile with him. "The Boudoir was one such time." She flushed as he watched her with pride.

"Ye are a resourceful lass. I should be thankful ye've never brandished such a knife on me." He chuckled when she nodded her agreement. "What will ye do?"

"Wait him out. He won't remain here long. He believes himself too essential to his company and his career in New York City to spend any appreciable time here." Her jaw firmed. "I will not be on that train with him."

He watched her with concern, unable to hide the caring in his eyes. "I ken ye well enough to understand that ye'll do what ye wish."

She flinched and looked down. "I didn't mean to hurt your feelings, Ewan."

He snorted. "What else could ye have meant?" He shook his head in confusion. "Ye made yer wishes plain enough. I ken I'm not the man ye're lookin' for." He smiled, any trace of hurt or anger hidden in his jovial expression. "Ye'll find someone worthy of ye, I'm certain."

She glared at him and pulled her hand from his hold. "How can you profess to care for me and then happily discuss my future relationship with another man?"

"It's because I care for ye that I wish to see ye happy. If it's no' with me, it will be with another." The flush on his cheeks belied his agitation. "Ye have no right to doubt the depth of my feelings, Jessie."

She dropped her gaze, her hands clenched together on her lap. "Forgive me for being so prickly," she whispered.

He chuckled. "It's as Bears said. Ye are fine as long as ye are in control. When ye are no', ye become feisty."

She glared at him. "*Feisty*? I'm not one of your brothers' beasts!"

He laughed and swiped a finger down her cheek. "Aye, I ken that well enough. I would no' have ye other than ye are, Jessie." He watched as she battled tears at his words. "Will ye be safe here tonight?"

She nodded and brushed a hand at her cheeks. "Yes. There is no need for any concern. I'm being foolish." She bit her lip as he rose.

"Well then, I must leave. I dinna wish to harm yer reputation further." He bent and kissed her on her forehead before unlocking and leaving through the back door.

She locked it after him and then leaned against it, fighting the impulse to race after him and beg him to stay. To never leave. After many moments she pushed away from the door and walked to her desk.

She sat and tapped a pencil on a piece of paper. Finally, after nearly an hour, she began to write.

The following day, a new edition of the paper was available for purchase. Jessamine took a deep breath and wiped at a piece of copper-colored hair as she battled exhaustion. Dark circles underlined her eyes, and she could not stomach any more coffee to keep her awake.

She smiled as one of the townsfolk jerked to a halt as he read her headline and then entered her shop. When he bought four copies, she smiled and handed them over. She had printed an extra twenty-five copies, unable to print anymore and have them ready for the day's publication. Soon the townsfolk streamed into her office, and, within two hours, she had sold out.

After locking the front door and pulling shut the curtains—even though she had missed both breakfast and lunch—she moved to her cot where she collapsed into a dreamless slumber. Her last thought before she fell asleep was that of Ewan kissing her forehead.

CHAPTER 14

*E*wan glared at his men as they whispered over a copy of the newspaper. One of the men had brought it back after running an errand midafternoon, and it had been passed from man to man since his return. He shook his head as Ben stood next to him. "I had hoped, when I made ye foreman, that this sort of mischief would cease."

Ben cleared his throat and whispered, "The article is all about the journalist. Her past. Her challenges with her father. Her father's cruelty. And his presence in town."

Ewan froze a moment before striding across the room and grabbing the paper from one of his workers. He managed to extricate it from his grasp without rending it in two. He returned to the table with Ben and set it in front of him.

"*True and Tantalizing?*" he asked with a raise of his eyebrows.

"That's what she's calling this section that will become a frequent feature, similar to the *N&N* and the *F or F.*" He grinned at Ewan. "Besides *T&T* has a nice ring to it."

"Aye. We all like to believe our lives are interesting enough to be explosive." Ewan shrugged and then focused on the paper.

True and Tantalizing

There once was a girl who believed in fairy tales and princes. She believed that mothers loved their daughters and that fathers protected them above all else. She caught fireflies in summer, wandered barefoot in the grass in city parks, and listened to a neighbor playing the violin as though it were a full symphony performing. Life was filled with joy and endless opportunities.

Then, one day, a man in a gray suit visited. He wanted her to abandon her magical life and forget the only mother she knew. Soon her life was filled with tutors, whacks on the hand when she failed to sit straight, and an empty belly for speaking out of turn. No time for laughter, exuberance, or joy existed in the glacial mansion she was to call home.

The pretty girl transformed into a beautiful woman, and men vied for her attention. However, the man in the gray suit insisted she marry a man three times her age. No act of rebellion, save one, would prevent her from suffering the fate the cold-hearted man planned for her. After her final act of defiance, born of desperation and determination, she survived on her own with only her wits, her talent, and her tenacity.

Now the gray-suited man has returned. Should the woman yield to his demands or continue to forge her life on her own? Should the heroine of this story be forced into a loveless marriage arranged by a calculating, cruel father with no regard for her? I believe not.

Ewan let out a deep breath as he read and then reread her words. "Well, she is good at garnering sympathy." He set aside the paper and stared at the workbench.

Ben snorted. "That's all you have to say?" He waited a moment, focusing on the clenching and unclenching of Ewan's fists. "Why aren't you over at her shop now, speaking with her?"

Ewan exhaled again, this time closing his eyes while he breathed out. "I'm certain she has plenty of admirers to fend off." He glared at Ben when he began to argue. "I willna beg. She kens ..." He looked at his men who were busy at work, ignoring his conversation. "She kens, aye?" He pushed past Ben and stormed from the workshop.

He stomped down the alley, past the rear of the school, and then slipped onto the main road that led to the valley. When he was nearly to the sawmill, he slowed his frenetic pace. He shivered, despite the sun in the sky, as he had not brought his jacket, and winced at the mud seeping into his boots.

He walked the rest of the distance to the sawmill, focusing on the intense blue of the sky, the white clouds in the distance, and the trees with a few golden leaves clinging to the branches. Fluffy snow sat atop many of the limbs, filling out the branches and preventing them from looking as skeletal. The scent of woodsmoke wafted through the air, and he smiled as he approached the sawmill.

"Miss Ericson," he called out. "What are ye doin' outside? 'Tis too cold today."

She laughed and waved. "Hello, Mr. MacKinnon. There are always chores to do." She frowned when she realized he only had on a long-sleeved flannel shirt. "Where is your jacket? Come. Nathaniel is inside."

He accepted her fussing and followed her into the house after kicking off his boots at the front door. He set them in front of the fire to dry and then held his hands out as he shivered as the warmth seeped in. He jerked as Nathaniel slapped him on his shoulders in welcome.

"Ewan! I never expected to see you today." Nathaniel's jovial smile faltered as he saw his friend without a coat and huddled in front of the stove.

"I'm fine," Ewan said. "I was a fool. Upset about something and stormed out of the worksite without grabbing my jacket."

"Well, let Leena warm you up with some food and hot apple cider, ya?" Nathaniel sat at the tall square table pushed against the wall of the room near the kitchen area. He smiled in welcome as Leena set out steaming bowls of stew, thick slabs of bread, and mugs of cider from a pot on the stove.

Ewan joined Nathaniel and Leena, sighing with contentment as he took a sip of the cider. "Heaven. You should sell your baked goods to the townspeople." He watched as the siblings shared a long look. "Has Anna or Cailean spoken with you yet?"

"Ya," Nathaniel said. He waited as he nodded for Leena to speak.

"I want to become her partner," Leena said as her cheeks reddened with her enthusiasm.

"That's wonderful!" Ewan said. "It will mean a lot to Cailean to know you are there and to ease Anna's worries after the bairn arrives." He frowned as Leena shrugged.

"Karl doesn't want me to accept such a position."

Ewan frowned. "I dinna understand."

Nathaniel chewed a carrot and then set down his stew spoon. "He thinks Leena should continue here, helping me, and then focus on the home they will have together."

Ewan saw any excitement in Leena's expression fade as her brother spoke. "Why can ye no' do both? I ken most men want their wife at home during the day, but Karl should be proud of yer abilities." Ewan shook his head. "And that ye can alleviate the financial concerns." He watched as the siblings shared a long look.

"Karl is not as … progressive as you," Nathaniel said. "He believes any financial solution should be resolved by the men of the family."

Ewan snorted. "That's rubbish, and ye ken it. I've hardly been accused of bein' a champion of advancin' women's freedoms, but ye canna allow Karl to prevent ye from doin' something ye desire. Somethin' ye and yer brother need." He shook his head in confusion. "I must admit I'm flummoxed." He paused. "Miss Erickson, what is it ye want? Not what ye worry others want, but what ye want?"

She smiled. "An easy question to answer. I want to work with Mrs. MacKinnon. I want to help Nathaniel after all he has done for me."

Ewan waited for Nathaniel to speak. When Leena's brother remained quiet, Ewan spoke. "I ken what it feels like to be in a sibling's debt. However, I'd no' recommend ye live yer life attempting to repay a debt. Repaying the debt is no' what will bring ye peace." He met Leena's confused gaze. "I hope ye can decide for yerself what ye want."

Nathaniel cleared his throat, and Ewan ate the bowl of stew in front of him. He complimented Leena for the delicious bread and gobbled down a piece of apple crumb cake. "Have things slowed down at the sawmill?" Ewan asked.

"Ya." Nathaniel swiped at his face with his napkin. "Winter came early, an' none other than you planned by framing buildings before the cold weather arrived."

Ewan shrugged. "The others constructing buildings in town are amateurs." He shared a grin with his friend. "I shudder to pass their buildings when a strong wind blows."

They shared a laugh, and soon Ewan departed for town. As he passed the livery, he ventured inside to speak with his eldest brother. He walked to the small office in the back of the livery and poked his head in. Cailean sat with a ledger in front of him, a lamp illuminating the rows of numbers and his brother's frown. "Money problems?"

Cailean looked up and smiled. "Nae. We're prospering, and it's all due to our partnership. Alistair has more time to work as a farrier, and Bears …" Cailean smiled. "He's a wonder with horses."

"Why were ye frownin'?" Ewan sat on an overturned box, his fingers tracing the rim of his hat.

"I've wondered for the past few months, but especially since we were full past capacity with the Harvest Festival, about when we'd have a rival livery. I fear we'll need to expand soon or another shop will open."

Ewan looked over Cailean's shoulder, his gaze distant. "They willna build over the winter, an' I willna build it for them." He smiled as he focused on his eldest brother. "Ye'll give me somethin' to focus on this season, plannin' the expansion of the livery."

Cailean smiled. "Thanks." He set down his pencil and ignored the ledger book as he looked at his brother. "What brings you by?"

"I spoke with Miss Ericson today. I hadna realized ye and Anna had discussed a partnership with her."

Cailean nodded. "We visited her and her brother yesterday. We planned on discussing it with you tonight." He raised an eyebrow. "You were absent from supper last night."

Ewan shook his head, ignoring Cailean's silent question. "She wants to be a partner, Cail."

His brother sighed and rested his head on one hand. "I know. It's convincing her dimwitted fiancé that's the problem." He shrugged.

"Now that Belle is willing to have a partner, I hope Miss Ericson joins her."

Ewan nodded. "I hate that there's nothin' more I can do to help ye."

With hazel eyes shining with gratitude and love, Cailean smiled at his youngest brother. "You've done plenty, Ewan. You've brought Belle's sister home. You've opened Belle's eyes to the possibility of a partnership. She hates the idea of closing the bakery, but I fear that would have occurred had she remained obstinate in her desire to run it alone."

Ewan nodded, tapping his hat between his legs and hitting the side of the box a few times. "How are ye, Cail? Now that the bairn grows and the birth approaches?"

Cailean ran a hand through his hair and leaned forward as though in prayer. "Terrified. Excited. Determined to enjoy every moment I have with Belle." He shrugged. "I imagine I'm like most husbands."

"Aye, but ye ken what it is to lose everything." Ewan cleared his throat, changing the subject for his brother. "Have things calmed here for Bears? I witnessed a man treating him with disrespect last week."

Cailean sighed, his finger tapping at the desktop in agitation. "Aye, it's no different now than before the article. Her apology"—he raised his eyebrows at the dubious use of the word—"appeased many of the townsfolk. There were enough here, who, after they calmed down, remembered the relationship Jack had with Bears." His jaw tightened for a moment. "There will always exist those who wish ill on others or act like idiots."

Ewan nodded. "I'm glad 'tis no worse than it ever was." He rose. "I'll see ye at home for supper." He slipped out the door and returned to the worksite, ignoring his desire to stop by the print shop to see how Jessamine fared.

～

Warren rapped on her door the following morning and waited for her to unlock it. He smiled when he let him in. "How does it feel to be the talk of the town?"

She shuddered. "I'm the talk of the town for all the reasons I dreaded." She glared at the one copy of the last paper she had kept. She always printed herself a copy and had a large file where she stacked them on top of each other. Soon it would be covered by the latest edition. "I had hoped I was vague enough that the townsfolk did not realize I was referring to myself." She shared a chagrined smile with Warren. "They are more astute than I gave them credit for."

Warren moved to the small potbellied stove in the center of the room and played with the slumbering coals inside. He then added a little fuel, closed the stove door, and held up his hands in front of it to warm them. "Ah, there's nothing I like better than a well-built fire."

She watched him curiously. "When you decide to make your story public, will you allow me to publish it?"

Warren flushed and turned to look out at the town where a fresh coat of snow covered the boardwalk and street. "Oh, there's little of interest to tell. Nothing to tantalize the townsfolk."

Jessamine shook her head. "I hardly believe that's true. You're one to know secrets but impart your own very reluctantly."

Warren shrugged. "With stories like the ones you have recently published, you are regaining the townsfolk's regard. However, I do not know how you will ever undo the damage you did to Bears' reputation."

She turned to fiddle with blocks of letters and failed to meet his gaze. "There is little I can do to make amends. I will continue to hope I can write something that will change the townsfolk's perception of him."

Warren nodded. "I could ask for no more." He clasped his hands behind his back. "I know I have been a constant irritant to you and that you must often wonder why I pester you as often as I do." He met her gaze. "However, it was due to my recommendation and pressure that you were offered the job. I convinced the committee that they could do no better than hire you."

Jessamine flushed and shook her head. "I don't understand. I was an unknown when I arrived."

Warren smiled. "I have friends all over the country. After you applied, I sent an urgent telegram for information." He lifted one eyebrow and shoulder. "I knew you were a woman. And I knew your penchant for stirring up trouble."

She pointed at him. "It's why you were dissatisfied with my articles. You had vouched for me and were worried I would be a disappointment."

He rolled his eyes. "You could never disappoint as a reporter. However, it's what you chose to report that rankled." He waved his hand. "Enough about the past few months. It seems you are turning a corner." He took a deep breath. "I need a favor."

She frowned and nodded. "What is it?"

"The town needs money. There are projects that must be completed if we are to remain a viable, desirable place for people to live. However, one of our committee members"—he pointed to the bank next door—"refuses to consider plans we have for raising taxes."

"*Taxes?* That's the most hated word, besides *war.*"

"Perhaps, but you can't live in a civilized place without some sort of inflow, and taxes are the fairest way to ensure revenue. We already know our most wealthy will not willingly pay for what we need."

Jessamine chuckled. "No, Mr. Finlay is too busy guarding his wealth." She furrowed her brows as she watched Warren. "How would I be able to help you?"

Warren sighed. "The townsfolk voted him onto the committee, but I fear they are not hearing the truth about what is occurring at the meetings. When they visit the bank, or see him around town, he spreads the tales of how much he is doing, but that he is hog-tied from accomplishing all he would like."

Jessamine shook her head. "What amazes me is that people believe him." She shared a look with Warren. "Why not have another meeting at your office and have me present?"

"That would never work. He'll act differently when he realizes you are there."

She smiled. "Leave your small office door open, and I'll sit back there, away from the three of you. If there is one constant, besides his frugality, it's his booming voice." Her smile spread. "That is one exposé I would relish publishing."

"I'll let you know of our next meeting date." Warren laughed and nodded, his shoulders relaxing as though a weight had been lifted. "Thank you, J.P. I've been unable to think of a way to bring about real change with him impeding us at every turn." He headed for the door but paused before opening it and faced Jessamine. "I know you'll hear this news soon enough. Once you released your paper yesterday, your father's welcome here became more tepid."

Jessamine sighed. "He won't like that. He expects to be celebrated wherever he goes."

Warren laughed. "Well, you should have seen his cold reception at the café last night. From what I was told, Irene gave him an earful."

Jessamine laughed. "I almost wish I had been there to hear it." She wrapped her arms around her middle and rubbed her hands over her upper arms. "If there is one thing he despises, it's publicity that makes him appear less than gallant."

Warren shook his head, his smile pleased. "Well, I'd say public opinion turned against him even more when he snarled at Irene." He nodded as Jessamine gasped. "Yes, he's not as astute as he likes to believe himself if he didn't know better than to treat her poorly in her own café."

"What happened?" Jessamine asked.

"From all accounts, he was thrown out on his hind end by a pair of miners who are fond of Irene and Harold. They were the first to react as it seems all the men in the café stood, ready to defend Irene. Harold was held back, with his rolling pin in hand, by one of the hands at his grandson's ranch."

Jessamine let out a sigh of relief. "Thank God my father can't complain to the sheriff and press for charges against them."

Warren chuckled. "His pride and pantaloons were damaged." He fingered the doorknob. "Lock up after me, J.P. I fear the man has yet to see sense. He's still at the Grand."

Jessamine nodded, locking the door after Warren. She pulled the curtains before collapsing on her small cot, a pillow hugged to her chest.

~

That evening Warren sat in his parlor, sipping an amber glass of spirits when he heard the knock at his front door. He groaned and rose. Long shadows filled the front door area, and he held a lamp up as he opened the door. "Come in," he murmured to the man on his front step.

"I dinna mean to interrupt yer evenin'," Ewan murmured.

"I was thinking about impossibilities," Warren said with a self-deprecating smile. "Come. Join me by the fire. It's cold tonight." He led Ewan into the parlor where he motioned for Ewan to sit in a high-back chair. He raised an eyebrow as he approached the decanters.

"Nae," Ewan said with a grimace. "I've a mind to drink stronger spirits than yer inclined to imbibe."

Warren nodded and sat, lifting his tumbler and swallowing a long swig of his amber-colored drink. "What brings you by tonight? Anyone with sense is buttoned down at home."

Ewan laughed humorlessly. "Aye, that's always been my problem. I'm too often without sense." He pinched the bridge of his nose and then squared his shoulders as he took a deep breath. "Do ye mean to ask for her?"

Warren squinted at Ewan after the question and shook his head as though he were hard of hearing. "I'm afraid I don't know what you are talking about."

"Dammit, man, must I spell it out fer ye? Do ye plan to marry Jessie?"

Warren choked on the sip of his drink he had just swallowed. "J.P.? Why on earth would I wed her?" He held up his hand to placate Ewan. "I meant no offense. She's a fine woman, but she's not for me. She never has been." He fought a smile before he saw Ewan's torment, and then he sobered. "She's never seen me that way either."

"Ye're at her shop constantly. Ye had dinner with her the other night. Ye … Ye …"

Warren raised his eyebrows as Ewan stuttered to a halt. "You're as bad as the gossiping biddies in this town. And you can't even come up with more than two reasons for why she and I would be courting. Which we aren't." He shook his head emphatically. "We are friends."

"Friends?" Ewan asked.

"As of today we are. Before now I was someone she put up with who criticized her soundly for her publishing mistakes." Warren took a deep breath. "I have my sights set elsewhere."

Ewan leaned back in his chair, mollified for a moment before he stiffened. "If ye mean Sorcha, ye'd better have only honorable intentions in mind."

Warren pointed a finger at Ewan. "It's none of your business who I intend to pursue. And no need to be insulting in your petulance at your inability to convince J.P. to marry you." He raised an eyebrow. "Plus I am as honorable as the situation requires."

Ewan snorted. "Said like a damn lawyer. Either ye are or ye are no' honorable. There is no' much room for prevaricatin'."

Warren laughed. "I'm afraid you have a lot to learn. There's always room for evasiveness, especially in the courtroom. Or love." He watched as Ewan fidgeted across from him. After taking a deep sip of his drink, Warren let out a satisfied sigh. He met his guest's surprised stare at his action and smiled. "Why should you care who pursues J.P.?"

Ewan shrugged.

"It's not as though you are still interested in her." He fought a smile as Ewan stiffened and gripped the arms of his chair. "J.P. told me today she's had no contact with you in days. She believes you are content to be pursued by the townswomen."

"Would serve the daft woman right if I married the Jameson girl." He frowned as Warren flinched.

"What about Fidelia?" Warren asked. "How is she since she left the Boudoir?"

Ewan shook his head and frowned. "Terrified. I dinna ken what to do for her. She hides in her room, refuses to see anyone until Anna forces her way in. She's no' like the woman I remember seeing at the Boudoir. Confident and sassy."

The lawyer stared into the fire for a long moment before sighing. "Perhaps adjusting to life away from such a place is more of a burden for her than could have been expected."

Ewan hung his head as though in shame. "I never meant to harm her. When I had the chance to free her, I took it. I thought of Anna, of what I would want were Fidelia my sister. I never considered what Fidelia wanted."

Warren sat in quiet contemplation a moment. "Perhaps she is having a difficult time due to the lack of a certain liquid the new doctor seems only too eager to supply the Beauties. I had hoped he would have greater expertise than he has thus far exhibited." He raised an eyebrow as Ewan snorted.

"The new doctor, Doc Chester, kens less than I do about medicine. I dinna ken where he went to school, but he was no' much of a student. I pity anyone in town who needs his services."

Their gazes met as though sharing their worry about Cailean and Annabelle as the birth of their child approached. "There's always the midwife," Warren whispered.

"Aye, that's what Alistair tells Cailean daily at the livery. An' what I tell Anna whenever I see her alone without Cail. But the anxiety is mounting for them, in case a doctor is needed." He tapped his thigh in agitation. "They should be lookin' forward to the birth of their bairn, not dreadin' it. Anna must force joy into her expression, and Cailean watches his wife as though he's tryin' to fill a lifetime of memories into these months."

"It isn't fair," Warren muttered.

"Nae, it isna. If that *bluidy* Doc had no' been intent on travelin' to Butte, we would continue with a competent man now." Ewan shook his head in disgust.

"If the new doctor is found to be incompetent, he will be replaced." Warren's jaw twitched as he clamped it shut.

"Aye, but who has to suffer afore then? Who must die?" Ewan

stared into the flames and then stiffened his shoulders. "I'm sorry to interrupt yer quiet evenin' at home, Warren. I'll see myself out." He rose, clapped Warren on the back, and strode to the front door.

Warren followed him, locking the door after him. He returned to the parlor, his thoughts even more muddled than before Ewan had arrived.

CHAPTER 15

*T*wo days later Jessamine pulled on a heavy shawl and slipped outside her print shop. Her paper was ready for the following day, and she had little to do. As she walked through town, it was largely quiet with most townsfolk inside as dusk arrived earlier as the winter solstice approached.

Tobias stood on the boardwalk in front of his General Store, a broom in one hand as he watched her approach. "Well, if it isn't the town crier," he said with a snide smile.

"Mr. Sutton," she said with a lift of an eyebrow. "I hope you have a good evening."

He laughed. "I hope you are as intelligent as you proclaim yourself to be. I'd hate to see you as disillusioned as the other misses in this town, played false by that rascal MacKinnon."

"I'm afraid I neither need your warning nor care what you have to say."

He laughed. "Then I suppose it makes no difference to the likes of you that your favorite newspaper subject is holed up at his latest project with his newest paramour." He watched her with feigned sympathy. He called after her as her pace away from him increased. "I look forward to reading about their wedding announcement in the paper!"

She walked with such alacrity she was soon out of breath. After a few minutes she groaned inwardly to realize she had arrived at Ewan's worksite. The small one-story home with glass windows on either side of the front door seemed cheerful to her just as it made her want to weep. She turned to leave but paused as she heard voices raised from inside.

The well-oiled front door eased open without a squeak, and she tiptoed down a hallway through the center of the house. The front room was empty, but she heard voices from a back room.

"Just imagine, Ewan. This could be our room," said a youthful, hopeful female.

"Ye are as daft as a donkey if ye believe for one moment I'll marry ye. I've told ye ten times already. Get out of my house!"

Jessamine shivered at the anger in Ewan's bellow. She peeked around the corner just in time to see Helen Jameson throw herself in the direction of Ewan's arms. Rather than catch her, Ewan side-stepped her, and she fell to the floor.

"I will no' have ye fabricatin' a story, sayin' I touched ye. Sayin' I wanted to be with ye. That we were alone in this house due to my desire for ye." He glared at Helen as she began to sob on the floor. "I will never say I understand all that ye are sufferin' at yer mother's house, but ye have to know I'll never wed ye."

Jessamine's sharp intake of breath was covered by Helen's howl of rage.

Helen raised her tear-ravaged face to meet Ewan's glare. "You and your family are not so special! Someday you will be brought low. Not everyone will love you." She pushed herself to her feet and rubbed at her skirt.

"I ken not everyone will love me, Helen. I'm sorry to cause ye pain, but I will no' marry where I do no' love." He met her pleading stare. "Nor should ye." He sighed as she barreled out of the room, glancing up at Helen's squeal of displeasure at the sight of Jessamine.

His shoulders stooped, and he pinched between his brows. "Of course ye'd be here to witness that." His pleading gaze met hers. "Will ye please no' write about that? 'Twould only harm Helen, and I will no' marry her."

Jessamine nodded. She swallowed as she took a step into the room. "This is a lovely house, Ewan."

He nodded as he glanced around. "Aye, 'tis. I'll find someone to sell it to."

She shivered at his hopeless tone and at the fact he moved away, rather than toward, her. "I've missed you." The anger in his gaze caused her shiver to turn into a shudder.

"Ye have no right to say such things. I ken ye have no regard for me. Ye never have, other than as a way to sell yer papers." He ran a hand through his long blondish-red hair. "I'll soon resume my disreputable ways, an' ye'll have plenty to write about."

"Ewan," she whispered.

"Never worry. I've a whore of my own now, so I'll have no reason to bother ye further." His bitter words sounded through the room as he turned away from her and stared at a bare wall.

He stiffened as she ran a hand over his back. "Ewan," she whispered again. "I ... I'm sorry."

"For what?" he asked, his shoulder muscles tightening under her touch.

"For thinking you were like my father. Like my old editor. For not realizing you were a different sort of man." She let out a deep breath. "I should have known. That first night you stayed to ensure no one broke in and harmed me, you gave me the clues to your true character then."

He shook his head in confusion. "I dinna understand."

"That night you told me that you'd thought about our earlier interaction. About what you could have done to have provoked my actions at the town dance. Rather than blame me, you looked to see what you could have done wrong and to fix it." She let out a stuttering breath. "You are honorable." She leaned forward and kissed him at the base of his neck. "You are loyal." She kissed one shoulder. "You are trustworthy." She kissed his other shoulder.

She squealed as he spun and hauled her against him. She barely had time to take a breath before he kissed her, his mouth moving over hers as pent-up passion and desire burst forth.

After a minute he pushed her away. "Dammit," he rasped as he caught his breath. "Forgive me. I should ken better with ye." He frowned with confusion as she smiled at him.

"No, I want your touch," she whispered, flushing at the admission. "I can't begin to describe how it pleases me to know how much you desire me." Humor lit her eyes. "And I'm a journalist." At his low chuckle, she relaxed marginally.

She shook her head as he moved to kiss her again, confusion clouding his gaze. "No, Ewan. I have to tell you something." At his nod, she took another deep breath. "I'm terrified of putting my life in another's hands. Of trusting that he will see me for me, not as a possession to be profited from."

Her face tilted into his touch as though against her will as he stroked her cheek. "But I've been miserable without you. And it's not only because I miss your touch, the passion you can evoke." She raised fearful eyes to meet his. "I miss our conversations. Your jokes. You." She blinked rapidly, but two tears slipped from her eyes. "I don't want to live without you."

He remained silent but shook his head in confusion.

"I ... I love you." She bit her lip and then cupped his face with her hands, running her fingers through his beard. "Will you marry me?"

He gave a small *whoop* before bending forward and capturing her lips in another kiss. He backed her until she was against the wall, his body bracketing hers as the kiss deepened farther. He raised his head, only to slip kisses along her neck. When she shivered as he nipped her earlobe, he murmured, "That's yes, in case ye were confused."

He pulled back when she burst into tears. "Jessie?" he whispered as his thumbs attempted and failed to swipe away her tears as quickly as they fell. He pulled her to him and cradled her.

"I thought you wouldn't want me. Not after all the horrible things I've written about you." She sucked in a stuttering breath.

He chuckled. "Ye've no' said anything horrible, love. Ye were courtin' me in yer own way. I was too stupid to figure it out in the beginnin', but I did eventually." His fingers tugged and pulled at her hair, freeing it from its pins. "This is our house, Jessie, if that is acceptable to ye. I built it for me, but, after only a few weeks, I couldna come here without thinkin' of ye."

He sobered as she remained quiet. "I ken 'tis not as grand as the homes ye are accustomed to. I ken ye are used to mansions. When I'm able, I'll build us a bigger home."

She slapped her fingers over his mouth and shook her head, sniffling as tears continued to cascade down her cheeks. "No, Ewan, you will not. You built this home for us. This is our home. Will be our home." She leaned forward until her forehead rested against his. "I love it."

He pulled her close, sighing with contentment to have her in his arms again. "It may prove too small once we have bairns," he murmured.

"Let's worry about that when the time comes," she whispered.

After a moment he straightened, kissing her on the top of her head. "Will ye come home with me? Have dinner at the house?" He watched as trepidation clouded her eyes. "They will accept ye because I love ye." He smiled as her breath caught at his declaration. "They will adore ye if ye promise to cease writing snide articles about the townsfolk."

She smiled. "I make no promises." She gripped his hand as he chuckled and followed him from what would be their home.

"When do ye want to wed?" he asked as they headed toward the home he had shared with his siblings since he had arrived in Bear Grass Springs three years ago.

"I don't care as long as it is soon."

He slipped her hand through his bent elbow as they walked from the smaller house he built near Alistair and Leticia's. He led Jessamine to the boardwalk, rather than along the alley, as the pathway was muddy after a late-November snow squall had melted. He nodded, unable to hide his smile of contentment when the townsfolk watched in shock as they traveled arm in arm down the boardwalk. After they passed the Odd Fellows Hall, he helped her down the boardwalk steps to cross Main Street to Cailean's house.

He paused as her steps slowed. "It will be all right, Jessie. I promise." At his encouraging nod, she took a deep breath and walked beside him, up the steps through the front door. He helped her out of her shawl, hanging it and her hat on a peg. His eyes lit with joy to see her hair remained mussed after their kisses, and he stifled a chuckle as she hastily poked in pins to give it a semblance of order.

When Ewan entered the kitchen, holding Jessamine's hand, the soft hum of conversation slowed to a halt.

Annabelle, who stood at the stove, was the first to approach and to smile at Jessamine. "Hello, Miss McMahon. What a pleasure to have you join us for our evening meal."

Cailean shared a long, hard look with his brother before nodding. "Aye, welcome, Miss McMahon." He stood behind Annabelle with a hand placed on her shoulder. "Alistair and Leticia are joining us tonight."

Ewan smiled, ignoring the subtle warning in his brother's tone. "Wonderful." He gave Jessamine a gentle nudge, and she stepped farther into the kitchen. Soon she was seated at the table with Ewan beside her.

Sorcha burst into the room, her gaze on Cailean and Annabelle, ignoring those at the table. "Can ye believe the daft woman has yet to act?" she asked as though in the middle of a conversation.

"Sorch," Ewan said in a deep voice.

She turned to him, her face reddened and her hands waving about as she expounded her point. When she saw Jessamine seated beside her brother, her eyebrows rose, and her eyes widened. "Oh, so ye did act!" She smiled as she sat beside Ewan and gave him a gentle nudge.

"We'll talk later," Ewan whispered in her ear.

"There's nothin' to talk about," Sorcha said. "I advised the reporter how she was a daft fool, and it seems she's come to her senses."

Alistair and Leticia arrived with Hortence, Leticia's gait hitching as she caught sight of Jessamine at the table. She turned to Alistair and shook her head. Alistair spoke soothing words to Leticia, before sending a searching look at Ewan. At his shrug, Alistair half smiled. "So ye finally convinced her?" He focused on Leticia who remained stiff as a board, any pleasure at the family meal diminished by Jessamine's presence.

Alistair ran a hand down Leticia's back and settled her far away from Jessamine, although that meant she was across the table from her. She leaned into his touch a moment before stiffening her spine and sitting with her shoulders back.

Hortence stared at Jessamine and scrunched up her face, as though deep in thought. "Why do you print lies?" She looked at her family members at their collective deep indrawn breath. "Jake at school says you can't help it. It's what all reporters do."

Jessamine flushed, her hands gripped together under the table on her lap. "I am not a liar."

"Is it because you have red hair? That's what the boys tell me at school. They think I'm a liar too." She fingered the end of her long braid, her red hair shimmering in the light.

Jessamine's gaze softened. "Your hair color has nothing to do with truthfulness. Does having blond hair make Mrs. Jameson an oracle of the truth?"

Her question earned startled giggles from the adults and a puzzled expression from Hortence.

"I don't know what an *ore ankle* is, but I know you wanted to print lies about my mama," Hortence said. "I heard Mama and Papa whispering about it when they thought I couldn't hear. Mama and Papa don't lie." She tilted her chin up in defiance like she'd seen her aunts do and stared down Jessamine.

"I never published anything about your mother. I was ... persuaded to see another point of view." She met the little girl's eyes and smiled. "You're very brave."

"I have to be brave. If I'm to marry a chief's son, I must be."

Leticia sputtered, and Alistair's eyes bulged as the others laughed. "Hortence, you just turned seven in September. You aren't marrying anyone!"

"But Mama, Bears is wonderful! He's as good with horses as Papa."

"Yes, but he's like an uncle to you. That's all he is or can be, darling," Leticia soothed. She speared Jessamine with a severe glare. "If you print any of this, you will wish you were dead."

Jessamine shook her head. "No, I am here as a friend, not as a reporter." Her flush heightened. "I know that I betrayed Ewan's trust once when I told him that before, but I truly mean what I say here today."

Hortence sat, deflated in her chair. "But Bears is wonderful, Mama. He listens when I talk and talk." She frowned when her uncles laughed.

Alistair ran a hand over her head. "Someday ye'll meet the perfect man. For now, enjoy life. Enjoy bein' seven."

Hortence grumbled her agreement, only perking up when Annabelle whispered she had apple pie for dessert.

Annabelle smiled at Jessamine. "We all know you acted as you did because you knew of no other way to maintain your courtship with Ewan." She bit her lip. "I beg your pardon. I spoke out of turn."

Ewan shook his head and smiled. He gripped Jessamine's hand under the table. "No, ye are correct, Anna. Jessie and I are to wed. As soon as possible." He and Jessamine shared a gaze filled with longing and love, missing his family's shocked expressions. He faced Annabelle. "Will ye make us a cake?"

She moved to him and hugged him and then Jessamine. "Of course I will. We'll have such a celebration for you both!"

Annabelle's ready acceptance induced similar reactions from the rest of the family, and soon they stood around the table, embracing and laughing.

Leticia was the last to approach Jessamine. She met Leticia's wary gaze and nodded. "I know you have no reason to trust me, but I promise I will never publish that article."

Leticia watched her with a concerned expression. "The fact it exists at all concerns me."

"I know. It would worry me too." She took a deep breath. "I will give you the proof copy. Give you my research notes. You can decide what to do with them. Keep them or burn them. It will be your decision."

"Why?" Leticia asked, unable to hide the surprise from her voice.

"I've learned that I don't need to be a heartless reporter. I can be something else and still be successful," she whispered.

Alistair joined them and wrapped an arm around Leticia's waist after she leaned into him. "If ye keep writing like yer last paper, ye'll have the town excited to see ye."

Jessamine grimaced. "Rather than fearful, you mean?" At his shrug, she smiled. "Well, as of now, that is my plan, although I will continue to report on local and national events."

Alistair's serious gaze met hers. "If ye are no' serious about Ewan, dinna play him false."

She took in a startled breath at his words, then looked at Ewan speaking with Cailean near the stove. "No, no. I cannot tell you how much I care for him." Her eyes glowed with sincerity.

Alistair nodded. "Good," he whispered. He turned as Cailean raised his voice in a toast to his brother and his fiancée, and Jessamine moved to stand beside Ewan. She tucked herself into his side.

"Are ye all right?" Ewan whispered. "I thought I should leave ye alone to speak with Lettie."

"I'm fine." She breathed as she pressed herself farther into his embrace. "It's a little overwhelming being surrounded by your family."

He chuckled. "Ye'll accustom yerself to us."

She heard the hope in his words and snuggled closer. "I will," she promised.

Cailean cleared his throat again, and she focused on the eldest MacKinnon. "To Ewan and Jessamine. May you only know joy, health, and harmony in the many years you have together." He beamed at his youngest brother and then at Jessamine.

The family raised their glasses and said, "Aye!" or "Hear! Hear!"

Cailean cleared his throat again, and the impromptu celebration paused. "I have it on good authority that Mrs. Jameson has left town for a few days. Seems a cousin is ill in Helena. If I were you, I'd wed while she is away."

Ewan gave a grunt of agreement. "Aye. We'll marry with all haste. The gossips be damned."

CHAPTER 16

The day before his wedding, Ewan worked in the home he would share with Jessamine. He whistled while he hung curtains, frowning as he backed away. "I think they're crooked," he muttered to himself. He shrugged and moved into the kitchen area where he unpacked a box of foodstuffs from the Merc.

"I always find it disappointing to see a man doing women's work." Mr. Abbott stood in the doorway to Ewan's house, his long black coat buttoned shut with a red scarf around his neck. He held his black top hat in his hand, and his brown hair was shellacked in place with a thick layer of pomade.

"Mr. Abbott," Ewan said. "Close the door behind ye as ye leave." He glared at the man as Mr. Abbott entered, closing himself inside the space with Ewan. "Ye are no' welcome here."

Jessamine's father chuckled as he wandered the small living area. "You actually believe my daughter would be content living in such a pathetic little home? She is accustomed to a mansion, my dear boy." He smiled as he saw Ewan stiffen. "Not some patched-together shack by a second-rate carpenter."

"I'm excellent at my trade," Ewan snapped.

"Ah, yes, a tradesman. Just what any father should wish for his only daughter." Mr. Abbott fingered the yellow curtain Ewan had just hung and wrinkled his nose in distaste. "You'd have to expect a father to object to you. A drunkard. A gambler. A whoremonger."

Ewan stiffened. "I am none of those things." His nostrils flared as he fisted his hands, and he faced his adversary.

"Yes, you are—and worse. You're a defiler of innocents." Mr. Abbott held up his hand. "I know you believe Jessamine's story that she was taken advantage of by that editor, but you should know she has always been adept at fabricating tales. It's why she has had such success as a newspaperwoman."

Ewan half smiled. "I think I have a better idea than ye if what she told me were true or no'." His mocking smile acted as fuel to her father's ire, and her father grabbed Ewan's collar. However, they were nearly the same height, and Ewan was accustomed to hard work on a daily basis. He pushed Mr. Abbott away, his eyes flashing a warning.

"How dare you imply that you have defiled my daughter!"

"Dinna think to touch me again, old man. I'll no' show ye respect the next time." He let out a deep breath. "Say what ye've come to say an' then leave."

Mr. Abbott ran a hand over his coat and picked up his forgotten top hat. "I would offer you financial compensation to forego this foolish notion of marrying my wayward daughter." He paused as he saw interest in Ewan's gaze. "I will be most generous."

"How generous?" Ewan asked.

"How does $10,000 sound?" Mr. Abbott asked.

Ewan ran a hand through his hair and turned away from Jessamine's father. He took a deep breath and then another. "Meet me at the lawyer's in an hour." He spun to glare at the man before Mr. Abbott clapped him on his back.

Ewan watched Jessamine's father depart, and he perched on a windowsill, his mind racing. After a few minutes he rose to prepare for his meeting with her father.

~

"**Y**ou're certain you want to do this?" Warren asked Ewan, rubbing at his temple. They sat sequestered in his private room at the back of his office with the door shut. "It could prove disastrous."

"Aye. 'Tis a gamble. I ken that. But I need to do it." He met Warren's troubled gaze. "I need ye to be as wily as Alistair said ye are."

Warren nodded and then motioned for him to move to the front room. "He'll be here soon." They settled into chairs at the table near the potbellied stove. Warren rose with deferential grace as Mr. Abbott entered, extending his hand and taking his coat to hang on a peg near the warm stove. When Jessamine's father sat at the table, Warren cleared his throat. "I need you to understand, Mr. Abbott, that Mr. MacKinnon has already explained the particulars of your request to me and that I have been retained by him."

Mr. Abbott smiled. "That is fine. Saves me the expense of lawyer fees."

Warren extracted three pages. "I always like to have a duplicates in case one is destroyed." He turned them so they faced Ewan and Mr. Abbott. *"I hereby declare, as witnessed by my hand and date below, that I will no longer pursue Miss Jessamine Phyllis Abbott McMahon. I will exert no influence over her future decisions and said decisions are hers alone."*

Warren continued to read the contract about the terms, where the money was to be deposited, and the loss of funds should the contract be violated. After a moment, he raised guileless eyes to Mr. Abbott. "Is this satisfactory?"

Mr. Abbott chuckled and grabbed the pen, inking his name at the bottom. He waited as Ewan did the same to the three copies. "I assume one of these is mine?" At Warren's nod, Abbott rose, grabbed his coat, and marched out the door.

Ewan sat back and let out a deep breath. "Thank ye, Warren."

"Don't thank me yet. You don't know if Jessamine will see through this."

Ewan rapped his fingers on the table. "When she calms down from her anger, I hope she will." He stood. "I hope I'm not the only one arriving at the church tomorrow."

～

Jessamine glared at the door as it burst open and then glowered at who stood in the doorway. "I thought you had the good sense to leave town."

Her father laughed as he waved a sheet of paper at her. "No, I would never admit defeat, daughter dear. You know me better than that." His polished shoes made a *click*ing sound on her wood floors. "If you believed those pathetic café owners would force me to leave, then you've forgotten who I am."

"I'm not alone here, Father. I have friends. I marry tomorrow." She paled as her father laughed.

"Yes, I imagine you consider that lawyer your friend. I wonder what you would think were you to know how eager he was to write up a contract between your supposed fiancé and me, making null and void any engagement." His smile broadened as she paled to the point she looked gutted.

"Give me that," she said, grabbing the document from his hand. She read it through twice, tears falling over her cheeks by the time she had finished the second reading. "He couldn't. He wouldn't," she breathed.

"He did. Seems he's more sensible than I gave him credit for." Her father leaned forward and gripped her shoulder. "Money wins out, Jessamine. It always will." He looked around her small shop and shook his head in disgust. "We will leave tomorrow on the train."

"I …" She shook her head as she wrapped her arms around her waist. "Please leave."

Her father plucked the contract from her numb fingers and smiled jovially at her. "This was an important lesson for you, Jessamine. Men will only ever want money. They will never want you."

She sank to her knees as the door closed behind him, her body racked by sobs.

～

The morning of her wedding, Jessamine entered the livery wearing a heavy wool cloak. She paused at the entrance, then firmed her shoulders as she approached Bears. "Mr. Bears," she whispered around a throat sore from crying, "I would like to hire a horse."

Bears turned to face her and frowned. He noted her reddened eyes and nose before focusing again on the desolation in her gaze. "There's no horse strong enough to help you escape your demons."

"Damn you, I must leave town. And I refuse to leave with my father on the train." She pursed her lips together as though battling another sob.

"You will be missed today at the church. I know Ewan will be waiting for you." He watched her with concern as she flinched at Ewan's name.

"Ewan is more concerned about my father's money than with me."

Bears smiled and shook his head. He ran a hand over the head of a fidgety mare as though he wanted to soothe Jessamine in such a manner but was unable to. "No, miss, you've got it backward."

"I know what I read." She jutted out her chin like an obstinate child.

"From where I'm standing, there's reading and then there's understanding. Seems to me, Ewan knows you better than you know him." He met her furious gaze. "You're marrying a gambler, miss."

"He hasn't gambled since he won Fidelia from the Boudoir."

Bears shook his head as though surprised at her obtuseness. "He gambles every day but in different ways." He sighed when he saw confusion in her gaze. "What did the words say?"

She bit her lip and then swallowed. "That he would no longer pursue me. That he would not exert influence over my future decisions." She blinked rapidly, but tears fell.

Bears grunted. "Just as I thought." He watched her for a few moments. "Think, miss. Think."

She shook her head and sniffled.

"Why would Ewan still wait for you at the church today?" Bears' deep-brown eyes were filled with sincerity.

Jessamine closed her eyes and took a deep breath as she thought. Suddenly she gasped. "He's giving me the choice, giving me the decision."

Bears smiled. "Yes, miss. So you aren't a porcupine after all." He chuckled when she looked at him in confusion. "If I were to marry today, I would not be in a cold livery. I'd be readying my wedding finery."

She gripped his arm. "Thank you, Bears. Thank you so much." She spun, racing for the exit and home.

E wan paced at the front of the church and ignored the smug smiles his brothers exchanged. "I ken I teased ye when ye were marryin' …" His voice trailed away as he heaved out a deep breath as though attempting to relax himself. He ran a hand over his groomed beard and then through his trimmed hair.

"But ye never thought ye'd be fortunate enough to marry," Alistair said with a smile. "I willna tempt ye with a dram of whiskey, the way ye did me."

"Quit ruining your clothes," Cailean said as Ewan tugged at the uncomfortable suit jacket.

Ewan dropped his hands. "I hope she comes."

Alistair and Ewan gave him curious glances, before shaking their heads and smiling. Soon all the guests were settled in the pews, but the bride was still missing. Ewan stared at the church entrance with such intensity as though attempting to conjure her appearance through sheer force of will.

Just as he turned away to speak with his brothers about canceling the wedding, the door creaked open. He spun to face the entrance to find Warren entering with Jessamine on his arm. Ewan sucked in a deep breath at the sight of her in a cream-colored dress with a bustle at the back and lace on the collar and wrists. Her red hair was loose over her shoulders.

Warren whispered something in her ear, and then closed and barred the door behind him. As they walked up the aisle, a pounding at the front of the church was heard, and Ewan saw Warren murmuring something to the crowd that elicited laughter.

"There must always be a spectacle with a MacKinnon wedding," said someone near the front in a carrying voice, causing Ewan to smile. He shared a glance with Alistair, and then he focused all his attention on Jessamine.

He frowned when he saw her reddened eyes. When she finally reached him, he traced a finger under one of her eyes and whispered, "Forgive me, my love."

She shook her head and smiled joyously. "No, my darling, we are together." She jolted as a resounding crash sounded at the front of the church. "That will be my father, attempting to gain entrance."

Ewan laughed. "I wouldn't expect him to back down without a fight."

The pastor stood in front of them and began the ceremony, pausing as the church door burst open. He glared at Mr. Abbott as he marched down the aisle. "You are indecent, sir. This is an honorable ceremony."

Jessamine's father waved the paper over his head. "I have a contract stating that he will not pursue her. That he will forego her!"

Jessamine laughed. "You were outsmarted by the town gambler, Father. Your contract says that *he* will not pursue me and that *he* will not influence my decisions. However, it says nothing about me pursuing him. Please desist in interrupting our wedding."

She watched as Frederick Tompkins and Warren hauled her father out of the church and then propped up the splintered door. Jessamine faced Ewan with a resplendent smile. "Shall we?"

"Oh, we shall, my love," he murmured as he squeezed her hand and faced the pastor.

~

E wan stood next to Jessamine, his smile both delighted and holding a warning to the townsfolk. He hoped they understood that Jessamine was a MacKinnon now. He would brook no disrespect of his bride. Although some appeared nervous to approach her, most were delighted and slapped him on his back. The majority were happy that the reporter's wedding to the last MacKinnon male was as entertaining as anything she had printed in her newspaper.

Ewan held up his hands and whistled for attention. He beamed at the crowd of townsfolk gathered in the Odd Fellows Hall to celebrate his wedding. "I want to begin by thankin' all of ye for comin' today to celebrate our weddin'. 'Tis a fine thing to see so many of our friends together, and I canna tell ye how much it means to have ye with us today."

He gripped Jessamine's hand. "Jessie an' I would also like to thank the MacKinnons for their support as they helped us prepare for our weddin'."

Someone called out, "And in such haste!"

He laughed and pulled Jessamine closer to his side. "If ye had any sense, Olaf, ye'd find yerself a good woman an' marry her afore she kens better." He felt Jessamine's body shake with her giggles, and he squeezed her hand.

Jessamine added in a loud voice, "We hope you'll enjoy the celebration, and we thank you for celebrating with us." She ignored the surprised looks as she spoke, refusing to remain mute beside her husband.

When the MacKinnons surrounded them to give them hugs and to congratulate them, the townsfolk broke into small groups, and a low, murmuring hum was heard throughout the room. Soon a small group of musicians began to play, drowning out the wild speculation as to the hastily arranged marriage.

Irene and Harold pushed their way to the front of those congratulating the newlyweds. "We couldn't be more delighted for you," Irene said. "And you must come by the café and explain what truly transpired at the church today." She waited until Jessamine nodded. "Although we won't expect you for a few days."

Ewan laughed as Jessamine blushed.

Harold nodded as he gave Jessamine a hug, then turned to Ewan with a smile. "I told you the fall was a time for great change." His expression sobered. "No more of your wild ways, young man. Treat her well."

Ewan laughed and nodded. "I've no need of those ways now, ye ken." He laughed harder as Irene batted him on his arm at his impertinence.

"Now there will be no talk of a *chivaree*," Irene said as she tapped her husband on his arm. His disgruntled moan met her glare. "The young ones have thrown a wonderful party, and that should suffice for the townsfolk. When they leave, you must let them be."

Harold grumbled but nodded. "Fine, Irene. But that means you can't stop me from having another glass of punch!" He laughed with glee as she shook her head in consternation at him as he walked toward the drink area where the majority of the men had congregated.

"What did she mean by a *chivaree*?" Jessamine asked Ewan, her brows furrowed in confusion. "I don't know what that is."

"It's when the townsfolk come by after you've settled in for the evening on your wedding night, demanding food and drink," Irene explained. "The newlyweds are expected to interrupt their … activities and attend to their uninvited guests. The carousing can last long into the night."

Ewan growled his displeasure. "I dinna want any unwanted visitors tonight, Irene."

She smiled and squeezed his arm. "I know, dear. It's why Harold is over there talking with the men, informing them that they must enjoy themselves here and leave you alone. Few would countermand him."

"Why is he no' mayor?" Ewan asked.

Irene laughed. "Oh, he prefers telling others what to do without the weight of responsibility that comes with such a position." Her smiled broadened as she saw her grandson. "Frederick! What a surprise to see you in town today. I didn't know you'd be here until I saw you in church at the ceremony."

Frederick Tompkins stood nearly a foot taller than his grandmother, but he bent to her will as he swooped down and kissed her cheek. He held a wide-brimmed hat in his hands, and his black hair was disheveled. "We needed supplies, and there was a break in the weather." He nodded to the newlyweds. "Congratulations. You'll be happy, I'm sure."

Jessamine fought a giggle. "Please don't sound so certain, Mr. Tompkins. And thank you for your help earlier with my father."

"You're welcome." His lips curled up at the corner, but he failed to fully smile. "I've yet to see the need for marriage, but I do wish you all happiness." He nodded again and turned away to join his grandfather.

Irene huffed out a breath as she watched him depart. "I swear I'll never understand that boy. He's growing too content with his own company on the ranch." She shook her head and forced a smile. "But that's a concern for another day. Congratulations, my dears. I wish you every joy." She squeezed their arms. "I must ensure those without sense understand your need to marry when a certain member of our esteemed town is absent." She headed to the food tables, calling out to friends and acquaintances.

Ewan laughed as Jessamine shook her head. "I could never match her for strategy," she whispered.

"She's as cunning as they come but serves it all with a warm meal and a smile, so ye dinna ken how much ye've been manipulated." He watched as the smiles in their direction became more genuine and less filled with intrigue.

Alistair and Cailean approached with glasses of punch in their hands. They attempted to block their view of the doorway, but Ewan frowned as he saw a disturbance there.

"What's goin' on?" He nodded to the door.

Alistair sighed. "We'd hoped to spare ye." He frowned as he met Jessamine's worried look. "Yer father showed up an' wanted to cause problems. He's bein' shown the door."

She gasped. "He won't like that."

Cailean smiled at an acquaintance. "No, but Warren is with him, and you know how persuasive he can be. Seems yer father dinna like being tricked by that contract." He shared a look with his youngest brother, and Ewan nodded his understanding.

"Well, ye should ken better than to make an agreement with a gambler." Ewan nodded to Warren who now stood near the door as though ensuring her father did not attempt to reenter. "An' Warren writes contracts that can make yer head spin if ye dinna ken what ye're about."

Cailean smiled. "He's a lawyer. As long as he advised Mr. Abbott that he was representing you?" Ewan nodded at Cailean's question, and Cailean relaxed. "Then Mr. Abbott will have to be disappointed that he was outmaneuvered."

"Aye," Ewan said before he focused on his wife. "Come. Dance with me afore I twirl ye out the back door."

She giggled, her concern about her father forgotten, before her eyes widened. "You're serious? We can't sneak out of our own wedding celebration. It would be scandalous!"

He wiggled his eyebrows at her. "Aye. An' few expect any less than that from me." He laughed as she shrieked when he spun her into a fast twirl, joining the dancers on the floor.

～

Helen Jameson stood with her shoulders straight and a blank expression on her face as she watched Ewan and his bride twirl around the dance floor. Helen ignored the pitying stares cast in her direction and stiffened her jaw as her brother snickered.

"Seems you'll always be the pathetic one in the family. Too fat and stupid to amount to much," her brother, Walter, sneered as he leaned against the wall on one shoulder, gazing out at the crowd, while also keeping an eye on his sister. He preened as he saw her stiffen at his barb.

"It's amazing that one such as you ever thought that you'd amount to anything. You're pathetic, and you'll never be important to anyone." He nodded to a woman across the room, hitching a thumb in his new sky-blue waistcoat.

"I am more than what you think of me." Her breaths emerged as shallow puffs. "I will not always be around for you to abuse."

He snickered. "No one will marry you, sister. Haven't you learned that after three MacKinnons have married other women? Not even your pathetic attempts at throwing yourself at them could induce them to marry you." His gaze raked over her. "And it isn't hard to see why."

"How dare you!" she snapped as she spun to face him. "I'm your sister. You should protect me and care for me."

He shook his head. "No. You are nothing to me. You never have been, and you never will be." He laughed as he looked out at the dance floor. "Look. It seems not even that lawyer wants you anymore."

She turned to face the dance floor and clamped her jaw tightly closed as she saw Warren laugh at something Sorcha MacKinnon said while he held her close in his arms. Although she attempted to refrain from showing any expression, Helen knew she had failed when she flinched at her brother's mocking laugh.

"You'll lose another one to a MacKinnon." He shook his head in disgust. "I told Mama not to go to Helena, but she wouldn't listen."

Helen froze. "She went because our cousin is ill." She shivered when her brother moved closer and whispered in her ear.

"No, darling sister, she went to convince him to come to town and to marry you. And you know Mother. She can be quite persuasive." He chuckled as she tensed at his words. "Enjoy the party." He pushed off from the wall beside her and sauntered into the room.

She blinked away tears, her desolation magnifying with every turn around the ballroom that Warren made with Sorcha MacKinnon in his arms.

∾

E wan clutched Jessamine's hand as he led her to their house. Soft light shone through the front windows, and he swooped her up into his arms after opening the front door. He kicked it shut behind him and set her down. Curtains hung across the windows, and a few pieces of furniture sat in the large room that served as the living room, dining room, and kitchen.

"I hope ye dinna mind that it's open. I liked catchin' the light at various times of day, and a wall separatin' the dining area from the livin' room would have made it dark."

She shook her head as she traced a hand over the worn green velvet of the settee. "I love it. It's ours."

She smiled at him, and his breath caught at the wonder and joy in her gaze.

"We can make this our home, with little mementos."

He tugged her to sit next to him on the settee. "Can ye forgive me?" He traced his fingers over her cheek.

She took a deep breath and laced the fingers of one hand with his. "Why do such a thing and not tell me? You had to have known how much it would hurt me. I was so confused."

Ewan cupped his palm to her face and stared deeply into her beautiful cognac-colored eyes. "I dinna ken what I would do should yer da confront me, until he visited yesterday. He came here, filled with insults and this superiority over ye. Over me." He flushed. "An' I wanted to find a way to humiliate him." His thumb rubbed over her cheek. "I'm sorry to have hurt ye. To have caused ye to doubt me."

She nodded. "I cried all night."

"Oh, Jessie. Ye ken I love ye. Ye an' no other." He leaned forward and kissed her lips. "If we dinna receive a penny of his money, that is fine."

"Why did you care about his money?" She ran her free hand through his trimmed beard.

"I hated that he thought ye expendable. That because ye were a woman, a daughter, that ye had little worth. I wanted ye to receive part of what was yer due." His eyes glimmered with anger. "He stole yer childhood. Yer joy. Yer mother." He let out a deep breath. "I wanted him to pay something for what he'd done."

"Oh, Ewan," she whispered. "He almost won. When I read that contract, all I saw was your deceit. I didn't understand what was written."

"When did ye understand?"

"I went to the livery this morning. I wanted to rent a horse to escape town and my father." She held fingers to his lips and shook her head. "I spoke with Bears. He helped me understand what I had been too blind to see."

"What was that?" he asked as he kissed her fingers.

"That you gave me the freedom to fully choose what I wanted. What I needed." She leaned forward and kissed him. "That you never intended to abandon me for money."

"Never," he growled as he pulled her close. "Ye are more precious than any amount of gold."

She clung to him for a few moments. "Show me the rest of our home, my love."

"Aye," he whispered. He grabbed her hand as he stood. "I ken ye'll want to continue to work at the print shop, an' that does no' bother me. But I ken ye often work late at night, craftin' yer tales." He smiled as he opened the door to a small front room off the main living area. "I thought ye could use this as an office. 'Tisn't a bad view."

She curled into his arms after she beheld a desk sitting in front of the window with paper, pens, and a dictionary set out as though waiting for her. "Oh, Ewan."

"I ken ye love yer work, but I hoped ye'd work where I could be with ye," he whispered.

She cupped his face. "Thank you. And you are always welcome at the print shop." She caressed his cheek. "What's in the other rooms?" She smiled as his gaze darkened with passion.

"Come," he whispered. After showing her a small room with a single bed set up for a guest, he led her to the bigger back bedroom with a large bed with an iron headboard. A bureau with a bouquet of dried flowers was against one wall with a lantern gently illuminating the room, while curtains covered the back windows. "I wanted this space for us, aye? The view in the morning is beautiful. And 'tis quieter here in the back of the house."

She wrapped her arms around his waist and rubbed her cheek against his chest. "Oh, Ewan," she whispered. "I love you. Thank you for building this home for us. For preparing it tonight for us." She squealed as he spun them, and she landed with her back against the bed with him alongside her.

"I love ye, Jessie. Ye an' no other," he whispered as he caressed a finger down her cheek. He kissed her, groaning as she pushed him back and leaned over him. Her small hands ran through his hair and beard before loosening his tie. She backed away, her breath emerging in pants as she tugged off his tie and then freed the buttons on his waistcoat.

He chuckled, pushing off his waistcoat and tossing it on the floor before working on the buttons on the front of her dress. He growled when her dress remained as tightly fastened as before, even with the loosened buttons.

"You have to unhook me from behind. Those are merely decorative." She hopped down from the bed and stood between his legs, facing away from him as he undid the small buttons down her back. His fingers caressed her exposed flesh, and she shivered at his touch. She giggled when his beard rasped over her bared skin as he kissed down her spine.

When her dress gaped open, he pushed it down her hips, unceremoniously dropping her wedding gown to the floor and turning her to face him. She crawled onto his lap, her lips meeting his for a deep kiss as his fingers dug through her fiery hair.

After many minutes he lifted her chemise and then loosened her corset. After helping her out of the rest of her clothes, he rolled until she lay on the bed. He heaved himself up, peppering kisses along her arm, belly, and leg until he stood long enough to shuck his pants.

He paused before joining her in their bed, his gaze glowing at the love and joy in her eyes. "I promise to love ye and no other until I take my last breath." He crawled onto the bed, his warm touch eliciting a gasp from her.

"And I you, my love," she whispered before tugging him down for another drugging kiss.

CHAPTER 17

The morning after their wedding, a loud knocking woke them a little after dawn. Ewan kissed Jessamine's shoulder and grabbed a pair of pants and a shirt, shrugging into them before marching down the hallway.

He flung open the door with a growl and then jerked his head back as he was slapped soundly across the face.

"How could you?" Mrs. Jameson shrieked. "You defile my daughter and then marry another." Her face was reddened with anger and by the cold wind blowing off the mountains.

"I never defiled anyone," he snarled. "How dare ye say such a thing." He stood in front of her, preventing her from entering his home even though she pushed at him in an attempt to gain entrance.

"I know she visited you at your worksite. At this very home. That she spent time with you." She took a deep breath.

"Aye, an' I ken ye are the type of mother who would encourage your daughter to take such actions. Ye are shameless in yer desire to obtain a husband for yer daughter. An' ye are blind."

She flushed but thrust her bosom out in righteous indignation. "I have perfect vision." Her glare intensified as he rolled his eyes at her for taking his words literally.

"I will sue you."

"For what? Havin' a conversation, unwanted on my part, with yer daughter?" He shook his head. "Ye're daft."

"How will you prove it was unwanted?" she asked, her eyes lit with triumph.

"Yer daughter was no' subtle. She spoke loudly enough my men heard her. They'll bear witness to the fact nothin' happened."

"You'd have your men lie for you?" she asked.

He bent over and yelled into her face. "They are no' liars!" He stood up, the tension easing slightly as a soft hand traced down his back.

Jessamine poked her head out to one side, her red hair a riotous mess after their night together. "How lovely of you to come wish us well on your arrival into town." Her eyes held a subtle warning. "I will be sure to remark upon it in my next publication."

Mrs. Jameson paled and then straightened her shoulders. "You won't always be able to use the press to your advantage."

Jessamine smiled. "Perhaps not. But, in this instance, it's valuable. If you don't mind, I'd like time with my husband." She pulled Ewan off the front step and shut the door in Mrs. Jameson's face. She fell into Ewan's chest, giggling as she heard the sputtering outrage on the other side of the door.

"What will ye write?" he whispered into her hair.

"I don't know, but something with a touch of sarcasm that the more astute townsfolk will understand." She kissed the underside of his jaw. "Come to bed, husband. I don't want to waste our time away from work thinking about such a woman."

He chuckled. "Nae, nor do I."

The following day Ewan sat at the small square table in the dining area of the large room, his hand clasping Jessie's as they talked about upcoming story ideas for her paper. She glowed with a silent contentment as they discussed options and seemed to relish his reaction to her scandalous suggestions.

"Now I ken ye're just tryin' to shock me," he said after she suggested a salacious story about Tobias. When she watched him with a twinkle in her eyes as she took a sip of coffee, he frowned. "Dinna tell me that it's true?"

She shrugged. "I've already said more than I should. And you have to promise that what we share is between us." She relaxed when he nodded. "I know you're loyal to your family—"

Ewan set aside his coffee and cupped her jaw. "Ye're my family now, Jessie. Aye, I'll always be close to my siblings, an' there is little I wouldna do to help them. But ye come first. Ye'll always come first." He looked at her as she bowed her head and frowned. "Jessie?"

"It will take me time to understand that I come first for you. I've never come first for anyone."

He shook his head as his gaze filled with tenderness. "Ye ken that's no' true. Yer mother loved ye, more than all else. She refused to give ye up, even though yer father wanted ye from the moment ye were born. 'Twas only due to his deceit that ye were ever separated from her." He traced her cheek. "Never doubt how much ye were loved, Jessie."

He waited a moment as she fought tears and failed. He rubbed them away as his thumbs caressed her cheeks. "Never doubt how much I love ye."

"Oh, Ewan," she whispered, leaning forward to kiss him. "Please continue to be patient with me."

"I understand insecurities, love." He squeezed her hand as he rose to answer the knock at the front door. "'Tis most likely Alistair or Annabelle with a basket of food for us." He winked. "They think we are no' able to leave the house to fend for ourselves."

He opened the door with a broad smile that turned into a snarl when he saw who stood on the doorstep. "What are ye doin' here?" he demanded. "There's nothin' more to say between us."

"Might I be allowed inside?" the man asked.

"Nae, ye will no'. Ye are no' welcome here." He stood tall, with strong arms crossed over each other and legs spread, blocking access to the house.

"I want to speak with my daughter. You have no right to separate me from her." Lawrence Abbott stood at the same height as Ewan, dressed immaculately in a heavy black wool coat with burgundy scarf, gray slacks, and polished black shoes.

"I have every right. I am her husband, and this is our home." Ewan shared a long glare with the man.

"I am working to have the marriage annulled. There is nothing legal about it. You broke the contract you signed with me," Mr. Abbott said. He gasped when Ewan gripped the two ends of Abbott's scarf and tightened them, cutting off his access to air.

"This wedding, my weddin', was legal. She used her name, which unfortunately meant yer name is on the certificate. It has been witnessed. An' consummated." Ewan glared at her father before releasing the scarf in disgust, watching the man bend over at the waist as he gasped for air.

"I will fight this. I will drag your name through the court and beggar you. I have lawyers!"

"Ye are a bully, who thinks he can prey on those weaker than him. Ye canna have a lawyer any more proficient than Warren Clark of the Philadelphia Clarks." He smiled with satisfaction as Mr. Abbott paled. "Aye, ye dinna ken we had such a prestigious man in our little town, did ye? Ye allowed yer prejudices to blind ye."

"You'll get none of my money! I'll give it all to charity before I see any of it go to you and this money-grubbing Scot!" he yelled into the house through the open door.

"No need to yell, Father. You should have your knuckles rapped and your supper taken away for a week for such behavior." Jessamine stood behind Ewan, her hand on his shoulder as though supporting him and also grounding herself.

"You have no right to reprimand me on proper behavior, young lady. Not after what you did to disgrace yourself and our family."

She stood with pride as Ewan stepped aside and gave her room to stand next to him to face her father. "Yes, how terrible for you to be denied the creation of a financial dynasty. You should have learned, Father, that women are more than objects to be displayed at social gatherings. We have opinions and thoughts independent of yours."

Her father flushed red. "You have no need for your own thoughts or opinions. You need only think what I or your husband tell you." He pointed at Ewan derisively. "And I do not mean this man."

Jessamine smiled. "He is my husband. You have no control over me. That contract you unwittingly signed gave *me* control of my future. Not you, Father. And I chose Ewan." She smiled in triumph. "It's remarkable you ever thought you could control me." She met her father's malevolent stare and nodded. "I'll be sure to print your congratulations in the next edition of the paper, Father. And, if you fail to meet the terms of the contract, I'll send a duplicate of it, signed by you, along with an article to my former editors in Saint Louis and New York. It's the sort of story that will generate good copy and scandalous interest."

He glared at her before spinning on his heel and storming away.

Ewan waited a few minutes to ensure Abbott had truly left before shutting the door and locking it. He pulled a quivering Jessamine into his arms. "Are ye sure ye are all right, love? That was no' pleasant."

She choked out a sob as she attempted to laugh, burying her face in his chest. "I think he'll finally leave me alone, Ewan. I'll no longer have to look over my shoulder."

"Aye. Ye ken I dinna care if we dinna receive a penny of his money?" He relaxed as she nodded her agreement against his shoulder. "I think having Warren here helped dissuade him from attemptin' to annul yer marriage."

"*Our* marriage," she whispered as she kissed the underside of his jaw.

"Aye, our marriage." He lowered his face and kissed her before holding her in his arms for many long minutes.

~

A week after their marriage, Jessamine and Ewan joined the family for dinner at Cailean's home. Steam coated the kitchen windows, giving the room a cozy feel, while the scent of freshly baked bread warred with the smell of roasting chicken, enticing the family to sit for dinner.

"Leena Ericson is going to start working with me," Annabelle said. "She convinced her fiancé that there is no shame in working as a baker. He seemed mollified when he understood she would not be a full partner and that she can cease working at any time."

Leticia sighed. "I doubt she'll want to quit once she realizes how much fun she'll have working with us. Poor man." She shared an amused smile with Annabelle.

Annabelle giggled.

Fidelia sat in a chair at the table, her hair listless, her clothes hanging off her, and her gaze downcast as the MacKinnon family sat around her for dinner. She shrugged her thanks for the food placed in front of her but refrained from raising her fork after the simple prayer.

"Also Dee is to start working at the bakery next week."

She jerked as Annabelle said her name.

"She'll help out front and with washing dishes. With two bakers, there will be too much work for Leticia." Annabelle cast a quick glance at her despondent sister. "I will be reassured to know that they are there to help Leticia when I am taking care of my baby."

"Anna, no," Fidelia whispered. "The townsfolk …"

"Are accustoming themselves to the fact that you are no longer at the Boudoir. You are no longer one of the Madam's Beauties. You are now your own beauty, and you need to find something to do, like continue with your embroidery again. You are a free woman. Able to choose for yourself. Until that time, this will help you as it helps me." Annabelle beamed at those around the table.

Her sister shook her head. "You will drive customers away, just as you are trying to accustom them to a new baker."

"Dee, you are family. The town has been aware of that since I moved here."

Ewan chuckled, his hand playing with one of Jessamine's as he ate his stew. "Besides they will become as addicted to Miss Ericson's baked goods as they did to Annabelle's that they will gladly approach Fidelia to obtain an apple cake."

Fidelia frowned at those she was expected to consider family. "Is it so easy for all of you? To consider me one of you when I know what I am? A dried-up whore strung out on laudanum?"

At Annabelle's cry of distress, Jessamine cleared her throat. "You were addicted to that horrible potion given to you by the wayward doctor. However, I think you are improving and that you will not have any setbacks as long as you refrain from using it in the future."

Annabelle had yet to calm herself, but she seemed pacified that Fidelia hadn't left the table.

"What's the latest news, J.P.?" Cailean asked when Fidelia studiously stared at her plate again.

Jessamine cleared her throat. "From what I hear, between the recent … tax, the big poker match, and the loss of income from a certain … asset," she flushed, "the Madam is desperate for an influx of cash."

Fidelia grunted. "She's always desperate. This time it's worse. She's facing bankruptcy. She needs an infusion of cash, and she needs it now."

Ewan frowned. "There's little that will cause her to receive such a sum now. The town is shuttered up for winter."

"She'll have her virgin auction." Fidelia met their worried gazes and watched as Annabelle paled. "She'll publicize it as something to entice the men before Christmas. As though it were their Christmas present." Fidelia shuddered as she kept her head bowed. "I hate to think what will happen to that poor girl."

"Who would agree to such an auction?" Sorcha whispered. She saw her siblings exchanging glances with their respective spouses and sputtered, "Helen? She's no' daft nor as desperate as that."

Jessamine nodded. "I'm afraid she might be. Her mother is outraged at my marriage to Ewan."

Cailean shared a long look with Alistair who was present without Leticia as Hortence had a cold and did not feel well enough to join the family. "Which one of us should inform Warren?"

~

Later that evening Ewan held Jessamine in his arms, cradled on his chest. He ran his fingers over her shoulders and upper arms. "Yer skin is like silk."

She chuckled and snuggled closer. "When have you had much opportunity to touch silk?"

He snorted. "I may no' have partaken of the Beauties in the Boudoir, but I know well enough what satin and silk feel like." He kissed her head. "I promise I willna go there in the future."

She stiffened in his arms, and he frowned. He pushed her back until he could see her worried expression in the faint light from a lamp on a far table. "What is it? What have I said that was wrong?"

"Did you pay back the Madam? After you won all that money, did you repay her what she thought you owed her for the broken furniture?"

He nodded. "Aye, because, if I hadna, she said she would come to you for it. I couldna allow her to badger ye or to involve Warren in such an affair."

Jessamine smiled. "So you are allowed to enter the Boudoir again?"

He frowned. "Aye, but I dinna want to. I have no need to enter there. Fidelia is safe, and I have ye in my arms every night."

She arched up and kissed him on his lips. "I ken," she said with a teasing smile. "But I know *I* will never be allowed in the Boudoir again, and I refuse to lose the knowledge of what occurs there. I need you to return and then report back to me."

His brows furrowed as he stared at her with his mouth agape. "Ye want me to spy for ye?"

She giggled. "No, I want you to be my junior reporter. And it can be our secret, when the townsfolk are confused because we appear so content, but you continue with your visits to the Boudoir."

He shook his head in dismay. "Nae, Jessie, I dinna like the idea of them, of anyone, speakin' poorly of ye. Of thinkin' I do no' respect ye as I should. As I do."

"Wasn't it you who told me that it doesn't matter what everyone else thinks? It only matters what we know to be true?"

He nodded, although his body remained tense with reluctance.

"I need to know what happens in the Boudoir during the virgin auction. Because I am a reporter at heart, and I hate being banned. Having you there, someone I trust"—she smiled as his eyes flared with delight at her words—"will ease my torment at being denied entrance."

He growled and toppled her to her back, looming over her. "Ye will no' go there during the auction. The men will be fired up enough as it is. I canna protect ye, Jessie, under those circumstances." His eyes gleamed with fear and passion. "I couldna bear it were something to happen to ye."

She ran her fingers through the hair that hung over his forehead and then through his beard. "I know." She leaned up and kissed him. "It's the only reason why I will promise not to attend."

He smiled. "Ye promise?"

"Yes, as long as you will act in my stead as my reporter."

"Aye, 'tis an easy thing to agree to." He rested his forehead against hers a moment before rolling to his side. Then he whispered, "What is it that ye ken to be true?"

She turned her head and met his guarded gaze. "What?" She ran a finger over his brow, and some of his tension eased. "Oh, ... I know many things to be true. That my father never loved me as anything more than a pawn. That my mother's need for her next bottle of laudanum does not mean she did not love me. That I am a very good journalist." She took a deep breath, and her voice dropped to a whisper. "I know that I love you. I never knew I could love as much as I do." She smiled. "I know that I was wrong about many things. The love and support of a good, loving family makes everything better."

"Jessie," he rasped, pulling her toward him as he kissed her deeply. "I love ye, almost more than I can bear. The thought of any harm comin' to ye ..." His eyes sparkled with unshed tears. "I canna even bear the thought of it."

She kissed his jaw and then his cheek. "I know. Because that is exactly how I feel." She smiled at him. "I never thought my husband could understand me, accept me, even help me with the work I do." She rubbed her nose against his. "I'm so glad to be proven wrong."

He chuckled as he pulled her tight against his chest. "I'll be happy to continue to prove ye wrong for the next fifty years."

"Only fifty?" she whispered as her smile spread. "I want forever."

"Gladly," he agreed before he kissed her.

SNEAK PEEK AT MONTANA RENEGADE!

CHAPTER ONE

December 1885, Montana Territory

"When is the virgin auction to take place?" Warren Clark asked. Dusk was falling, and an oil lamp on the corner of his tidy desk cast light onto a small portion of the front room of his office, enhancing the shadows in the corners. A pot bellied stove in the corner emitted much needed heat in the frigid December evening. He paced behind his desk and kicked one of its legs for good measure. As the only lawyer serving Bear Grass Springs, he was used to knowing all of the intricacies of small town life and little surprised him.

A cold wind howled on this mid-December evening and snow threatened. The front windows, currently steam covered, prevented any hardy townsfolk from peering inside. However, those with sense were inside around a warm fire. Those without sense could be found at one of the town's four saloons. Or at Betty's Boudoir, the town's brothel. Warren sighed and scratched at his head. At thirty-seven, his hair remained brown with no hint of gray.

Alistair MacKinnon sat in a chair across from Warren's desk and rubbed at his temple. "I kent ye'd be shocked. I never thought ye'd be distraught she'd given herself to the Madam." Alistair, the second of four MacKinnon siblings at thirty-three, ran the livery with his brother, Cailean. The two eldest brothers had left the Isle of Sky thirteen years ago, and, after years traveling around the United States together, they had settled in Bear Grass Springs in 1881. Their two younger siblings—Ewan, thirty; and Sorcha, twenty-four—had followed them over in the subsequent years. Alistair frowned at his friend as Warren collapsed, holding his head in his hands.

"I hate her mother," Warren rasped, provoking a startled laugh from Alistair. "Shouldn't come as much of a surprise as half the town does too."

"I'd say 'tis more than half. She's despised by all, except her sniveling son." Alistair tapped a finger on the arm's chair. "As to the auction, 'tis tonight. Seems a few big spenders are in town for the holiday season, and the Madam wants to see how much she can obtain for fresh flesh." He shrugged at Warren's daggerlike glare. "Or so says Ewan."

"And Ewan's rarely wrong when it comes to the bloody Boudoir," Warren hissed. "I hate this."

Alistair canted forward, his brows furrowed with confusion. "I'll never understand why ye feel such a … a tenderness for Helen." He shrugged as Warren stiffened at his word choice. "I've seen how ye argue with her, but I can tell when a man is dancing around in the middle of his courtship."

"You're insane if you believe I've been pining for the likes of Helen Jameson all these years." The red flush on his neck put the lie to his words.

Alistair studied his friend. "Must have been hard to swallow, watching her throw herself at my brothers and me." He sobered further when he saw the hastily hidden agony in his friend's eyes. "Ye ken I never sought her company?" He relaxed when Warren nodded.

Warren rose and paced again. "Why would she go to the Boudoir?" He shook his head. "It makes no sense."

"From what J.P. learned, Helen had a monstrous fight with her mother after her return from Helena. She either left or was thrown out. I dinna ken which, and J.P. couldna discover which was true." He shrugged as he considered what he had learned from Ewan's wife, Jessamine, nicknamed J.P., who was also the town's reporter. "An' the homeless lass doesna have many friends in town."

"No," Warren whispered. He ran a hand through his brown hair. "She has not been so fortunate as to form friendships." He raised tormented blue eyes to meet Alistair's confused gaze. "I know you don't understand my need to aid her."

"No, I've never understood your fascination with her. Since we traveled to Helena this past summer, your interest in her has seemed to only grow." After a long pause, Alistair asked, "What will ye do?"

Warren eased back into his chair. "What else can I do? Save her. As I should have done years ago."

Alistair fought, and failed, to hide a smile. "I fear she'll fight ye tooth and nail. For she seems like one intent on savin' herself."

⁓

Helen Jameson stood in a small room upstairs in the Boudoir. She had walked past the tiny rooms called cribs where the women lived and entertained the men of the town. She fought nausea as she considered living in such a confined space and sharing her body with another. Anyone other than …

"Get her dressed," the Madam shrieked, interrupting Helen's thoughts.

Helen was jerked forward, her arms slung upward so a flimsy white nightgown could be tugged over her confining corset. Her generous curves were made more abundantly obvious by the tortuous contraption, and she had to fight her natural inclination to cover her breasts with her hands. They seemed about to burst from the corset.

"Perfect," the Madam said with a sigh. She cinched the nightgown with a red ribbon around the waist, further accentuating Helen's bust, small waist and generous hips. She pushed Helen forward until she sat at a vanity table.

A woman dressed in scarlet with a low cut bodice moved to her side and brushed makeup on her forehead, cheeks and chin. Her gaze flit from Helen to the Madam, her posture relaxing when the Madam left the room for a moment. "Are you sure you want to do this?" the woman whispered.

"I have no choices left," Helen murmured. She watched the doorway in the mirror.

"There are always choices. But once you spend a night here, they are drastically reduced," the woman with blond hair and brown eyes said. "If you stay, pick a name for yourself. I'm Grace. Never use your real name. Never let them touch you in that way." She met Helen's terrified gaze. "For they'll touch you in every other conceivable way."

Grace, who would place the role of mentor to Helen, frowned as she stared into Helen's gaze. A gaze filled with too much understanding. "You're playing a dangerous game," she breathed. She clamped her jaw shut as the Madam bustled in. Grace puckered her lips, nodding with satisfaction when Helen mimicked her movement. She slathered on a thick coating of red lipstick and backed away, awaiting the Madam's verdict.

"More rouge. More kohl around the eyes. We want all the men in the room, even those at the back, to be tantalized by her." The Madam squeezed Helen's shoulders as she leaned against her back, meeting Helen's gaze in the mirror. "You will be my next Charity. You will restore my fortunes, and I will be the talk of the Territory."

Helen shivered. She knew of Charity, also known as Fidelia Evans. She had escaped life in the Boudoir last month when the Madam had bet her—and lost her—in a hand of cards. The man who won her, Ewan MacKinnon, saw her as a sister, as his sister-in-law Annabelle was Fidelia's sibling. Fidelia had been welcomed back into the MacKinnon family with open arms, an uncommon occurrence for a reformed whore.

"Never forget. I own you now. You are nothing without me. You are only as important as the next man who wants you. Tonight, your innocence is what is valued. Tomorrow, I will expect you to learn from those who've been here for years." The Madam patted Helen's shoulders and departed, calling the names of the other girls to ready them for the procession downstairs.

"I don't believe in God or good fortune, but, if I did, I'd pray for you," Grace whispered as she rose. Her work was done and she exited the room.

Helen sat a moment, staring at a stranger in the mirror with a prostitute's face paint. "I am a whore," she whispered to herself. Rather than bolstering her failing nerves, she fought tears. She dug her nails into her palms and rose as the Madam called her name. It was time to face her destiny.

~

Available May 2018

AFTERWORD

Thank you for reading *Montana Maverick*! I hope you enjoyed Ewan and Jessamine's story as much as I enjoyed writing it.

Are you curious about the *Fact and Fiction* sections? The idea for this section came about on a plane ride when my brother was bored and he started spinning yarns to kill time. I wrote them down, and I then embellished them and turned them into tales. Thanks, Bar!

There is a legend about Liver Eating Johnson, but from my research it is just that: a legend.

ACKNOWLEDGMENTS

Thanks to the best fans! I love hearing from you and your enthusiasm for my novels keeps me writing.

My beta readers push me to write better and more interesting novels-thank you!

Thank you to my editor, DB. I couldn't do this without your insight and help.

Jenny Q- you created another beautiful cover- thank you!

I couldn't do this without the support, faith and encouragement of my family. Thank you!

ABOUT THE AUTHOR

Ramona Flightner is a historical romance author. She lives in Montana, and is the author of the Bear Grass Springs Series and the Banished Saga.

Made in the USA
Middletown, DE
20 October 2020